PRAISE FOR CAROLYN HAINES AND THE SARAH BOOTH DELANEY MYSTERIES

STICKS AND BONES

"Many well-drawn charaters . . . help bring this Southern tale to colorful life."
—*Publishers Weekly*

ROCK-A-BYE BONES

"As usual, Haines crams a lot into her latest cozy, aiming at readers with a taste for levity rather than restraint."
—*Kirkus Reviews*

BONE TO BE WILD

"Haines shows Sarah at her madcap best . . . in this clever adventure. This is a crazy cozy with a little something for everyone: paranormal doings, plenty of Evanovich zaniness, and a cast of eccentrics."
—*Booklist*

"Engaging."
—*Publishers Weekly*

BOOTY BONES

"Delightful . . . [a] satisfying beignet of a mystery."
—*Publishers Weekly*

"[Haines] delivers a riveting love story alongside the mystery, leaving her readers in hot anticipation of her next novel."
—*Mississippi Magazine*

"Entertaining."
—*Booklist*

SMARTY BONES

"Raucously entertaining. This entire series is filled with mystery, humor, and more than a touch of the romantic South . . . not to be missed."
—*Criminal Element*

"If you enjoy mysteries with rich Southern settings, fascinating history, and quirky characters, you'll devour this one quicker than a plate full of buttermilk biscuits."

—*Mystery Scene* magazine

"The South's answer to a feminine Sherlock Holmes, the marvelous and smart Sarah Booth Delaney is on the trail of another fun and fascinating mystery." —*Fresh Fiction*

"A satisfying mystery framed by a well-drawn small-town Southern setting." —*Booklist*

BONEFIRE OF THE VANITIES

"Delightfully fun." —*New York Post*

"Wildly entertaining." —*Criminal Element*

"We have to admit being hooked by the title, but even urbane Tom Wolfe would get a kick out of this delightfully fun twelfth installment of Haines's Southern mystery series."

—*New York Post*

"An entertaining romp with enough twists to hold interest to the end." —*Booklist*

BONES OF A FEATHER

"A lesson in lying, Mississippi style . . . Haines diverts the reader . . . with great dollops of charm." —*Kirkus Reviews*

"Entertaining . . . Sarah and Tinkie must strive to thwart a plot of brilliantly diabolical proportions." —*Publishers Weekly*

"Sarah Booth Delaney has a funny way of ending up in extremely strange situations . . . a perfectly written mystery with a cast that is humorous, charming and deadly. Haines certainly is one of the best mystery writers working today."

—*RT Book Reviews*

BONE APPETIT

"Distinctive characters and a clever cooking background make Haines's tenth Sarah Booth Delaney mystery the best yet in this Southern cozy series." —*Publishers Weekly* (starred review)

"A whole lot of Southern sass . . . Haines's novel is definitely a page-turner." —*Jackson Free Press*

GREEDY BONES

"The cast is in fine form (including the helpful ghost, Jitty), and it's good to be back in Mississippi . . . One of the more entertaining episodes in the series." —*Booklist*

"Captivating—readers will enjoy *Greedy Bones* from cranium to phalanges." —Don Noble, Alabama Public Radio

"Jitty, Dahlia House's wonderfully wise 'haint,' [is] one of the best features of this light paranormal mystery series infused with Southern charm." —*Publishers Weekly*

WISHBONES

"Funny, ingenious . . . and delightful." —*Dallas Morning News*

"*Wishbones* is reminiscent in many ways of Janet Evanovich's Stephanie Plum novels, only fresher with a bit more of an edge. Light, breezy, and just plain fun. Call Haines the queen of cozies." —*Providence Journal-Bulletin*

"Stephanie Plum meets the Ya-Ya Sisterhood! Non-Southerners will find the madcap adventure an informative peek into an alien culture." —*Kirkus Reviews*

"Sarah Booth Delaney heads for Hollywood in Haines's entertaining eighth cozy . . . The chemistry sizzles between Graf and Sarah Booth." —*Publishers Weekly*

A Gift of Bones

CAROLYN HAINES

St. Martin's Paperbacks

This is a work of fiction. All of the characters, organizations, and events portrayed in this novel are either products of the author's imagination or are used fictitiously.

Published in the United States by St. Martin's Paperbacks, an imprint of St. Martin's Publishing Group.

A GIFT OF BONES

For information, address St. Martin's Publishing Group, 120 Broadway, New York, NY 10271.

www.stmartins.com

Library of Congress Catalog Card Number: 2018025704

ISBN: 978-1-250-19363-6

Our books may be purchased in bulk for promotional, educational, or business use. Please contact your local bookseller or the Macmillan Corporate and Premium Sales Department at 1-800-221-7945, ext. 5442, or by email at MacmillanSpecialMarkets@macmillan.com.

Printed in the United States of America

Minotaur hardcover edition / October 2018
St. Martin's Paperbacks edition / November 2019

10 9 8 7 6 5 4 3 2 1

For Dean James, whose friendship is always a gift

Acknowledgments

So many people are instrumental in completing a book. As always, thanks to the St. Martin's team—Hannah Braaten, Kelley Ragland, Martin Quinn, and Nettie Finn. Always professionals, and always fun.

Many thanks to my agent, Marian Young. We've had a long partnership and no better agent could ever be found.

A big thanks to the readers who have made Sarah Booth and the Zinnia gang part of their literary family. I am a lucky writer to have a series going into the nineteenth book, and it is because of the readers who have made this long journey with me and Sarah Booth. Thank you.

And big thanks to the booksellers and librarians who recommend my books. You've spread the word about Sarah Booth far and wide, and I thank you so much.

1

"How can the holiday season be both melancholy and joyful?" I address the question to my Redtick Coondog, Sweetie Pie Delaney, as she snoozes by a crackling fire. Pluto, my black cat, is curled beside her. Outside, the night is chill but not bitter. It's winter in the Mississippi Delta and the weatherman has teased us with the possibility of the impossible—a white Christmas. I've already blanketed my three horses and given them hot bran mashes. It's time for Christmas cheer and a visit from my favorite lawman, Coleman Peters.

"Fa, la, la, la, lah!" I sing at the top of my voice, because I have to stop when Coleman arrives. I don't want to make his ears bleed with my caterwauling. I love to sing, but I have no talent for it.

"Fa, la, la, la, lah!"

Sweetie Pie begins a low, mournful howl. She does that whenever she hears a siren or me singing.

"Thanks for the commentary," I tell her. Instead of singing, I decide to check the bottle of champagne I have in the freezer chilling. It's a special occasion. I have a holiday gift for Coleman, a pre-Christmas present. One I think he's going to like.

"Put a bow on it!"

The command comes from the parlor near the Christmas tree. I whirl around and there, standing at attention, is a life-size nutcracker doll. Brightly painted and filled with the magic of my favorite ballet, he awkwardly steps forward, his wooden jaw opening wide. I could put my whole head in his mouth.

"That's rather ominous." I know it's Jitty, the resident haint of Dahlia House. Jitty was my great-great-great-grandmother Alice Delaney's nanny. The two women, one black, one white, survived the Civil War together, bonded by friendship and love rather than the law of property. Jitty has remained behind at Dahlia House to be my guardian. And tormenter, would-be boss, conscience, mother confessor, and keeper of the family history.

The beautiful music of the ballet comes out of nowhere, and Jitty the Nutcracker begins to limber up until he/she is moving with the grace and ability of a member of the Russian ballet. I had no idea that Jitty could dance like this. Perhaps it is just a spell cast by the mantle of Christmas, a time of wonder and possibility spread across my homeland. Whatever is happening, Jitty dances like an angel. She whirls and leaps and flies to the wonderful music that captures the essence of Christmas. Jitty brings to life the mystical land of sugarplum fairies, dolls who are alive, and one handsome prince. I have nothing to do but enjoy the show.

In the background is the beautiful cedar tree I cut out of a fence row and dragged back to the house by myself. It's thirteen feet tall, at least—full and fragrant. Tonight, Coleman and I will decorate it.

Jitty does one more flying leap and lands in a perfect bow.

"Brava! Brava!" I clap loudly and whistle when she is done. Sweetie Pie lifts her head and gives a big yawn. Millie's fine chicken potpie from the café has put her in a food coma. She is also no big fan of culture. If she's going to applaud dancing, the Boot Scootin' Boogey is more her kind of performance.

Pluto the cat stretches and rubs against my legs. It's a ploy for more catnip. I give it to him in a clever little elf cat-toy, even though he's done nothing to get such a reward. After all, it's the season for giving.

Jitty returns to the parlor, morphing back into the beautiful woman I've grown to love. She is still sporting the ridiculous fake beard. She puts her hands on her hips and looks me up and down. "Looks like you've been snackin' on the Sugar Plum Fairy. Girl, those hips could be deadly weapons. *Pa-boom!*" She cocks a hip at the dining room door and slams it with force.

Riding me hard is Jitty's favorite sport. "Not even Coker would kiss you sporting that pathetic clump of white hair on your face." I snatch for it, but she steps back. Jitty is quick.

"You leave my dead husband outta these debates. Coker and I had some mighty fine Christmases before the war took him." She grows suddenly melancholy.

"I'm sorry, Jitty. I miss my family, too. It feels like I've been on my own forever." In fact, I've been an orphan for a long time. My parents died in a car accident when I was twelve. My Aunt Loulane moved into Dahlia House and raised me until I went to college and then to New York City to try my hand at being a Broadway actress. That didn't work out so well and I came home with my tail between my legs.

"The holidays can bring on a mean case of the blues, and not the good musical kind." Jitty pulled the fake beard away from her face. "Lord, Sarah Booth, I hear in the Great Beyond that a white Christmas isn't out of the question for Sunflower County."

That news perked me right up. "The weatherman says the same. Snow! That would be awesome!"

"No promises, but it's definitely a topic of conversation up there."

"You know what I'd like for Christmas?" She knows what I'm going to say. A message from my mother or father, some sign that they're still around me.

"I'll do what I can, but no promises. There are rules, you know, and they're there for a reason."

"Five minutes. I won't ask for more." Sometimes Jitty can make that happen. Not often, but each minute is precious.

"Now what you got for that big lawman to chow down on? He's gonna be hungry when he arrives, and not just for lovin'. The way to a man's heart is through his stomach. An old saw, but true nonetheless."

"If you start quoting ancient axioms like Aunt Loulane, I'm going to run away from home."

Jitty gives me a dour look. "You'd better come up with

a more credible threat than that. Now finish puttin' up that mistletoe. There's a car comin' down the drive."

She was gone in a puff of cedar-scented smoke just as I heard Coleman's tread on the front porch.

"The door's open," I called, starting back up the ladder to hang more garland over the parlor arch. The door opened and I turned to give my winter date a smile, only it wasn't Coleman. Madame Tomeeka, aka Tammy Odom, plowed into the foyer and stopped. Tammy is a friend from high school who also happens to be psychic. Judging from the frown on her face, she had bad news.

"What's going on?" I climbed down. "Want some coffee?" Tammy doesn't often drink alcohol, but she is always good for caffeine.

"Yes. I need something to give me a boost."

I motioned for her to follow me into the kitchen, where I put the coffeepot on to brew.

Instead of sitting down, she paced the kitchen. "I fell asleep this afternoon watching a TV show." I'd left some Christmas-themed dish towels on a chair and Tammy folded them in a neat stack. "I had a dream."

"What kind of dream?" I busied myself at the sink. This was not good. Tammy's dreams were often prophetic. "What did you see?"

"I hate coming here, spoiling your holiday with dire warnings."

"You aren't responsible for what you see, but it's better for me to know." She had me really worried, but I downplayed my anxiety. "What was the dream?"

"Sarah Booth, something big and wonderful is coming, but at great cost."

I put a steaming cup of coffee in front of her. "Cost to me?"

"I can't be certain," she said. "You or someone you love."

"Tell me the dream."

Tammy eased into a chair, sipped the coffee, and sighed. "You were riding that big gray horse across the cotton fields. It was winter, the fields were bare, and you were flying. You had the biggest grin on your face, and I thought how much you looked like that tomboyish young girl I first met in grammar school. Hell-for-leather. That was how you did everything."

"The horses aren't going to be hurt?" It was my first reaction and worry.

"Oh, no. Not the horses."

"Then who?"

She shook her head. "The dream changed, and you were riding your horse into an empty town. The stores were all locked up. At the end of the street was a crèche, and you rode down there. It was so real. There were sheep and donkeys and three wise men with their camels. But the manger was empty. The little baby Jesus was gone!"

She was about to cry. I put a hand on her shoulder. "Hey, it's okay."

"You don't understand. Everyone was searching for the little baby, and no one could find him. The wise men were frantic. Sarah Booth, I'm worried sick that something dark is going to happen this Christmas."

"Now, Tammy, don't get yourself all worked up over—"

The front door flew open with a huge bang. I darted

out of the kitchen. If that was Coleman coming in, he was in a dither. But it wasn't the lawman standing in my foyer. Cece Dee Falcon, Zinnia, Mississippi's finest journalist and my friend, stood in the open door, her face drained of all color.

"Cece, what's wrong?" She looked perfectly undone.

"You have to help me, and you can't tell anyone." She thrust a gift-wrapped, padded envelope into my hand. "This came for me today."

I dumped the contents into my palm. A photograph of a pretty, pregnant woman looked up at me. A lock of dark hair tied with a ribbon fell onto the floor. And there was a note.

I unfolded the paper and stared at the typewritten words.

We have your cousin Eve. She is due to give birth Christmas Eve. We'll exchange her, unharmed, for $130,000. Do not tell the law or she will die.

I read the note twice before I remembered Tammy in the kitchen. "Uh, Tammy is here, and don't you think $130,000 is a very specific amount to ask for a ransom?"

"I knew something bad was going to happen." Tammy stood in the doorway. She'd heard it all—and there was no taking it back. "That baby is gonna be born, and the mama is missing."

"Hold on!" I held up a hand. They were both about to verge on hysteria. "This could be a setup." The note didn't have the feel of a real ransom demand. It was just . . . off somehow.

"Coleman is on his way—" I started.

"No!" Cece snatched everything from my hand and stuffed it back into the padded envelope. "No! I can't involve Coleman."

Tammy gave Cece a long, considered look. "Who is this Eve girl?" she asked.

"My cousin. It's Carla and Will Falcon's only child. When she was growing up, we were close, but I haven't seen or heard from her in . . . a while."

"So why are they contacting you for ransom money? Where's her mama and daddy?"

Cece's eyes filled with tears. "When I transitioned, Carla and Will thought I was Satan. They broke off all contact with me. And a few years ago, I heard that they turned Eve out in the street because she did something that disappointed them. I tried to find her and get her to move in with me. She couldn't have been over sixteen. But she was gone, and I never got a lead on her. I figured she'd changed her name and was living with some friends."

"So you didn't know she was pregnant?" I asked.

"I don't know anything about Eve anymore."

"Then why would the kidnappers contact you?"

"Some folks think I inherited the Falcon land and fortune, but you guys know better. I walked away with nothing."

I remembered the fight over the property. Cece had wanted to be herself more than she'd ever wanted money or land—even though she should have been entitled to it. She'd fought so hard to be Cece instead of Cecil, and the very people who should have cherished and helped her—her family—were the people who fought hardest against her dream.

"This girl sounds like trouble." I hated to say it, but

this kid ran away when Cece was going through hard times and could have used a loving family connection. Now Eve suddenly needed to be ransomed. I didn't want my tenderhearted friend to be used.

"If you knew Will and Carla, you'd have more compassion." Cece studied the picture of her cousin. "She's about to pop. It says she's due Christmas Eve."

"If the picture is even real." I sounded like such a bitter cynic.

"It's real, and that is Eve. I remember one Christmas when she was six, I got her a bicycle." Cece's face hardened. "Carla poured gasoline on it and set it on fire in the front yard. She said Christmas wasn't a time for gifts. To commercialize the Lord's birthday was just asking Satan to grab hold of Eve. The child stood on the porch until the bike was just a smoking heap. She never cried. When the fire was out she took the bicycle into the woods and buried it all by herself."

That memory was a perversion of Christmas. And what a terrible thing to do to a child. "You should have smacked that stupid woman in the kisser."

Cece's smile was tired. "It would only have made it harder on Eve. I bought another bicycle and kept it at my house for her. When she came over, I taught her to ride."

"Some people don't need to have children," Tammy said. "Some people should be sterilized."

Tammy was indeed in a dark mood. The whole missing-baby thing was preying on her mind. Tammy's dreams, while frightening for me, were more terrifying to her, because she knew the power of the images that came to her. She was still living in the moment of panic from the missing baby in the crèche, and now she was confronted with a real live missing mother and child.

"I have to help Eve," Cece said. "Whatever she's done, I have to help her."

"And we'll help. I have some savings." It was a paltry amount, but I would give it.

"Me, too." Tammy put an arm around Cece's shoulders.

"Scott and Jaytee said they'd send a bank draft. They're in Scotland doing that tour. I told Jaytee not to come home. There's nothing he can do."

"I'm sure Tinkie and Oscar will contribute." My partner in the Delaney Detective Agency and her husband would kick in. Tinkie and Oscar Richmond were loaded—and they were generous to their friends. "And Harold, too." Harold Erkwell worked at the Zinnia National Bank that Tinkie's family owned and Oscar ran.

"Why $130,000?" Tammy asked. "That is just a strange sum."

"Very specific," I said.

"Who knows why? Maybe Eve owes that much money to someone. Or maybe the person who abducted her has a specific financial need. All I know is I'll have that money by the time they call with the deadline. I'll give it without a second thought to make sure Eve is safe."

"Coleman is on the way here, and we really should bring him in." I said it softly.

"Absolutely not!" Cece was adamant. "We can do this without the law. The kidnappers will send more instructions for how to drop the money, and I'll get Eve back, then we can call in the law hounds."

Pushing Cece at this particular time would not be smart. To be honest, I didn't know what I would do in such a situation. If she brought in the law and something happened to Eve, she would never forgive herself. If she didn't . . . we simply had to get the young pregnant woman back without injury.

"Cece, why would anyone think you would pay that amount for Eve?" This was the key to figuring out who'd taken her.

"I don't know. Only Eve would be aware how much I'd do to save her. She knew I loved her like she was my own."

And yet she'd left town without an attempt to stay in touch with Cece. "We can assume that Eve told the kidnapper to contact you, because she believed you could— and would—help her."

Cece nodded. "What hell it must be that she knows she can't contact her parents for the ransom. She knows they won't help her. How must that feel?"

Not very good. But Eve's parental rejection wasn't my biggest concern. Getting her and her unborn baby to a safe place for delivery and care was at the top of my priority list. "Cece, forget all of that. We have to make sure the money is raised and try to figure out who took your cousin."

"That's right. And I'm not much help. I haven't been in touch with Eve for several years. Her parents said I was a deviant and a freak and that God would punish anyone who associated with me. They told me to stay away from her, and I did. I shouldn't have listened to them."

I glanced at Madame Tomeeka and read the same reaction on her face. There was a very good chance we might beat the eternal snot out of Will and Carla Falcon when we ran across them. Cece was one of the finest people I'd ever met. She'd suffered through high school and college, forced into a gender that didn't fit her. And she'd saved her own money and taken action to change from Cecil to Cece. No living person had a right to judge her for that choice.

"Do you know where Eve lives?" It was a start.

"No, she left the area after her folks put her out. I never knew what the disagreement was about, and by the time I learned what Will and Carla had done, Eve was long gone. She was only sixteen. I hunted for her, but I never found her. I guess she changed her name and started a new life. Now she's pregnant."

"That was how long ago?" Tammy asked.

"About four years." Cece paced the room. "I hate to dump this on you at Christmas, Sarah Booth, but can you help me?"

My friends would show up to help me even if hell was freezing over. "You know it. Tinkie and Oscar are in Memphis at a party. I'll get her on the case first thing tomorrow."

"And you won't tell Coleman?"

"I won't." My gut clenched because I knew the high consequences I might pay. I'd hidden things from Coleman in the past, and we'd vowed not to do that anymore. But Cece was my friend. She was asking me to do something that she felt was necessary. I was caught between a rock and a hard place. "When this is over and Eve is safely back, Coleman will understand why I made this choice." I said it with certainty, but it was more prayer than fact.

Footsteps coming across the porch told me the lawman had arrived for our rendezvous. He swept into the foyer on a wave of cold air and the smell of cut pine and wood smoke. I ran into his arms. "You smell like a camp out." I burrowed close and inhaled. Coleman's scent always contained a sliver of my childhood.

"Group of teenagers decided to start a bonfire at the Olson farm. Without permission." He took off his hat and shucked out of his heavy jacket. "Tammy, Cece, happy holidays. It's good to see you."

"We were just leaving," Tammy said. She was a worse liar than Cece, who was pretty awful. If Coleman asked what they were up to, they'd be hard-pressed not to tell the truth.

"See you at Harold's dinner," Cece said as she and Tammy rushed out the front door and closed it behind them.

"What are they up to?" Coleman eyed me. He knew suspicious behavior when he saw it.

"Oh, Cece has some bee up her bonnet and she's got Tammy involved. Every holiday those two have to stir something up."

Coleman went to the bar in the parlor and poured us both a Jack Daniel's on ice. "Jaytee is out of town, so Cece is at sixes and sevens."

"Yes." I'd learned not to add more detail when fibbing. Just to roll with the minimal lie.

"You're not going to tell me, are you?"

And when confronted with a chance to tell the truth, to jump on it. "No."

He pointed at the mistletoe I'd hung over the doorway arch. "Is that for me or some other man you're expecting?"

"Not telling that either." I slowly began to back away, but Coleman was quicker, and the truth was, I wanted to be caught. I melted into the heat of his kiss.

"Happy holidays," I said when he finally released me, breathless.

"I thought we were going to finish decorating the tree

tonight." He looked at the big cedar he'd put in the stand. We had the strings of multicolored lights installed. Now it was time for the three hundred or so ornaments that were the Delaney family treasures. They'd hung on every Christmas tree since Dahlia House was built, the current generation adding more and more ornaments. I thought briefly of Aunt Loulane and how she'd insisted on following the traditions my parents had set—even when I'd tried to stop her. At the time I hadn't realized what a kindness she was doing me. She kept up the chain of simple holiday traditions that connected me to my past. I owed her far more than I could ever say.

"Sarah Booth, are you okay?" Coleman brushed the hair from my face. "You look pensive."

"I'm very happy, Coleman. I just miss the things I lost so young."

"Your parents."

I nodded. "Yes."

"Let's finish the tree." He took my hand and led me into the parlor. In a few moments, he had me laughing as we hung the ornaments, each with a story. When we were finished, he pulled me against him. "Let's go to bed."

It was the promise of a night of sweet intimacy. "I second that motion."

I locked the front door, using the chain I'd installed after Tinkie's unexpected entrance had left both Coleman and me in an exposed and embarrassing situation. I needed no urging as I followed him to my bed and into his arms.

The next morning, I woke before Coleman and dream-walked to the kitchen, remembering some of the highlights of the previous evening. Coleman was a take-charge man, and he knew his business. When I'd first moved back to Zinnia, I'd almost climbed in the sack with him. He'd been married then, and thank goodness we'd sidestepped that situation. I'd learned that for Coleman, honor was imperative. He would never have forgiven himself, or me, if he'd broken his marriage vows to the wackadoodle Connie. His ex-wife had even faked a pregnancy in order to keep him. By the time Coleman had learned the truth about her, it was too late for us. My wounded heart had festered, and it took a lot of time to heal. Now I was ready.

Sweetie Pie came down the stairs behind me and plopped under the kitchen table. "Aunt Loulane always said that things happen when the time is right," I said to the dog, who gave a low, garbled little howl, and settled into a heap. She was snoring before her head touched the floor.

I put coffee on to perk and bacon to fry and then called my partner. Tinkie was an early riser, and she answered on the second ring. "We have a case. It involves Cece." I looked furtively around the kitchen as the bacon sizzled. "And we can't tell Coleman."

"I knew it. I just knew it." Tinkie was working up a head of steam. "I knew you couldn't keep your word about being honest with Coleman. You know this will blow up your relationship."

"Wait a minute—"

"No, you listen to me. Whatever secret you're keeping, you'd better tell him. I mean it."

"Come over. And keep your lips zipped if he's here." I hung up and sat down at the table. Tinkie sucked the energy out of me when she got in one of her moods.

No matter that I was annoyed, the smell of the frying bacon teased my appetite and I got out eggs and grits and bread for toasting. Nothing like a big breakfast on a cold December morning. Biscuits would be better than toast, but for some reason, whenever I stirred up a batch of cathead biscuits, they turned into hockey pucks. Safer to make toast.

The kitchen door swung open and Coleman, hair tousled, sat down at the table. "Something smells good."

I passed by him and paused long enough to kiss his cheek. "Breakfast fit for a king."

"You're in a good mood."

"How could I not be?" I felt a tiny flush as I remembered the past evening.

"I have to escort a prisoner to the Hinds County court today. I'll be gone until about four."

"Harold's party," I reminded him.

"Wouldn't dream of missing it. What's your plan for today?"

"Oh, not much. I'm sure I'll get into something with Tinkie." I forced a smile. The doorbell rang and I was, literally, saved by the bell. "That's probably Tinkie at the front door. I left the chain on this morning." I rushed out of the kitchen to let her in.

Tinkie stood on the porch in a gorgeous russet duster-type coat. She wore tall boots, tight jeans, and a beautiful forest green sweater. She looked like the colors of fall walking through my front door.

"Glad to see you learned to use a door lock." She breezed past me and went to the kitchen, where Coleman was stirring scrambled eggs on the stove. "Yum. I'm glad to see Sarah Booth finally got some competent kitchen help." She looked him up and down. "And help in other departments, too. She looks like you worked out a few of her kinks."

"Tinkie!" I exchanged a look with Coleman as the blood rushed to my cheeks.

"Oh, don't play innocent." She laughed. "You two have been lusting after each other for weeks. You know the old saying. 'If you got an itch, you just need to scratch it.'"

"There is no such saying." I had to get in front of this train wreck of a conversation. "What's Oscar getting you for Christmas?"

"He won't say. What's Coleman getting you?"

"I don't know." I was dying to find out, though. I loved presents. It was just the idea of a surprise that someone else picked out for me. My family had never been much for huge expensive gestures. We focused on intimate gifts with meaning.

"I hope it's more of what he gave you last night. You look more relaxed than I've seen you in days. But how in the world is he going to put a bow on that?"

Coleman had toasted some bread and he quickly made a bacon, egg, and cheese sandwich and filled a go cup with coffee. "I'm out of here. You women are too bawdy for a man of the law. I don't want to have to arrest Tinkie for lewd and lascivious behavior."

"Oh, you'd love that." Tinkie held out her hands. "Sarah Booth tells you her fantasies of handcuffs, doesn't she?"

"Tinkie!" I was going to gag her on the spot. "Give it a rest."

"Did you say arrest?" She almost cackled.

"I'll call later." Coleman took his coffee and his sandwich and beat a hasty retreat.

"You practically drove the poor man out into the cold morning without breakfast," I told her.

"Don't act so innocent. At least I'm not deceiving him like you are."

And she had me there. "Cece won't let me tell him and it involves her relative." I gave her the details of Eve's abduction. "Cece is afraid that if I tell Coleman, the kidnapper will know she brought in the law. She's afraid Eve will be hurt."

Tinkie's foolishness had evaporated. "This is serious," she said. "Cece has put you in a bad spot."

"And one I'll honor. She's my friend and has been for many years."

"And Coleman is your lover and the sheriff." Tinkie didn't mince any words.

"And he would do exactly what I'm doing—honor his word to his friend." That was one thing I knew about Coleman.

"Okay, so then what are we going to do?" Tinkie asked. "After we eat this sumptuous breakfast." She got a plate and began to help herself.

I followed suit and then we both sat at the table and ate. "We have to pay a visit to Carla and Will Falcon, Eve's parents. And then we'll find out where she lives, where she's working, and backtrack from there. We have to find out who knew enough about her to believe Cece would pay a ransom for her."

2

The farm where Will and Carla Falcon lived sprawled across forty acres of freshly turned land. Will farmed as a hobby, growing row crops that Carla put up and pickled and sold at local markets during the summer months. Will's primary job was as a data analyst for a financial company. He fit the stereotype to a tee. Nerdy glasses, inkblot on the pocket of his long-sleeved plaid shirt, rumpled khakis, and hair askew. Carla, who was thin and bitter, did all the talking.

"We haven't seen Eve in years. She has nothing to do with us. Whatever she's done is her own problem." Carla blocked the door like a ninety-pound woman of steel. "Go away."

When she tried to slam the door in Tinkie's and my face, I'd finally had enough. I grabbed the door and stepped into the entrance of the house. "We came to talk about Eve. She's been kidnapped and we're trying to help her."

"Kidnapped?" Carla looked completely blank, as if she'd never heard the word. "Who would take Eve? She's useless. Are they asking a ransom?" She snorted. "Good luck with that."

Standing beside me, Tinkie grew angrier and angrier. I could practically feel her swelling with fury. Any minute she was going to bust. And it would not be pretty.

"Do you know where Eve was living?" I pushed ahead with my questions.

"She dropped out of high school and took off. I heard she was in Memphis with a bunch of those horrid people wearing black clothes and piercing their lips and nipples." Carla was almost as angry as Tinkie. I was standing next to two time bombs.

"Do you have relatives in Memphis? Anyone she might have contacted?"

"No. She is the devil's spawn. As far as I'm concerned, whoever has her can keep her and good riddance."

"Ma'am, she is your daughter. Your *pregnant* daughter." Tinkie was standing on her tiptoes to get in Carla's face. I put a hand on her shoulder and felt coiled steel. She was ready to spring.

"What would you know about it?" Carla said. "She was a disappointment from the day she came into this house. She's a little slut with the morals of a cat in heat. Right, Will?"

Will was staring out the door as if he was listening and watching an entirely different scene unfolding. He didn't respond to Carla's question, but that didn't slow her down with her complaints against Eve. "We gave her every chance, and she blew every single one."

"Like Cece, she's just a terrible disappointment to your family?" Tinkie's fists were clenched. I was prepared to tackle her if she took a swing. "You judge people harshly, but can you stand up to such rigorous scrutiny?"

"I obey God. I fear no man's judgment because I will be judged by the Lord himself, and he will find me righteous."

"But not very loving," Tinkie said.

I had to get my partner out of there before she did something that would land her in the hoosegow. And likely sued for a ton of money.

"You get out of my house." Carla pointed at the door, her bony little finger shaking. "Out!"

"Gladly," Tinkie said, marching out the door and down the steps so fast I had to run to catch up with her. Will followed me outside.

"We'll check in at Memphis. See if we can pick up her trail."

"She was good with numbers," Will said. "And smart. Eve is smart. She'd be a good bookkeeper or maybe—"

Before he could finish, Carla screamed for him to come back inside. As soon as he cleared the jamb, Carla slammed the door.

Tinkie spun like a dervish. Digging into her purse, she pulled out a long, wicked nail file. Before I knew what was happening, she ran across the yard to the Falcons' nice new car and began to stab the front tire with her nail file. "Take that!" She stabbed as hard as she could.

I got to her in time to pull her back before she punctured the tire. I didn't think it was possible with a nail file anyway, but I didn't want to take any chances of having her arrested for destruction of property.

"I should have stabbed her in the throat!"

I couldn't argue that, but I also had to calm Tinkie down. "Look, let's find Eve and then worry about beating up Carla Falcon."

"You promise we can beat her up?"

I considered. "Yeah. I promise. I'll help." In the months of our work as detectives, our roles had slightly reversed. Normally I was the emotional one, and Tinkie was the responsible, calm, ladylike partner. Now she was almost frothing at the mouth.

I managed to get Tinkie in my car. While I drove, Tinkie put her phone on speaker and called Cece. "Carla is a piece of work," Tinkie said. "What kind of job do you think Eve might have taken?"

"She was good with numbers." Cece confirmed what Will Falcon said.

"Call the big accounting firms and the banks in Memphis, please," I requested. Cece had a computer and a phone at her desk at the *Zinnia Dispatch*. "It's like a needle in a haystack but if we can find where she worked, we'll have a hot trail, I hope. Carla and Will were useless."

"Worse than useless I suspect," Cece said. "Will has no backbone and Carla has no heart. Anyway, I talked with Zeedie Adams, one of Eve's childhood friends. She said Eve had gotten her GED and had gone into banking. She worked as a loan officer at a branch of the Bank of the Deep South in Cleveland, Mississippi."

"Thanks." That was a big help. "Did Zeedie know anything else?"

"No," Cece said. "They haven't spoken in a while. She

ran across Eve in Memphis, where Eve was training at the bank and going to night classes."

"Then Zeedie doesn't have a clue who the baby's father might be?" Tinkie asked.

"No."

"Thanks, Cece." Tinkie hung up and when we came to a juncture of two county roads, I took a left to head for Cleveland. It was as good a place as any to start looking.

"I didn't ask Cece about the ransom money," Tinkie said. "Oscar has agreed to give her as much as she needs, but I didn't want to put her on the spot."

I reached across the seat and patted Tinkie's shoulder. "You and Oscar are the most generous and kind friends."

"You would do the same."

I had to chuckle at that. I lived on a month-to-month basis of paying house repairs, taxes, and bills. It would be a miracle if I ever had ten grand I could give away, much less more than a hundred thousand. "Hopefully we'll figure out who has Eve and rescue her without having to give them a dime. Their payoff will be a long prison term."

We rode through the flat Delta in silence for a while, passing wrought-iron archways to plantations decorated with magnolia and cedar garlands, colored lights, and in a few instances the blow-up Christmas characters that Tinkie loathed. She called them cartoon Christmas.

"They're an example of what's wrong with our society. Folks buy some crappy decoration at the store and stick it in the yard and think that's a good thing. Decorating is supposed to be family and friends gathering, good times, making memories. What kind of a memory can you make by taking two minutes to stick a bloated, ugly Santa on the grass and turn on something to fill him with air?"

I couldn't—and wouldn't—argue with her. I preferred tradition to convenience myself.

"Those ugly things are almost as bad as people who keep their outdoor Christmas lights up year-round. There are just certain holiday things that a Daddy's Girl cannot stoop to do."

"Toss the DG rule book at them, Tinkie." I wasn't kidding, though I was teasing her.

We arrived at our destination to find that Cleveland had a city tree on the verge at the entrance to town. An old-fashioned tree. I loved the colorful ornaments and baubles that had been used to adorn it. In fact, I loved the holiday season, and this year, I had very warm thoughts of Coleman Peters. The mistletoe had been a wonderful jump-start to a fine holiday tradition that we'd started on our own.

"Thinking of Coleman, are you?" Tinkie asked. She was watching me closely.

"Of course not."

"Liar!" Tinkie smiled at last. She was over her fury at the Falcons and low-class decorators.

"Okay, so yeah. I was thinking about where I might attach a bow to—"

"TMI!" She held up a hand. "I don't want to know what you do with bows or handcuffs or anything else."

"Oh, so now you're too delicate to get the details you're always clamoring for."

"I'd rather tease Coleman. He's an easier target. He gets all red in the face and flustered."

"He does." I had to laugh with her. For two grown-ups, we acted like high school kids caught kissing under the bleachers.

"It's good to see you happy, Sarah Booth." Tinkie had grown suddenly serious.

"I am happy." It was something of a revelation I realized as I pulled into the bank parking lot.

"I know it's hard to trust in happiness." Tinkie waited for me to stop the car. "You've lost so many people that you loved. Your parents, Aunt Loulane, even Graf, though he's still alive. It's hard to trust that happiness will stay, but Coleman won't abandon you."

The truth of her words was an arrow in my heart. I hadn't consciously worried about Coleman "leaving," but it was there, burrowed deep in my subconscious. What if something happened to Coleman? I couldn't take another loss. Tinkie saw it long before I did.

"There are no guarantees, Sarah Booth. I remember the Christmas we were in ninth grade and you had a crush on Bobbie Ladd. You wouldn't even admit it to yourself. Your aunt Loulane tried to talk to you, but you shut her down. She said something that day that stuck with me."

"What?" I had to ask around a lump in my throat.

"Remember she made us cocoa with the green and red Christmas marshmallows in it and we were sitting in the parlor looking at the beautiful tree that her beau had cut and brought in."

I remembered that tree and the day very well. I'd worn my favorite red-and-white-candy-cane-striped sweater to school. Bobbie's friends had teased me about what those horizontal stripes accented. I'd been mortified, but they were only teasing me to get a rise. I could almost smell the gingerbread cookies Aunt Loulane had baked and put on a plate for us to have with our cocoa. And I knew a few things about Tinkie, too. "You'd just kissed Frank Basco. It was all over school."

"Yes." Tinkie laughed. "I thought I was very brazen. We both had braces so we were afraid to do more than touch our lips together, but we said it was a passionate kiss."

"What did Aunt Loulane say?" I wanted to hear her say it.

"She said that you could go the rest of your life afraid to love anyone, or you could be brave and hurl yourself at love. I remember those exact words. 'Hurl yourself at love.'" She sighed. "She's right, Sarah Booth. That's what you have to do. Hurl yourself. Don't hold back. Just leap at it with all the faith you can muster."

A tear slipped down my left check, but I brushed it away before Tinkie could see it. The holidays made me sentimental. "Aunt Loulane had a marriage proposal that she didn't accept so she could take care of me. She didn't want to uproot me from Dahlia House."

"She was a remarkable woman. And she knew every wise old saying that had ever been created."

"And didn't hold back with any of them." We both laughed and I opened the car door. "Let's find Eve."

Allspice candles burned in a lovely floral display in the bank's lobby and the scent of Christmas wafted out to us as we walked through the front door. A young male teller was open, and we went to Danny Clay's station. I noted the heavy name holder that told folks who he was.

"Hi, we're looking for Eve Falcon," I said.

"You and everyone in the bank. She hasn't shown up for work for the past three days."

That wasn't what I wanted to hear. "Is she sick?"

He shrugged. "Who knows."

"You don't seem too worried," Tinkie said.

"Eve is the golden girl. She can do whatever she wants and never gets in trouble. So, she doesn't come to work. Who cares? She'll still get the next promotion."

"Check your teeth," Tinkie said. "There are fragments of sour grapes caught in them."

I laughed. I couldn't help it. Which only made Danny Clay angrier. "Maybe she's off with the boss. They seem to need a lot of time together."

Now he was making a serious accusation. "Danny, are you saying that Eve and the bank president are having an affair?"

When I put it in bald terms, he backed down. "They're mighty chummy, and Eve gets all the promotions. I have a bachelor's degree in banking, and guess who gets promoted to loan officer. The girl with a GED and the nice rack. Not to mention that she's incubating someone's bastard."

Danny Clay was an insecure and bitter young man. "I see that you feel left behind. Could it be because you're an asshat?" Tinkie asked.

His only response was a glare.

"Danny, I need to know. Do you know for a fact that Eve and the bank president are involved? Or are you just spreading rumors?"

"I don't have proof, but everyone knows. Ask the other tellers." He waved at several women who'd overheard the conversation. They all turned and edged away.

They were not nearly the fool Danny Clay appeared to be.

I glanced at the big door to a private office. FREDDY TEDDY BELVUE was the name on the door. Whoever had christened the bank president had a cruel sense of humor. "Where is Mr. Belvue?" I asked.

"Playing golf. Where he is every single morning of every workday."

Danny was carrying a bucket load of spleen. "I'm going to ask him if he's having an affair with Eve, and I'm going to say you told me it was true."

"Like I care." He stood up from his stool. "I've had it with this place. Eve sleeps her way to the top and I get in trouble for pointing it out."

"You'll get sued for slander if what you're saying isn't true."

He leaned into the window. "Eve was a little slut when she trained at the Memphis bank. We were hired at the same time. She got off at three so she could take her GED classes. I was going to college, and I couldn't catch a break on scheduling. It took me six years to get through school because of it. She only had to bat her eyelashes and she got an amended schedule. And then when she showed up pregnant and unmarried, no one said a thing. How is that right?"

"Maybe she does a better job than you do," I said softly. "And maybe she doesn't whine all the time."

"Right. Well you should try being a white male in the banking business."

"Oh my god," Tinkie said, putting the back of her hand to her forehead. "I am going to swoon. Poor, poor you." She brightened. "I have it. You should try stand-up comedy. Instead of the blue-collar comedy act, you could be the entitled white male privilege comedy act."

"Tinkie!" I needed a muzzle for my partner. This case had her wound up and she wasn't holding back.

"Maybe if I slept with the boss, I'd get the advantages, too," Danny said. "Even better, if I got pregnant and then could blackmail my way to a promotion, I'd be on Easy Street."

I looked past Danny out the bank window and saw a Jaguar tearing out of the parking lot. While Danny Dufus had been diverting our attention, the bank president had made a clean get-away. He'd been in the bank all along.

"Dammit." Now I wanted to punch the teller as bad as Tinkie did. "Let's go."

We left the bank and were getting into the car when the bank's back door opened and a young woman ran over to us.

"Eve wasn't like that. Not what Danny was saying. He hates her because she's smart and works hard. She wasn't sleeping her way into promotions."

"And you are?" I asked.

"Dawn Hasiotis. Eve and I are friends."

"Do you know who the father of her child is?" I asked.

She shook her head. "Eve was already pregnant when she moved down here from Memphis. I got the impression it was one reason she left the Memphis area. She's never mentioned anyone she was romantically involved with. I was concerned that maybe she was . . . raped or something."

"She isn't involved with Freddy Teddy Belvue?" Tinkie asked.

Dawn looked at the parking lot. "I don't know anything for a fact, but she isn't that kind of person. Life happens to people. Especially people like us, who don't have family or resources to fall back on. Eve's been on her own since she was sixteen. Me since I was seventeen. Things don't ever come easy to someone without an education and with no safety net."

"I can understand that," Tinkie said. "Thanks for talking to us."

"Mr. Belvue is probably playing golf. He comes in every morning and leaves. You know, so much business is done on the golf course." Her sarcasm made me smile.

"So I've heard."

"I'm worried about Eve," she said. "She always comes to work. She's reliable. And when she didn't show up and didn't call, I knew something was wrong. Has something terrible happened to her?"

"We only know she's missing," I said. "Her cousin hired us to find her. So if you see her, give us a call." I handed her one of the nifty business cards Tinkie had printed for Delaney Detective Agency.

"She'd be at work if she could," Dawn said, her eyes misting over. "She's responsible like that." She glanced at the door. "I have to go. My break is over." She took off jogging across the parking lot and disappeared into the bank.

"It's clear Eve has one enemy here at the bank," I said.

"I suppose Danny Clay is on the suspect list, but he's such a loudmouth. And not all that bright," Tinkie said. "He's the type who blames everyone because he isn't top dog."

We got in the car and I turned the heater up to full blast. It was a cold day even though the sun was shining.

Clouds were building to the north, and the weather forecasters were gleeful at the 20 percent chance of a white Christmas for the Delta. It would take a miracle to get Christmas snow in upper Mississippi, but the thought was tantalizing.

"The best golf course is at The Club. Let's see if we can run Teddy Freddy Belvue to ground there."

"Good idea, but it's Freddy Teddy. His name is Frederick Theodore," Tinkie said. "We can grab lunch if you want."

My answer was the loud rumble of a hungry stomach and an eye roll at the man's name.

Tinkie and Oscar were premium members of The Club, and as such Tinkie easily sweet-talked the manager into loaning us a golf cart. We set out around the course to track down Belvue. His Jag was in the parking lot, so we knew he had to be on the links.

Tinkie had looked up Belvue on the internet so we could recognize him, and we found him at the third hole. He was playing with another man. Tinkie stopped the golf cart thirty yards back so as not to interfere as they teed off, and then we hurried to catch up with him before he started chasing his ball that had gone into the rough.

"I'm in the middle of a game," he said as soon as he saw us. "Mrs. Richmond, I know you know better."

So he knew Tinkie. That was telling. "And we're in the middle of a case that involves one of your employees. Eve Falcon is missing."

"Eve? Missing? How so?" He put the head of his club on the ground and leaned on it.

"Her family is looking for her and she can't be found."

"Have you checked hospitals? She was about to give birth."

"We have," I said.

"That's what I know. Sorry I couldn't be more helpful." He got into the cart and motioned for his golfing partner to pull away.

"Mr. Belvue, are you the father of Eve's baby?" I had to stop him, and it worked. He got out of the cart and came toward me, still holding a club.

"What are you saying?"

"Are you sexually involved with Eve Falcon?"

"I will have you in court on slander charges. How dare you accuse me of such a thing! I do not sleep with my employees."

Righteous indignation mixed with an inability to meet my gaze told me Freddy Teddy Belvue was a liar, and not a very good one. I'd be willing to bet he was sleeping with someone who answered to him.

"If you're involved with Eve, just say so." Tinkie had picked up on his deception, too.

"I don't have to answer to you. Get off this golf course. You aren't playing. You're violating The Club's rules, and you know better, Mrs. Richmond." He ignored me.

"I haven't violated any rules."

"I'm going to report you to your husband."

Oh, boy, that was a bad misstep on Freddy Teddy's part. Tinkie didn't cotton to being treated as Oscar's property.

"You can tell Oscar whatever you desire. And I'll make a call to the Institute of Certified Bankers and the American Bankers Association. I think they'd love to hear about what's happening at the Bank of the Deep South in Cleveland, Mississippi."

Tinkie had pulled out the big guns.

Freddy Teddy slid his cell phone out of his pocket and dialed. "We have vandals on the golf course at the third hole. Please send security to escort them off the property."

Tinkie signaled me into the golf cart, and before I could say anything, we were flying across the green. "Oscar will kill me if I make a scene at The Club." She was driving that electric cart like a NASCAR entry.

"A little late in the game for that concern."

"If we don't get caught, we don't pay the penalty."

And she was right about that. I had a little truth, too. "They can't catch us if we're dead." I grabbed hold of the sidebar and hung on for dear life.

When we screeched into the cart barn at the country club, Tinkie barely let the buggy stop before she was out and running toward Belvue's Jag in the parking lot. I'd never seen anyone with such short legs run so fast wearing high-heel boots. It brought to mind a fact I'd learned about alligators—they could run sixty miles per hour on six-inch legs for a short distance. I pursued Tinkie for all I was worth.

I caught her just as she pulled out her nail file and went after the tires on the Jaguar.

"Stop it! Now!" I pulled her to her feet. "What is wrong with you?" I took the file from her and put it in my back pocket. "You've been irrational all day today. What the heck, Tinkie?"

"I'm completely rational. I'm just sick of mean, bullying people."

"You cannot slash their car tires. Especially not with a nail file. It won't work."

"Sugar in the gas tank? I could get some packets from The Club."

"No. No property damage. I'm serious. And no, you can't physically attack Belvue. You know this; why are you acting like you don't?"

"I've had every privilege that a white female can have. The best schools, the best clothes, the best extracurricular activities. I was loved and coddled. The only thing that could have been better would have been to be a boy. Then I would have owned the world."

"You've been really lucky, Tinkie."

"I have and I know it. But people like Freddy Teddy Belvue have had all the advantages, and they aren't even aware. It pisses me off. I was thinking about what Dawn the bank teller said. And I was thinking about what Eve has surely confronted as a single woman trying to hold down her job, advance her career, and have a baby. That little prick Danny Clay believes he's entitled to the promotion Eve got simply because he's a man. Qualifications be damned. With all of my advantages I don't know that I could manage what Eve has on her plate. And she had none of my good fortune. It just makes me really mad."

Tinkie was a champion of the underdog and, speaking of dogs, we needed to head back to Zinnia and check on Sweetie Pie and Tinkie's little Yorkie, Chablis. All of the animals got along fine, but Pluto the cat was big enough to eat Chablis.

I steered her toward my car and I just about had her seated when someone tapped my shoulder. I turned to confront a man I couldn't place but knew.

"Ms. Delaney," he said, "Mrs. Richmond. Could I buy you ladies a holiday poinsettia?"

"No, thank you. Poinsettias are poisonous to cats."

He laughed and Tinkie joined him. "We'd love a drink, Cameron. He's offering us an adult holiday beverage. Sarah Booth, this is Cameron Phillips. He's one of the vice presidents at the bank."

I placed him as soon as I heard his name. "Thanks, Mr. Phillips."

Tinkie took the arm he offered and fell into step with him. "I'm assuming you saw my little tantrum in the parking lot and that you'll be discreet?"

"Of course. I happen to know Freddy Teddy Belvue, and I've wanted to slash his tires a number of times."

We were already in the stewpot. Might as well have a libation. I dropped in behind them and headed into The Club. I'd wanted to see the Christmas decorations. Cece had done a spread on them in the newspaper.

We walked into The Club and I stopped. The place was beautiful. They'd opted to decorate as an old-fashioned Christmas and had pulled out the stops with a lovely tree, hand-strung popcorn and cranberry garlands, and antique Christmas toys, from dolls to a sled and old cruiser bicycles. It was an instant taste of my past.

"This is wonderful."

"It is," Tinkie said. "The theme was Oscar's idea. Sometimes that man surprises even me."

When we were seated and on our second poinsettia—champagne and cranberry juice—Cameron leaned forward. "What has that moron Freddy Teddy Belvue done now?"

"Nothing we can prove," Tinkie wisely answered. "What's his reputation with female employees?"

"That he likes them. A lot."

I wondered why Cameron was so free with his gossip. Bankers, like doctors and lawyers, often stuck together.

"Belvue screwed me out of a business deal last year that I'd worked on for months. It was a big project for the bank, and he lied and snatched it out from under me and Oscar. I'd like to get a little payback if I can."

Ah, revenge. Always a great motive. "Is there a specific girl you can point us to?" I asked. We needed exact details, not gossip.

"In fact, there is." He pulled out a checkbook and tore off half a check to write down a name. "Jodie O'Neill. She lives in Greenville now. I think she's working at a local credit union. She'll tell you the truth."

"Thanks, Cameron." Tinkie gave him a big smile. "Thanks a lot. I'll be sure and tell Oscar I ran into you."

"Just so you know, Oscar is not a fan of Freddy Teddy." Cameron grinned. "He accused Oscar of marrying the boss's daughter just to get ahead. There's plenty of bad blood there."

"Thank you, Cameron." I wasn't sure I really thanked him for that because now Tinkie was really out for blood. "You have a good holiday." I maneuvered Tinkie out of The Club and into the parking lot. "Drat, I left my cell phone at his table. I'll be right back."

I rushed inside and picked up my phone, thanking Cameron for the drinks again as I left. When I got back to the parking lot, Tinkie was gone. I looked around and finally heard a strange huffing sound, like someone who needed the Heimlich maneuver in a bad way. I followed the sound around three cars and found Tinkie on her knees, stabbing the tires on Belvue's Jag with her nail file. She'd somehow managed to pick it out of my pocket without me even suspecting. She was giving it everything she had, but the thin file couldn't puncture the rubber. I pulled her to her feet.

"Stop that. It won't work and you look silly."

"Belvue is a bastard."

"Yep." I pointed to my car. "He is. Let's go."

"What if he impregnated Cece's cousin?"

"Then he'll pay child support until the baby is twenty-one." I had to be practical or Tinkie would really lose her temper.

"What if Eve and the baby are dead?"

I stopped. "We can't think like that. We have to find that girl and her infant. And we have to do it now. We don't have time to poke at car tires. We've got serious work to do. Cece is counting on us."

Tinkie nodded. "You're right. Let's find Eve."

3

We hit Greenville just in time for hot tamales at Doe's Eat Place. The former grocery and honky-tonk, now a famous eatery, was highly lauded for the best steaks in the region. The restaurant business had grown out of a tamale recipe Mamie Doe had found and added her own special touch to. And I loved them. Tinkie was no slacker in the tamale-eating department.

While Elvis, B.B. King, Ella, and other blues greats sang holiday songs, we chowed down. All around us was the ebb and flow of Greenville residents. Eating and listening, we caught tidbits of conversations that could have been held anywhere in the Delta. Talk about the river, traffic, crops, weather. At one time Greenville had been a jewel in the crown of the Delta, but the city had fallen onto hard economic times. Still, the people who ate at Doe's held on to their spirits.

A table of young women on their lunch hour provided the opportunity I was looking for, and I stepped over to the table and asked if they knew Jodie O'Neill.

"Sure. I know Jodie," a pretty blonde said. "Why are you looking for her?"

"She may be able to help me find a young woman who's missing." I pulled out one of the new business cards. "We're private investigators and we're looking for Eve Falcon. Her cousin is worried about her. Eve is due to give birth any minute now."

"Jodie had a baby a year ago." The blonde considered me. "Let me give Jodie a call. If she says it's okay, I'll give you her address."

"Good enough."

I went back and filled Tinkie in on what I'd done, and in a moment the young woman came to our table with a slip of paper. "Jodie says she'll help you. She knew Eve a little. They had some training sessions at the Memphis bank together."

"Thanks." I took the address, and Tinkie and I paid the tab and left. Thirty minutes later I was pulling up in front of a clapboard house set on a slight rise not far from the river. Aunt Loulane had told me stories about the Mound Landing levee breach in 1927, when the Mississippi River had poured into the Delta and submerged part of Greenville. In the end, over two million acres were flooded and the water rose so high in the lowest portions of the city that some homes and businesses were completely underwater. The crevasse in the levee poured water for months, and numerous residents had been rescued while clinging to treetops and whatever else they could grab hold of. Until recent hurricanes, the Mississippi River Flood of 1927 was considered to be the nation's worst natural disaster.

Now Greenville suffered from an economic drought, not a river flood. Tinkie and I parked and went to the front door, where a pretty young woman met us with a toddler on her hip. "What happened to Eve?" she asked, pushing the door open for us to enter. She wasn't wary of us in the least.

"She's missing. Her cousin is trying to find her." We stepped into a neat house where clean clothes were folded and stacked on the sofa and baby toys were scattered about a scrubbed floor. In a corner of the living room was a small fir tree decorated with lights, ornaments, and tinsel. Christmas memories flooded me once again.

"Excuse the mess. I'm home today with the baby. She's teething, and I'm trying to catch up on chores. Eve's due to have that baby," Jodie said. "Her due date is Christmas Eve. I remember because we laughed about Eve and Eve."

It was good to know Jodie was friends with Eve. Perhaps she could tell us something that would help us find the girl. "Do you have any idea where she might be? Who her friends were? Was there anyone who might wish her harm?"

"Harm?" She was quick on the uptake. "Is there a reason to suspect she's been harmed?"

"Please tell us what you know," Tinkie said gently. "We just want to find her. Cece Falcon is very worried about her."

"She mentioned her cousin Cece." Jodie nodded. "They were close once. But Eve isn't close to anyone in her family as far as I know. Her parents are kooks."

"Yes, I agree." I gave Tinkie the stink eye to keep her from going off on Carla. I knew she wanted to—because I did, too—but it wouldn't serve us well. "Any friends or enemies? If she's picked up and moved, we just want to know she's safe."

"I haven't talked to Eve in the last three months." Jodie was rueful. "I haven't been a good friend, I fear. It's just so hard trying to manage my baby and work full time, go to school in the evenings. I stay on the verge of exhaustion. I haven't seen any of my friends unless they stop by here after work for a cup of coffee."

"How did you meet Eve?" I asked.

"We both had training sessions at the bank in Memphis. I was surprised when Eve said she was moving to Cleveland." Her brows drew together. "She knew what had happened to me. I'd already left the Cleveland branch by then." She looked at her baby, who was sleeping in her arms. "I wouldn't trade anything for my baby, but I hadn't expected to be pregnant and single. Freddy said he would leave his wife and marry me. I was a fool."

"Belvue is the father?" I felt compassion for her.

"Yes, Freddy promised me the moon, and all I got was ashes." She scoffed. "I was a kid and I believed every lie he told. He was this rich guy who drove a fancy car and took me to Memphis to fancy restaurants. He completely turned my head. I should have known better. I was raised better. My mama almost died of shame when I got pregnant. To this day she doesn't know little Brie's daddy was a married man. I can't ever let her know about Freddy Belvue." She put a hand over her eyes. "I'm just ashamed of myself."

Tinkie put a hand on her shoulder. "Everybody walking has made mistakes. You have a beautiful baby girl. You love her. That's all that matters."

"Thank you." Jodie straightened her posture. "But that doesn't help you with Eve and where she might be."

"Is it possible that Belvue is the father of Eve's child?" I asked.

She looked at Brie and her face softened. "I don't know. Eve never said. She was pregnant before she moved to Cleveland, but she could have met Freddy at a training session and gotten involved." She blew air out of her mouth in a sound of disgust. "He's slick when it comes to unsophisticated young girls. Especially girls who want to be loved."

"He hasn't hassled you about visitation with Brie?" I asked.

"Are you kidding? He signed over full custody—as long as I said I would never tell her he was her father and I would not attempt to gain anything financially from him."

"Wow." He was pretty damn cold.

"There's always a price," Tinkie said, and I knew she had an ultimate revenge plan cooking on the back burner of her brain. Freddy Teddy Belvue had made one solid enemy.

"Did Belvue threaten you to make you leave Cleveland and the bank?"

"No." She didn't hesitate. "Not in so many words. There was talk, and his wife came by the bank one day. She made it a point to come to my window. She remarked on my pregnancy and asked who my husband was. She said that a lot of women died in childbirth in the Delta. It was pretty clear she'd bump me off if she could."

"Very interesting." I made a note of Mrs. Belvue. I hadn't considered a jealous wife.

"Freddy has been coming around the credit union here for business meetings. I work in the back—I'm not a teller anymore. He pretends he doesn't know me."

"Class act," Tinkie said.

"It's fine with me. Brie and I don't need him. I'm terrified he'll change his mind and try to interject himself into Brie's life."

"But he signed papers, right?"

She laughed. "Sure. Like that would stop him. He's got money and lawyers and everything else. His name is on the birth certificate, if anyone really wanted to look. His wife knows. She made that clear." She shrugged. "Brie and I just want to live our life here, to work at the credit union and advance if we can. She'll be grown and off to college in a flash. She won't make the same mistakes I made."

"That's every parent's hope," I said softly.

"Did Eve ever mention anyone following her or watching her?" Tinkie asked.

"Now that you bring it up, when she first moved to Cleveland, we talked on the phone a couple of times. She said there was a young man. She saw him several times outside the bank, across the road at the farm supply place. Just parked there. Watching the bank."

"Was she afraid of him?" I asked.

"I don't know." She rubbed under one eye with a finger. "I wasn't a good friend. Not like I should have been. I didn't want to talk to anyone who worked at the bank in Cleveland because of Freddy. I didn't return her calls. We sort of drifted apart. I sure hope she's okay."

"We do, too." Tinkie patted her shoulder awkwardly. "Thanks for your help. If you think of anything . . ."

"I'll give you a call." Jodie pointed to the card. "Find Eve and her baby. They have to be okay."

Mrs. Belvue was a lead we had to pursue, and we had time. It seemed we'd driven in a triangle around the Delta. We cut back to the highway that would take us north of Cleveland to the address for Ricky Belvue. Tinkie had found the location by calling Harold at the bank. It was almost more than I could stand. Freddy Teddy and Ricky Belvue. Surely they'd violated some law of "Y" abuse. No two people should corner the market on Y's.

The Belvue house was on the highway that led to Zinnia and Cleveland, and we turned down the long drive bordered by crepe myrtles and hydrangeas. In the spring and summer, it would be gorgeous. Winter's look was barren, though. The house was a boxy Tudor that reminded me of New England instead of Mississippi. It was very upright and plain. "Is Ricky Belvue from around here?" I asked.

"She grew up in the Delta, but she went to Paris to attend fashion school. As far as I know she never worked in fashion. She married Freddy Teddy and joined all the social clubs. She's active in a lot of them."

"Do you know her?"

"Not really. We've attended some of the same functions, being banker's wives, but she's not my cup of tea."

Which meant Tinkie hated her guts. This day was just getting worse and worse.

A maid came to the door when we knocked, and I

took the lead, presenting our business card on the little silver platter the maid held out for our calling card. Where was Charlotte Brontë when I needed her? Maybe I should add Lady Sarah Booth or Her Royal Highness Tinkie to the cards. This calling-card silver platter was pretty pretentious stuff for the Mississippi Delta.

"Madam will see you," the maid said when she returned to motion us to follow her.

We landed in a lovely morning room with pastel wallpaper and wicker furniture. Ricky Belvue was seated at a small rolltop desk, working in a journal. "Hello, Tinkie. And you must be Sarah Booth Delaney." She dismissed me with a flick of her hand. "Make it quick. I'm taking notes on my life," she said. "It's going to be a bestseller. I've done everything a refined woman could ever dream of."

"And probably a lot more," Tinkie said under her breath.

"What?" Ricky asked.

"Nothing." I stepped between them. "You know Tinkie and now you've met me. We have some questions about some bank employees."

"Make an appointment with Freddy Teddy," she said, flicking that royal hand again like she could make us vanish. "He manages the staff and servants. It isn't a proper job for a lady."

I did want to bop her in the nose. Hard. It was remarkable in this day and time that an educated woman would cling to such conventions. Fitting for a lady. Oh, I knew some feminists who would thrash her. "We'd rather talk to you," I said. "We've heard that Freddy Teddy has been . . . too familiar with some of his young female employees." I raised a hand to shut her up. "There are ethics violations here. I'm perfectly willing to press this matter. If I have to."

"What do you want?" she asked, dropping all pretensions of the grand lady.

"Eve Falcon is missing. She's due to give birth Christmas Eve. Is your husband the baby's father?"

"Absolutely not."

Tinkie laughed, and it was not the soft, bell-like sound she normally made. "How can you be so sure?"

"I know Eve and I know my husband. Eve intimidates him with her intelligence." Ricky was blunt.

"You're saying he's innocent not because he wouldn't cheat, but because he wouldn't cheat with a smart woman?" Tinkie was mildly amused.

Ricky sighed. "You've had more than a thirty-second conversation with my husband? Not the brightest lamp on the street. Eve was pregnant when Freddy Teddy hired her. I told him to give her the job. She's smart. Smarter than he is, you're right about that. She's an asset to the bank and she keeps the other young tellers in line. She knows Freddy Teddy is a fool. And she knows that if she keeps him on the straight and narrow, I'll see that she is rewarded. Eve and I have an agreeable arrangement."

I hadn't seen that one coming. Eve had found a place at the bank and as an extension of the Belvue household. She was the wife's surrogate in keeping Belvue in line. My estimation of Ricky rose. She'd chosen her path and she'd also figured out how to make the best of it. Her intelligence also made her a suspect, despite her warm praise of Eve. "Do you know where Eve is?"

Ricky shook her head. "I don't know, and that's the truth. I've been looking for her myself. We were supposed to meet three evenings ago. I give Eve a little bonus every month or so for her help. I had cash for her, but she never showed. They said she failed to go in for work that day."

"She's been missing three days," I said. It was looking dire. A million things could go wrong with a pregnant woman due to give birth at any minute.

"Do you know of any reason Eve would voluntarily leave the area?"

"She had everything arranged for the baby's arrival. I don't." She swallowed. "Do you think the baby's father is involved?"

"We don't know," I answered, "but we're going to find out."

"I'm worried about Eve," Ricky admitted. "Freddy Teddy says she's just laying low, hoping to trick the baby's daddy into stepping forward. That makes no sense." She stood up. "You girls want some coffee or a drink?"

"No thanks," Tinkie said. "We're in a hurry. But thank you."

"Listen, when you find Eve would you give me a call?" She rang a bell and the maid arrived with another little silver tray with *her* calling card on it, including a phone number.

"Sure." Tinkie took the card. "And please call us if you hear from her. Her cousin is very worried."

"I'm not going to mention to my husband that you dropped by. He's made his mistakes in the past. I know about that young woman and baby in Greenville. I think Freddy Teddy will do the right thing . . . eventually. But you can't force him into a corner. I've tried that."

"Do you have any children?" Tinkie asked, and I admired her sudden perception of the situation.

"No. I can't have children. Freddy Teddy doesn't want

any. We travel a lot. He plays golf. He has the life of a privileged sixteen-year-old, playing games and doing exactly what he wants. His saving grace is that he's good at running the bank. The employees don't like him, but he has a talent for hiring women with good sense. Eve was one of them. And Jodie before her. With a smart woman at the helm, he was free to be that irresponsible boy."

We rose. It was time to go. She stood also, but it was the maid who walked us to the door and let us out.

"I wonder who really hired Eve and Jodie?" Tinkie asked as we pulled onto the highway. "I don't think it was Freddy Teddy."

"You think it was Ricky?"

"I do."

"I tend to agree with you. Iron fist in a velvet glove."

"And she likes the perks of her husband's job." Tinkie leaned back into the seat as I drove. "Do you think Eve is alive?"

"I do. The only lead we have right now is the young man who was watching her from the hardware store. We can go there and ask around."

"It's not a very substantial lead." Tinkie was nobody's fool. We were whistling past the cemetery.

"Chew the bone you've got," I said. It was an old law-enforcement saying. The truth was, we didn't have another bone. "Cleveland is only twelve miles down the road."

"Hit it." Tinkie pushed her sunglasses more firmly into place and leaned her head back.

I turned on the radio to a blues station and rode into Cleveland on the joy and sadness of Billie Holiday.

The bank was just where we left it, across the street

from the local farm supply store. My old antique convertible was pretty conspicuous—but so would Tinkie's new Caddy have been. I pulled around the building and we got out and sauntered inside.

I love old farm supply stores. I'm a regular customer at the Sunflower County Seed and Feed. I like the smell of the horse and cattle feed, and in the spring there are baby chicks, which I always worried about. They seem so fragile and frisky and helpless. The Cleveland feed store was no exception. I wandered through the aisles looking at gardening tools and weed killers, fertilizers and salt blocks. I kept one eye out on the parking lot, hoping against hope that our stalker would appear.

Tinkie had fallen into conversation with the clerk behind the counter, and they were laughing at some joke she'd shared. The clerk was an older man and it was clear he was smitten with her, in the most gentlemanly fashion. She used her feminine wiles to ask him questions that he didn't know he was answering, but it was also genuine from Tinkie's perspective. She liked men. She enjoyed their weaknesses and their strengths, and while she knew how to play one like a fine fiddle, she was never careless or cruel. It was a craft she'd been taught in the cradle. The art of being a Daddy's Girl, a woman who could bend a man to her whims and fancy and make him think it was his idea.

Long ago, I'd been contemptuous of such manipulations. I was an older and wiser woman now. Why battle with a man to prove a point? Sometimes you *could* catch more flies with sugar than vinegar, as Aunt Loulane used to say. Tinkie, with her sweet laugh and flashing blue eyes, was bringing in a swarm of flies.

I ambled a little closer to the conversation and learned

that the store owner had seen a young man watching the bank. He gave a pretty good description of a dark-haired, slender man in his early twenties. He'd applied for work at the farm supply store and Mr. Melton, the owner, was thinking of hiring him if he showed up again.

"Didn't leave a phone number or address," Mr. Melton said. "I got the idea he was looking for a job so he could find a place to settle. So many young folks today got no family to rely on. It's a shame. They're just out there on their own."

He was right about that.

"Do you remember his name?" Tinkie asked.

"Sorry, Mrs. Richmond, I don't. I should have written it down, but an eighteen-wheeler of fertilizer arrived and it was all hands on deck unloading it. The young man helped, and I was going to give him a ten spot because he threw in without being asked. I came in the store and got the money but when I went back out to give it to him, he was gone."

"And you haven't seen him since?"

Mr. Melton shook his head. "I haven't. That was three days ago."

"Did you know Eve Falcon from over at the bank?"

"Oh, yes. Pretty little thing, but she was about to pop the last time I saw her. She stopped by for some dog food. She said there was a stray dog near the place she rented and she wanted to feed it. Sweet woman." His mouth thinned. "That father of her baby wasn't around to help her. Some men should be horsewhipped."

Mr. Melton was old-school when it came to responsibilities. I liked that.

"Did Eve have a place in town here?" Tinkie asked.

"She rented a little apartment off Dawes Road. Cute

little green cottage set off the road in a nice residential area. I haven't seen her lately, so I assumed she was at the hospital having the baby." He was getting suspicious. "Is something wrong?"

"Eve's gone missing." Tinkie just put it out there. "Her cousin has hired me and my partner to find her. You've helped us a lot."

"What do you mean she's missing?" He was about to get upset.

"She hasn't shown up at work and her relative is worried. Because of the baby and all."

"You let me know when you find her, okay?" Mr. Melton wrote a number on the back of a receipt. "I'm fond of that young woman. Everyone who meets her is."

"Thanks, Mr. Melton. We'll let you know for sure." Tinkie took the number and soon after we left. We had one more lead—Eve's cottage. Cece hadn't known where Eve was living, but now we did. It wouldn't take but a minute to search through it to see if there was evidence of an abduction or a scuffle . . . or worse.

4

Eve's cottage was tiny—and absolutely adorable. It was almost a dollhouse, and somehow seemed so perfect for a soon-to-be mother. As Mr. Melton had explained, her landlady was an older woman who lived next door but "didn't pry."

"Mrs. Otis is a good soul," he'd said. "Outlived all her family, and I get the idea she really dotes on Eve. Might be good to check with her, too."

As we took in the cottage and the "big house" in front of it, Tinkie said, "Let's talk to Mrs. Otis first. I don't want her to think we're burglars."

A neat brick path led from the cottage to a large-frame house that would have been called a plantation owner's "town house" in an earlier time. When the Mississippi Delta was cleared and settled, wealthy planters often had a plantation house on the vast stretches of agricultural properties and another, smaller house in town for social events and soirees. The families stayed in town for the social season and for loading and selling the cotton that was harvested in the fall.

Tinkie had the whole registry of historic homes lodged in her brain. As the head Daddy's Girl in the Delta, she knew the pedigree of families and properties.

"Who built this house?" I asked as I took in the gingerbread trim around the curved front porch that graced the house on three sides. It was certainly a porch for sipping juleps and regaling guests with stories of the glory days.

"It's the Otis house. Been in the same family since it was built back in the 1850s. Myrtle Otis is the last of her line and she inherited this property plus five thousand acres of farm land. She sold the plantation to Chamblee Agricola about three years ago, and I think it's almost driven her insane. They're planting GMO corn and soybeans and she's been to several protests saying they're poisoning the crops, the ground, and the people. No one listens to her. They treat her like she's a crazy old lady. I feel bad for her. She couldn't keep up the plantation, but she never expected to see the land abused." Tinkie's expression reflected her sadness. "Time leaves us all vulnerable and outdated."

"I know what you mean." And I did. I lived with one foot in the past, and it was hard to straddle both worlds. "Let's take off the mourning clothes and have a chat with Myrtle."

"You're too perky for your own good," Tinkie admonished as we climbed the steps to the front door and rang the bell. Unlike our reception at Ricky Belvue's home, the owner opened the door. There were no maids or butlers or silver calling-card trays. It was Myrtle Otis who met us in a floral lavender dress that screamed 1960, a string of elegant pearls, and a smile.

"Ladies, what can I do for you?" she asked.

Tinkie gave her a business card. "We need your help, Miss Myrtle. Eve's cousin, Cece Falcon, has hired us to look for Eve. We're all a little worried about her. We wanted to ask if we could search her cottage and see if you might know where she went."

She pushed the door open. "Come in. Thank goodness someone is looking for her. I've been worried sick. I'm Eve's partner in the Lamaze classes. We've been working together for the past two months. I was supposed to go into labor and delivery with her. And then she just disappeared."

Myrtle Otis's home stopped me in my tracks. It held the warmth and love of history that I'd missed since my aunt had passed on. The gracious old furniture gleamed under a careful polishing. The crystals on a tasteful chandelier sparkled. A large fireplace centered the front parlor, and logs had been laid, ready for a match when the evening chill crept in. Even the smell of baking cookies floated from the kitchen.

"I was making a batch of Toll House cookies for Eve. She's had a real sweet tooth for the past three months, though she complained about the weight gain. I told her, 'Honey, you're carrying a baby. Eat.' So I decided to bake a batch today. I had to do something constructive while I was waiting to hear from her." She inhaled raggedly. "She's hurt, isn't she? Something has gone wrong."

"We don't know," Tinkie said. "She *is* missing, and we're worried."

"Sit and I'll get some coffee. I just made a fresh pot. And some cookies."

"I'll help," Tinkie said, giving me the eye. She wanted me to poke around, and I was happy to oblige. It wasn't that we didn't trust Mrs. Otis, but sometimes people knew things and didn't know they knew. If something was obvious, maybe I'd stumble across it.

I did a quick walk-through and found something extremely helpful—Myrtle had rigged her grounds with surveillance cameras. And one was pointed at the cottage where Eve lived. If I could work the conversation around to that, she might give us permission to look at any footage she had.

When Tinkie and Myrtle returned with a huge silver tray that held a sparkling coffee service, with lovely, fragile china cups, and a platter of cookies that made my mouth water, I was seated on a brocade sofa that was probably worth at least five grand. The house was furnished in antiques and artwork that even I recognized as valuable. Some of the portraits of Otises from generations long past were exquisite.

"That's my grandmother, Bella Schaffer Otis," Myrtle said as she handed me a cup filled with aromatic coffee. "She was from Virginia, and she was Wickham Otis's third wife. The first two died in childbirth. It was during Reconstruction, and times were hard. There was little food and worse health care. Pregnancy was a very dangerous time. It still can be."

"Eve was taking care of herself, wasn't she?" I asked. Tinkie looked too upset to talk. The whole pregnancy/

baby topic was tough for her because she wanted a child so badly.

"Yes, Eve made every doctor's appointment, took her vitamins, ate properly. I made sure of that."

"You were very good to Eve." I had to be blunt. "Why?"

Myrtle nodded as she passed the cookies around. I took one because I couldn't resist. I was still full of tamales, but the cookies smelled like heaven.

"My daughter was killed coming home from Ole Miss. Freak car accident. She was the light of my life. Eve reminded me of her."

I sipped my coffee, unable to say anything for a moment. Myrtle's grief and sorrow were palpable, but she was not a woman who would be beaten down by loss, no matter how acute.

"I'm so sorry," I said. "I didn't know."

"She was a remarkable young woman. You would have liked Rebekah."

Somehow, I thought I probably would have. "Did Eve ever mention the father of her child?" I asked. Tinkie was blinking back tears.

"I asked her, and she only said that he was a good man and that she was happy to have the baby on her own."

"Could the baby have belonged to her boss, Mr. Belvue?"

Myrtle almost snorted her coffee. "Absolutely not. Eve didn't suffer fools, and Mr. Belvue understood that she ran the bank. He was too smart to fart in his own scuba tank."

I almost choked on a bite of cookie. Tinkie put a napkin to her mouth to control her surprise.

"I'm twenty years older than you girls, but I still have vigor, and Freddy Teddy isn't brilliant, but he's business smart. Eve was his best asset. He took care of her."

"Then who might the father be?" Tinkie asked. At last she had gained control of her emotions.

"I don't know." Myrtle sighed. "I didn't want to know. I had this idea that Eve and the baby would live in the cottage and I'd keep the baby during the day while she worked. I had it all planned out in my head. To be honest, the daddy would have been an inconvenience, so I never pressed hard for information. I should have. I was selfish, and now she's been taken away."

Tinkie moved to the sofa beside Myrtle and put a hand on her arm. "She's not been taken away. She's just missing, and we're going to find her."

"There's been a ransom note, hasn't there?" Myrtle asked. She was sharper than anyone else we'd talked to.

When we didn't deny it, she continued. "I'll pay it. Whatever it is."

"We have the amount covered," Tinkie said. She glanced at me and I nodded. "It was an unusual amount. One hundred and thirty thousand dollars. Do you have any idea who might think Eve could raise that kind of money?"

She thought a moment, passing the cookies again. "Do you believe it's the father of the child?"

"Maybe," I said.

"It isn't. No, I can't see that. It's someone else."

"Who?"

"Someone who would risk Eve and her baby's well-being. I never got that impression about the father. Eve never said much about him, but she let me believe he was a decent man who might not know he was a potential father." She paused with the coffee cup almost to her lips. "But there was a young man lurking around her cottage a week ago."

"Tell us." I clicked on the recording button on my phone just to have a record if she happened to give a good description.

"I can show you. I have video."

And that was that. We followed Myrtle into the small office where she'd set up screens to view the surveillance camera recordings. "Before my husband died, he had these cameras installed. A lot of houses in this area were being burglarized and he was worried about me. At first I thought he'd lost his mind, but now this gives me a sense of safety. I know exactly who's roaming around my property. I even saw you two earlier."

She went back through several CDs. "I don't keep the footage, normally, but this bothered me. Eve said the same guy was watching her at the bank."

This was exactly what we needed. "Did Eve know him?"

"No. She said she didn't."

"But you didn't believe her completely," Tinkie said softly.

"She was curious about him. And not in the way you'd be if someone scared you. He was a puzzle to her and she was intrigued."

Oh, I knew that sort of curiosity and how dangerous it could be. Especially to a woman. We watched the video of a young man walking around Eve's cottage and peering in the window twice. There was never a clear view of his face, though. It was almost as if he knew where the cameras had been placed and could avoid them.

"I don't know him," Myrtle said. "I know most of the

younger people from the county, but not this man. Maybe if I had a clear view of him, but all I can tell is that he has dark hair and seems to be tall and slender. He has good posture."

"Eve said she didn't know him?" I asked again.

"I don't think she did, but she wanted to. That's what concerns me."

The guy didn't behave furtively, but he was poking around while no one was home. That in itself was suspect—even though Tinkie and I did it all the time when we were on a case.

"He's wearing that hoodie and we can't see his face," Tinkie said.

"I've studied the images," Myrtle said. "I don't know who he is."

"The morning she disappeared, was he hanging around?" I asked.

Myrtle expertly scrolled forward to the morning of Eve's disappearance. We watched Eve on the footage as she came out of the cottage, got in her car, and drove away. I noted she had a blue Ford Focus.

"May we have those CDs?" I asked. "We've been warned not to go to the police, but if Cece changes her mind, the sheriff might be able to enhance the images of the stalker."

"Sure. Take them." Myrtle popped them out and handed them to us.

"Is there anything else you can tell us?" Tinkie asked.

"Only that Eve loved that baby more than anything. She had everything arranged, planned out, ready. She'd even named her."

"Her?" Tinkie said.

"Yes, she was having a girl. Eve never missed her medical appointments."

"What was . . . is the baby's name?" Tinkie corrected, but we'd all heard the slip.

"Sally. She said it was an old-fashioned name for an old-fashioned child. She wanted Sally to grow up with all the love that she'd never had, with a mother and auntie who baked cookies and decorated for Halloween and made Christmas special. Eve never had that."

"Eve's mother doesn't believe in Christmas." I remembered the story Cece had told me about Carla burning the bicycle. "I think Carla Falcon doesn't believe in anything soft or pleasant. Eve really got cheated."

"That's why she's so determined that little Sally have all of that. Not material things, but the important things like time and love and knowing she's wanted." Myrtle stood up. "Please find Eve. I love her like she's my daughter. I'll pay any amount."

I put my arm around her and gave her a hug. I knew how hard it was to want to help a loved one and not be able to. "We'll do everything we can. And as soon as we know anything, we'll be in touch. Now would you mind if we went through her cottage? Maybe there's a clue as to where she's gone."

"Just leave the key under the doormat," Myrtle said, handing us a key painted bright red.

5

Eve's cottage was a pleasant contrast to Myrtle's home. The interior had been updated with a brand-new kitchen and laundry with all the latest gadgets—and a delightful nursery, painted lavender and with cartoon characters all over the walls. It was a room set up for a happy childhood.

Tinkie fingered a mobile of the planets and stars that hung over a bassinet layered in tulle and lace. The melody from "Dreamer's Holiday" began as the mobile turned. Stuffed toys lined one shelf, and below that was a large collection of Little Golden Books, the joy of my early years.

"We have to find her," Tinkie said as she touched a soft lavender blanket folded in the crib.

I nudged her with my hip. "We will. Now get busy looking for clues." I couldn't let her dwell too long on what might have happened. My friend was brilliant, but sometimes too tender.

"Do you think it's a sign that this baby is due on Christmas Eve?" Tinkie asked.

I knew exactly what she meant, but I wasn't stepping into that trap. "What kind of sign?"

"You know, a miracle. The baby is a miracle."

"All babies are miracles." I felt like I was being pulled deep into the ocean by an undertow. Tinkie was investing way too much in Eve's unborn child. She was beginning to think of it as a messiah or some kind of divine message. Which would be fine if the baby was cooing and gurgling in front of us. But the baby was missing, and I didn't want Tinkie imbuing the child with some kind of mystical importance. What if the child was hurt?

"I know what you're doing, Sarah Booth. Stop it."

Tinkie had an ability to suss out my motives, so I didn't bother denying it. "Please check the medicine cabinet in the bathroom."

She disappeared into the bathroom and I went into Eve's bedroom and started searching through her dresser drawers. I found all the normal things—and one thing extra. A photograph.

I studied the old and fading photo of two babies. The woman holding them was visible just from the torso and she looked to be wearing a hospital gown, as if she'd just delivered. Her head hadn't been included in the photo. Just two little babies, one in each arm, swaddled tightly. Newborns. Clutched among the infants were a rattler, a pacifier on a ribbon that could be pinned to a blanket, a baby's hairbrush, and, at the bottom of it all, a baby doll. It was almost buried in blankets and babies, but from what I could see it was exceptionally ugly. The blue glass eyes stared out blankly. The eyebrows had been drawn on. It was not only ugly but a little frightening. Then again, I'd never had a thing for dolls.

I wondered who the infants were and why Eve had this photo. As bad as I felt, I slipped the picture in my pocket. I would return it when we'd found Eve, but Cece might know who these babies were and if they somehow related to the case.

"There's nothing in the bathroom," Tinkie called out. "Not even a cobweb. Eve was a good housekeeper. She seemed to put a lot of love into this cottage."

I met Tinkie in the kitchen. When I pulled the photo from my pocket, she took it and studied it. "Who are the babies?" She flipped it over but the back was blank. I'd already looked.

"I don't know. I guess I think it may be relevant somehow."

Tinkie took the photo to the window. "This photo was cheaply processed. Back when everyone used color film, the big developing companies would run the film through in batches and then print at a standard exposure. This photo wasn't left in the fix long enough. See how it's fading."

She was right. "How do you know so much about film development?"

"One summer at Ole Miss I worked as an apprentice for a wedding consultant. My job was hiring photographers for the high-end weddings. I had to be sure the photographer used the best processing standards."

"Getting that Mrs. Degree did pay off," I teased her.

"You're just jealous."

I laughed out loud, because I was. A tiny little bit. Oscar and Tinkie had a great love. They'd overcome hardship and disappointment. They were forged in fire. My heart belonged to Coleman, but we hadn't been tested. Would we endure, or would we break? I had only hope and no answers.

"Did you find anything relevant to the case?" I asked.

"Her toothbrush and toiletries are in the bathroom. It doesn't look like she intended to go anywhere. I think she was snatched either on the way to work or while running an errand in the morning before work."

"That makes sense. There's a cereal bowl in the sink, like she had breakfast and then left home. She put out dog food at some point." I indicated the open bag of kibble against the wall.

We were at least establishing a timeline of her actions. On the morning she'd disappeared, she'd eaten cereal and then vanished. She hadn't shown up for work that morning, so somewhere between breakfast in this cottage and the bank, she'd been taken. There was nothing in the cottage to indicate that she'd struggled, and there was no footage of anyone assaulting her in the yard. Where had she gone after she left here?

"We don't have a clue what happened to her," Tinkie admitted. And she was right.

On the way back to Zinnia, Tinkie and I tossed out ideas that ranged from a gypsy abduction to aliens to a jealous boyfriend. Nothing seemed to fit Eve's disappearance. She'd been in Cleveland, headed to work on a normal day, and then she was gone. Her car had also disappeared.

"Maybe she was carjacked and they just took her," Tinkie said.

"A pregnant woman could be an impediment." We talked all around the idea that if Eve was too bothersome they might just kill her.

"What are you wearing to Harold's big dinner party?" I asked, changing the subject. I didn't want Tinkie falling down the baby well again.

"I have a really pretty white cocktail dress with pearls and crystals. I think I look a bit like a wedding cake in it, but Oscar picked it out. He says I look like a winter princess." She cast a knowing eye at me. "And you? What are you wearing?"

"Ummmm, red velveteen top with black jeans. And heels." I threw the last in as an attempt to save myself. I hated heels and dresses. After I'd been caught at one dinner party in a long skirt and had had to wade through cotton fields dragging that heavy wet skirt behind me, I'd vowed never to leave my more accommodating pants behind.

"You have to wear a dress, Sarah Booth. It's a cocktail party." She said it as if the rules of cocktail-party wear were inscribed in the Ten Commandments. And probably there were Daddy's Girls commandments of attire for every social occasion under the sun. I, though, had refuted the cult of the DG. I didn't have to abide by their dress code or any other rules. I would wear my red blouse and celebrate the holiday.

"Sarah Booth, don't bring any of those fruitcakes you soak in Jack Daniel's."

"Why not?" I asked.

"Those things are potent and Oscar is like an addict. Once he tastes them he can't stop himself."

"Which is the point of fruitcake, isn't it?"

"I'd like him sober enough for a little private celebration, if you get my drift."

I did but I wasn't going there. "Do you think Cece will come? Since Jaytee and the band are out of the country? I know she's worried."

"She has to attend. The kidnapper warned her to act normal."

That was true.

"But the real question is—can you behave naturally around Coleman?" Tinkie asked with a spark in her eyes.

"We'll just have to see, won't we?" I kept it light, though deep in my heart I was worried about Eve and her baby. And I knew Tinkie was, too. Funny how we'd ended up playing roles in an effort to do as Cece asked. It would take all of my acting skills to cover my worry, but I would give the performance of my life.

Once Tinkie departed, eager to get into her party duds, I started up the stairs. I was reluctant to think about finding appropriate wear for the gala. I'd missed the dress-up gene that so many of my friends had.

"Come and play with my dolls!"

I stopped in my tracks. The voice came from my bedroom—the voice of a child. I'd never played with dolls. In fact, they scared me. They always seemed on the verge of . . . coming to life. Chucky had cured me of ever keeping a doll in my house. I approached my room with caution. At the doorway I stopped in my tracks.

Shelves of dolls lined my room. Toys were scattered about the floor, and a pretty young girl sat cross-legged, playing a game of jacks. "Please, come and play. You can have any doll you want. It's almost Christmas and I'm sure to get something special."

I knew the child from the story of "The Nutcracker," who was leaned against the wall, his jaw a very sad mess. "Marie?" I asked.

"Masha, Clara, Marie," she shrugged. "I don't care what you call me if you'll just play with me. I'm not ready for bed and no one believes my dreams." She held up her bandaged arm. "But what I dream is real."

I struggled to recall the details of the story that I hadn't thought of in years. Why Jitty had decided to devil me with characters from a ballet, I'd never know. Jitty was wicked like that.

"Is it true love that brings the Nutcracker to life?" I asked Clara, aka Jitty.

"True love is the only magic that's real." The little girl began to grow and change until it was Jitty sitting on the floor. "I'm on fours. Come play."

I hadn't played jacks in decades, but I sat on the floor. Anything was better than getting duded up for a party. I scattered the jacks and started with one at a time, bouncing the ball and catching it until all the jacks were collected. I moved on to twos as she watched.

"I didn't think you were coordinated enough to play jacks," Jitty said.

"Surprise, surprise." I grinned. It was good to keep her on her toes. Sometimes she took me for granted.

"What does 'The Nutcracker' mean to you?" she asked when I missed and handed the ball over to her.

"It's a Christmas story for children. The ballet is lovely." I'd seen it in Jackson when the Imperial Russian Ballet was in town. "I love the idea that we can all escape our destinies to become something magical and loved."

"So you still have a bit of the romantic in you." Jitty stood up, done with the jacks and the floor. "You'd better get ready for that party. Your date will be here in twenty minutes to pick you up."

An hour had flown by. Time had passed so swiftly— it was incomprehensible. Ten minutes before, it had been dusk. Now, it was almost time to depart for Harold's. I stood up and headed to my closet for clean black jeans and my fancy red top.

"Stop!" Jitty was suddenly barring the closet door. "You are not wearing pants to this shindig."

"I haven't had a chance to go shopping." It was a dodge *and* the truth. I hated shopping, so I hadn't gone.

"Which is why I look out for you. Check to the left in the closet." She moved aside and curiosity prompted me to push the coat hangers around until I saw the dress. It was tomato red with sparkly fringe like a flapper's dress. I recognized it instantly. My mother had worn it to a holiday party when I was eleven. I'd thought she was a movie star.

"Where did you find it?" I asked.

"In the Great Beyond, we know things," Jitty said. "And your mama knew you'd try to wear some awful outfit so she put me on the case."

I might want to fight Jitty, but I couldn't go against the wishes of my dead mother. I pulled the dress out and felt a thrill of anticipation. I'd never in a million years buy a dress like this. My mother had panache and style. She would rock this look, but could I?

"Put it on and give it a chance," Jitty said. "Your mama would never lead you astray."

She was right. I slipped out of my clothes and into the dress. With the addition of some pretty high heels, which looked like new because I never wore them, I chanced a look in the mirror. For an instant, my heart stopped because my mother looked back at me. I hadn't realized how much I'd grown to look like her.

"Beautiful," Jitty said. "Now fix that mop of hair."

Mop was overly optimistic, but it was getting there. I'd had an unfortunate accident, but my hair had almost grown back out. I'd had it shaped and styled, and with a curling iron and a bit of care, I'd be party ready.

And just in time.

The front door opened and Coleman came into Dahlia House, calling my name.

"Give me three minutes," I said, hurrying to put the finishing touches on makeup and hair. As I rushed to the stairs, I felt a fluttery kiss on my cheek, but when I turned, Jitty wasn't there. I wondered if it might have been my mother.

"Merry Christmas," Coleman said when he saw me. "My god, Sarah Booth, you are stunning. I think I just got my present."

And I had also gotten something I'd wanted very badly—a few minutes with my mom, even if it was just her prodding me to wear a party dress. I glanced back at the empty landing. "Thanks," I whispered to my mama and Jitty. And I was down the stairs and in Coleman's arms.

Harold's house was ablaze with white fairy lights wrapped around the oak trees that stood sentinel along his curved driveway and lawn. Harold gave the most elegant parties on the planet. He had a flair for decorating and making each occasion special. He loved entertaining, and he was good at it.

Coleman reached across the seat of his private pickup truck and found my hand. "This is our first official party as a couple."

"I know." I kissed his hand and squeezed it. I couldn't help feeling like a cad. I sat beside him in the truck, going to a party as his partner, and I was lying to him. A lie of omission was still a lie. But I had promised Cece. As each hour passed, though, I questioned my decision to keep Eve's disappearance to myself. Especially as her due date drew closer. Where was she? Did she have medical care? My gut churned.

"Is something wrong?" Coleman asked.

"Yes." One lie was enough. "But I can't talk about it now."

"This sounds ominous." He parked under a low-hanging oak branch that glittered with white lights as though it had been sprinkled with fairy dust. He shifted so that he faced me, his knee on the seat between us. "Are you in trouble?"

"No, and I can't tell you any more. I promised. But I'm not in danger."

He nodded, and his hand touched my face. "Thank you for telling me this much."

I felt an irrational urge to cry. "I'm trying to convince my friend to tell you."

"That's all you can do," he said. "Now let's see what new delight Harold has in store for us."

We walked up the sidewalk together, his arm around me. The house was bright with lights. Christmas music and laughter filtered out to us. There was magic in the air. Coleman stopped me on the porch. "I remember a certain night when we shared a kiss on this porch."

I remembered, from the top of my head to my toes. Coleman had truly rung my jingle bells that evening with his kiss. "I think I've forgotten. Could I have a reminder?" I played coy to the hilt.

"I thought you'd never ask." He swept me into his arms and kissed me with jet-fueled passion. I couldn't breathe, but it wasn't necessary. All that mattered were his lips and arms. I wrapped my arms around his neck and twisted my fingers in his hair, holding on for dear life. I held nothing back.

The front door opened and I heard laughter, but I didn't care. Let them look and laugh! I was in heaven.

"Sarah Booth, come inside before that man gnaws your face off," Madame Tomeeka said. More laughter erupted, and Coleman eased back.

"Thanks, Tammy." I called her by her given name. "I was in the middle of something very important, in case you missed it."

"Lord help us, Sarah Booth, we couldn't miss it. If I'd stepped any closer I'd have been swept up into the vortex of that kiss and might have ended up in a black hole of the universe."

Now a crowd had gathered on the porch and everyone was laughing. Harold came to our rescue with two flutes of champagne. "Drink, Sarah Booth. That way you can blame your socially unacceptable behavior on the booze."

I drained the glass and turned back to Coleman. "I'll have another of those kisses, please."

And he obliged without a second's hesitation.

By the time we went inside to the party, everyone had

resumed chattering, drinking, and sampling the fabulous hors d'oeuvres. Harold had a battalion of caterers working, but he'd also made some of the fancy appetizers. And they were yummy.

Tinkie and Cece were huddled in the corner, and when they saw me, they waved me over.

"Glad to see you still have some lips left on your face," Cece said.

"Think of all the extra tooth care you'd have to do without lips," Tinkie agreed, baring her teeth. "Lips shouldn't be abused, Sarah Booth. They're important."

"Back off, wise guys." I didn't mind the teasing, but enough was enough. "I was reliving my past."

"My god, when she gets to the future she and that lawman might have enough friction to catch on fire." Tinkie was beside herself.

"What's the latest with Eve?" I asked. "Have they called about the ransom drop?"

"Nothing." Cece was suddenly serious, and I was sorry I'd brought up the subject of her cousin. "Not another word. Have you found anything?"

I'd kept the photo of the two babies, and I brought it out of my purse. "Does this mean anything to you? It really was the only photo in Eve's cottage. There was no other evidence of her past."

"With Carla for a mother, there probably weren't a lot of good memories. But I don't recognize these babies." She stared at the photo, and I realized Coleman was watching us. It wouldn't take him long to put two and two together. We had to break up the hen party.

"I need to get a drink and we need to mingle before Coleman is on to us," I said. "And, no, I haven't mentioned a thing."

Cece nodded. "Time for photos for the paper. I'll think about those two babies and see if my brain drops something out."

"Cece, she was taken on her way to work, we believe." I had to give her something. "There's no indication of foul play. And she had to have driven her car. There's no sign of it anywhere."

"She could be in labor without any medical help." Cece's face flushed and then went pale. "I can't stop thinking about that."

"And she could be sitting on a sofa drinking a glass of tea waiting for us to drop the money," I responded. "I still think you should tell Coleman, but it's your call."

"Please don't tell him," she said. "Now let's put some effort into this party. Harold is watching us, too."

We smiled and laughed and then I went for drinks. When I handed Coleman another flute of champagne, he merely looked at me, his blue eyes deadly serious as he sipped. He knew something was up. I hoped Cece would do the smart thing and include him, but I couldn't force her hand on this.

I made the rounds of the party, talking with people I saw only once or twice a year. Zinnia was a small town, but everyone led such busy lives that we headed in different directions.

"You look blissful, Sarah Booth." Harold kissed my hand. I loved Coleman, but my thumb had a will of its own and gave a sad little throb. I had feelings for Harold, too. But I'd made my choice.

"I am happy, Harold. Really happy."

"You deserve that for the rest of your life."

"The party is great. I haven't seen a lot of these people in months."

"The holidays are the perfect time for reunions and gatherings. I do love Christmas." He leaned closer. "What gives with Cece? She's like a cat on a hot tin roof, to borrow from old Tennessee."

"Family stuff." I was determined not to lie unless I had to.

"She only has that brother that stole everything from her."

"Can't go into it. Change the subject, please."

"Whatever you say. I—"

A gasp came from the bar area and I turned to see Cece, her face completely drained of color. She started to step forward, faltered, and then grabbed the bar to stay upright. I hurried to her side. "What is it?"

"Get me out of here."

I obliged, taking her into the kitchen and out the back door into the cold night. The freezing temperature seemed to revive her. "What is it?" I asked.

"It's Eve. I got a call. Someone found her purse in the mud on the banks of the river."

"Where?"

"Fortis Landing," Cece said. "There's no trace of her. Just the purse."

"We'd better go there. Let me get Tinkie." I looked around. Getting away from Coleman and Oscar was going to be a risky business. "Come on, we don't have time to waste. Meet me at your car."

I went inside and caught Tinkie's eye. A moment later she met up with me and Cece down the street where Cece had parked. As we drove to Fortis Landing, I filled Tinkie in. The purse in the mud wasn't a good sign at all. But it didn't have to be a bad sign—or at least that was my argument with Cece.

We'd just left the Christmas lights of Zinnia behind us when Cece's phone rang. She answered on the car's speaker system.

"You'd better get that money fast." The voice had been altered by some device. It was neither male nor female. "And now we need a hundred and fifty thousand. Get it. Don't call the cops. Don't act unnatural in any way. We'll call back with a place for you to leave the money and we'll leave the pregnant woman."

"I have the money," Cece said. "Where should I take it? Just let me speak to Eve. I want to be sure she's okay."

"Wait for my call."

And the line went dead.

6

For the entire drive to the river, Cece was fit to be tied. She white-knuckled it the whole way, and though Tinkie and I did what we could to put the events in the best light, she wasn't hearing us.

At last we pulled to a stop by the boat landing where there was a paved boat launch, a bait shop, and, about a hundred yards up the road, a juke joint. Scattered up and down the river were camps and houseboats where those who disdained unexpected visitors lived. I knew where I wanted to go—the jukebox in the bar was playing a tune I knew. I hadn't had a chance to drink nearly enough at Harold's party before we left. I'd walked out the door without even telling Coleman I was leaving. Same for Oscar. The menfolk were going to be on the warpath, and I didn't blame them one bit. Not much of a Christmas party if you were dumped and left behind.

"Who found the purse and how did they know to contact you?" I asked Cece. It hadn't occurred to me earlier that this was a pertinent question. We'd been so hell-for-leather to get to the river.

"Mr. Bromley. A man named Curtis Bromley. He lives right along the river around here somewhere. He recognized the Falcon name and figured Eve was a relative. He called the newspaper and they gave him my cell phone number."

I looked around and didn't see anyone. "Is he meeting us here?"

"He said he would." Cece didn't sound nearly as sure as I would've liked her to sound.

"Any time specifically, or just when he shows up?" I was a little snarky because I knew I would have hell to pay from walking out on Coleman. And I was standing in the freezing December cold in the mud beside a river in my mother's fancy holiday dress and heels. I knew I should have worn jeans. I would get even with Jitty, too.

"He said he would be here." Cece rounded on me. "I'm sorry. I shouldn't have brought you and Tinkie. It's going to make trouble for you, I know."

"We can manage our men," Tinkie said. "If Sarah Booth needs help, I'll just go visit the Harrington sisters and get another charm for her."

Tinkie referred to three Wiccan sisters who'd moved to the area to start a boarding school. Even months later, they were still the talk of the town. Yet their school was developing a terrific reputation for academics and nature-based learning programs. Tinkie had bought a charm for me to lure Coleman into my bed, and it had worked.

Or something had worked. Now she'd never let me forget that I'd had help from "the other side" to land Coleman in my bed.

"I can handle Coleman on my own," I said, and I was about as uncertain as Cece had been. "Look, headlights."

We turned to face the road and waited as an older model pickup came right down to the water. We couldn't see who was driving, but in a moment the lights were cut and two people exited the cab. A middle-aged couple came toward us.

"Mr. Bromley," Cece called out.

"Yes, it's Curtis and Matilda. We have that purse."

Cece walked to meet them and Tinkie and I fell in behind her. My teeth were chattering to the point I didn't think I could talk, so it was good Cece was taking the lead. Tinkie, in her beautiful white and glittering cocktail dress, was also shaking with cold. We'd been foolish— and in too big a hurry—not to bring our coats.

Matilda took one look at the three of us and nudged her husband. "Let's go to Bullwinkle's. These girls are freezing."

"Good idea," Curtis said. "Ladies, let's take this inside. It's cold out here."

"Where did you find the purse?" Cece asked, and her desperation was clear.

"Right here." Curtis knelt on the apron of the boat launch. "Right in the mud there. It was almost covered up, but I saw the pink leather. Then when I looked inside, I saw the driver's license for the young woman. Eve Falcon. You were the only Falcon in the area I knew about." Curtis stood up and put a hand on Cece's shoulder. "Wherever this young woman is, we'll find her. Now

I'm not saying another word until we're somewhere warm."

There was nothing to see at the riverbank. Whatever evidence had been there was now washed away by the wakes of boats coming and going. And we were freezing. Without complaint we walked up the hill to the juke joint we'd passed. Bullwinkle's was ablaze with strings of bright blue Christmas lights. There wasn't a band, but someone was playing Christmas blues on an old jukebox. Thank goodness the sound was low enough to talk over.

We took a table in the corner and I got a good look at Curtis and Matilda. They were salt-of-the-earth farmer types, or maybe river rats. The good kind. Folks who had grown up on the local waterways and knew them inside and out. The Tallahatchie River was a part of Delta legend and some families had lived on its banks for generations.

The waitress stopped by and took our orders—Jack Daniel's all around. This wasn't a bar that offered fine wines or martinis. It was a beer-and-bourbon kind of place. Someone put Elvis's "Blue Christmas" on the jukebox.

Cece made the introductions, and Matilda reached over the table and touched my hand. "You sure do look like your mama. Miss Libby was a wonderful person."

"Thank you." It was good to hear. "How did you know her?" My mother had been dead better than two decades. I was glad some people still remembered her.

"Everyone knew your mama," Matilda said. "She was a good person who went out of her way to help others."

"Tell me about the purse," Cece said. She was frantic, and I didn't blame her.

Matilda reached into her big coat and brought out a

pink clutch. "Here it is. Everything that was in it is still there." She pushed it across the table to Cece, who fell on it like it was a treasure.

Cece opened the snap and dumped the contents on the table. A lipstick, a pen, a billfold, some change, nothing else. She opened the billfold and saw Eve's driver's license and one credit card from the Bank of the Deep South. She flipped through several empty slots meant for photos or other forms of ID and found one photo. When she pulled it out, I recognized it instantly. It was a duplicate of the photo I'd found in Eve's bedroom drawer in the little cottage she rented in Cleveland. The same two babies, newborns, squinted up at the camera as a woman in a hospital gown held both in her arms.

"Who are these children?" Cece asked aloud.

Everyone at the table shook their heads.

"Did anyone happen to see anything at the landing?" I asked.

The waitress brought our drinks and for a moment no one said anything. The Elvis tune wound down and Koko Taylor cranked up with "Merry, Merry Christmas."

"We didn't see anything, but we asked around," Curtis said. "There was a boat here early this morning when it was still foggy. Came from upriver, and pulled into the landing. The man piloting it tied up and went up to the store for some supplies. When he came back, a truck pulled down to the landing and the two men unloaded something from the backseat. Looked like a rolled-up carpet." He hesitated. "Could have been a body."

Tinkie gripped Cece's hand and held it. "What did your eyewitness see?"

"The men put the bundle in the boat. It didn't make a sound. They unwrapped it, but it was down in the bottom of the boat and the witness wasn't close enough to see. The boat pilot took off upriver like the devil was on his coattails. The other man got in his truck and drove off. About ten minutes later, Matilda and I came down to the river, and I found the purse mashed into the mud by the launchpad."

"Who is your witness?" Tinkie asked.

"They don't want to get involved. They told me everything they saw. And they did say the men were very careful of the bundle—that they took care with it." Curtis was uncomfortable. He was caught in a bad spot, trying to do the right thing without giving up his friends. This was the time Coleman would have been invaluable. He could have gotten Curtis to give up the names of the witness or witnesses. Tinkie and I had no leverage to make him talk.

"Did they recognize the pickup that delivered the . . . bundle?" Tinkie asked.

"It was really early. Not quite light. They didn't recognize the truck, the boat, or the men. The bundle could have been a rug or something." He drained his glass and signaled for another. "No one gave it a second thought until I found that purse. Then we got to wondering."

And I was wondering if Curtis was the actual witness and had fabricated the ruse of his "friends." I wasn't in a place where I could make the accusation and gain a single thing. "How tall were the men?" I asked.

He shook his head. "Average, I guess. No one remarked that they were tall or short or fat or thin. Just average."

That didn't help at all. "Any chance your friends overhead them talking? Maybe they had an accent." I tried another tactic.

"They didn't talk. Or at least my friends didn't overhear them."

"And they headed upriver?" Tinkie asked.

"Yes, the one piloting the boat did."

"And the boat was what kind?" she continued.

"Flat bottom fishing boat. Had an 8 horsepower Mercury motor, like most every other fishing boat around here."

Matilda spoke up. "Look, Curtis just wanted to do the right thing and return this purse. And he knew Cece Falcon would be worried. We don't know anything else. If we hear or see anything, we'll call. You have our word."

And there was no reason to doubt them. They'd come forward of their own volition. We'd gotten what we could from them.

"If you see that boat or those men again, please call. And if you see Eve, please let me know."

"Sure thing," Curtis said. "You ladies stay warm. It's bitter tonight."

Tinkie went to the bar and took care of the bill, and we left Curtis and Matilda at the table. We high-stepped it back to the car because we were cold. The moon had come up and glinted on the narrow river.

"I hope Eve is okay," Cece said, and she was near to breaking down.

"We don't know anything worse than we did before we came here," Tinkie said. "And we know the kidnapper can get in touch with you. We just need to have that money ready for the drop when they call back."

"I've got the original amount. Now I'll need twenty thousand more," Cece said.

"First thing in the morning I'll go by the bank," Tinkie promised.

I knew it was not going to happen, but I had to try. "Please tell Coleman about this. Please. He has experience in these matters, and I know he wouldn't do anything to risk Eve's life."

"No," Cece said softly. "I can't. I'd never forgive myself if something happened."

"We're out of our depth," I said. "We don't have a clue who took Eve, and she's ready to give birth."

"That's the problem," Cece said. "I'm hoping to get her back before she goes into labor."

"Her due date is Christmas Eve," I reminded her. "And we're all expected to be at the pageant at the Methodist church. Coleman, Harold, and Oscar are playing the wise men. There is no way in hell we can miss that and not be strung up." I wasn't kidding. It had taken all of Tinkie's persuasive abilities to get the men to participate in the church pageant. We'd had other pageants in Zinnia, and some had gone terribly wrong with spitting llamas and runaway pigs, not to mention bad boys stealing the baby Jesus. This year the church had opted for adult players in the Christmas pageant that portrayed the birth of the baby Jesus. Now I wasn't certain involving the men had been such a smart idea.

"We still have a little time to find her," Cece said.

"Very little time, if her delivery date is accurate. I wish the kidnappers would set a drop place and time." I might be tempted to include Coleman if we knew far enough ahead of time.

"Do you think Eve was in that bundle?" Cece asked. "Mr. Bromley said they were careful with it. That's a good sign, right?"

"I don't know." Tinkie was firm. "We can't know. We can't speculate, either."

"How did her purse get dropped right at that place?" Cece persisted.

"We don't know that either," Tinkie said. "No one has found her car. Maybe she took some time off and she's fine."

"Then who's asking for a ransom?" Cece asked.

"I don't know." Tinkie sighed. "That's our problem. We just don't know much. Now let's get back to Harold's before they get a search and rescue out for us. It's too bad Curtis and Matilda cleaned up the purse or we could have tried for fingerprints."

"We still can," I said. "It won't hurt to try."

"But we'd have to ask Coleman, DeWayne, or Budgie to dust for prints, and we're not doing that." Cece's jaw was clenched. She was going to hold firm.

7

Our return to Harold's party was met with raised eyebrows and glares from the men in our lives. I judged that out of 100 percent, we were about 75 percent in the dog house. Tinkie and I would have some 'splaining to do. Cece's main squeeze was out of the country, and he was also in the loop. Jaytee knew about Eve's disappearance and had sent money, as had Scott. Oscar suspected something was wrong—I knew that because Tinkie had hit him up for a lot of money. To Oscar's credit, he never said no to Tinkie, and he didn't press her. Only Coleman couldn't be told what was going on, because, as a lawman, he would be obligated to do something.

Harold was curious about our departure, but not judgmental. He put a hand on my shoulder and gave me a word of advice. "I sent Coleman to the kitchen. He's in there alone. It might be wise for you to address this head-on. Right now."

The party was winding down. I followed Harold's sage advice and found Coleman in the kitchen, where he was getting more ice for the punch.

"I do have an explanation," I told him.

He slowly rose from the ice chest and studied me. "I'm trying to figure out where the line is, Sarah Booth. For me to leave you at a party, it would have to be something serious."

"It *is* serious. I swear it." I could tell him that.

"You were with your friends, who adore Harold and would never cut out on his party without good reason."

"True."

"Since Oscar isn't too upset, I suspect whatever this is has to do with Cece."

I pressed my lips together. Where was the line for me? "That's true, too, but please, no more. I promised I would let her handle this. I want to tell you. I do. But I gave my word."

"If someone is hurt or in danger, you should tell me."

"I know." I suddenly wanted to cry. What was the right thing to do? If I weren't sleeping with Coleman would I be so hesitant to tell him? The choice between friend and lover was truly cruel. And especially at Christmas. My plans for the holiday had included lots of snuggling, champagne, and passionate lovemaking. Not secrets. But I had to toe the line for Cece, no matter how much it chafed and pinched me. I would not let a secret come between us on this magical evening.

Harold had strategically hung mistletoe in several rooms, including the kitchen. In the parlor, the remaining guests were singing "I Saw Mama Kissing Santa Claus." My parents had acted out that song for me when I was a toddler, and I loved it. More than anything I wanted the kind of love my parents had shared. It was a now-or-never Christmas moment, so I took action.

I grabbed Coleman's arm and pulled him under the leafy green bundle and kissed him long and deep. At first he was a little resistant, but I burned that away with the power of my passion. I loved this man and I wasn't going to hold back and pretend otherwise because I risked getting hurt.

His hands settled at my waist and he kissed me back. Really kissed me with enough passion to make my legs weak and my head swim. When we finally parted, I knew the bump in the road was behind us. Coleman had chosen to trust me to do the right thing.

"Let's go home," I whispered. "Right now."

"I think so." He found our coats and we said our good-byes to the gang. When we stepped into the night, he kissed me again under the twinkling fairy glow of the tree lights. I closed my eyes and gave myself to the magic of the moment. I consciously chose to yield. When had I learned to be so guarded and so afraid of risking my heart? Courage was required to confront the barriers my heart attempted to erect. Once upon a time I'd been a lot bolder. I would find that place again. Coleman would lead me there.

"I love you, Coleman."

He swept me up and spun me in a circle until the beautiful lights danced in a blur. "I love you, Sarah Booth. More than you'll ever know. Now let's head back to Dahlia House. We need a crackling fire."

I jumped into the passenger side of his truck and in

no time we were headed to my home. Coleman drove down Main Street, where the lovely lights and decorations of the season sparkled. The storefronts had been staged for holiday scenes, some even sporting fake snow in the displays. I loved looking at them even if I wasn't fond of shopping. Zinnia was an old-fashioned Southern town, built around the courthouse square. The grounds were marked with oak and magnolia trees that were also decorated in light and tinsel. The lone statue of Johnny Reb wore a Christmas wreath.

"The city voted this morning to remove the statue," Coleman said. "They're going to take it down immediately."

"Where will it go?"

"They're still looking for a museum or park to place it in."

The statue was a part of my childhood, of riding my bicycle around the square and visiting my father in his law office, but I also understood how painful it was for others. "I have a compromise," I said. "Couldn't we commission more statues? A Union soldier, a black soldier, Medgar Evers, James Meredith, Dr. James W. Silver, that newspaper writer Jerry Mitchell, Michael Schwerner, Andrew Goodman, and James Chaney—the three young civil rights workers who were murdered and buried in a dam, the men and women who stood up to racism. Couldn't we learn from the past?"

"We don't seem to be capable of learning from history." Coleman put his arm around me and pulled me close. "The best we can hope is that you and I learn from our past mistakes."

He was right about that. I snuggled against him, silently vowing to do my best not to repeat the missteps

I'd made before. Perhaps it was an inch-by-inch learning process for everyone, just like me.

We arrived at Dahlia House to Sweetie Pie's happy howls and Pluto's cool disdain. He was in a snit because he'd been left behind. Pluto enjoyed a good party with fancy gourmet treats. I won the cat over with some of the snacks I'd put in a plastic bag and pocketed for my pets. Sweetie Pie and Pluto ate dog and cat food, but only under duress. Normally Millie or I cooked for them—healthy food, but still home cooked. Canned food was a last resort.

Within ten minutes, the animals were smacking down salmon puffs, scrumptious chicken salad croissants, and some curried shrimp to die for. Coleman pulled a bottle of chilled champagne from the refrigerator. He'd snuck it in without my knowing. He popped the cork and filled two glasses.

"What are we celebrating?" I asked as I took the flute he handed me.

"Us."

And so we did, with long, slow kisses, talk of dreams for the future, and Christmas wishes and memories of the small miracles that made the season so wonderful. I'd avoided a fight with my man, and I'd come up with another lead to pursue as soon as the sun rose.

The next morning, Coleman left at daybreak. An overnight burglary at the local hardware store had him on the job—before I could even make coffee. I was in the kitchen brewing a pot when Cece called. I wondered if she'd butt-dialed me because Cece was not a crack-of-dawn person.

"I couldn't sleep," she said. "Guess what I found out."

"What?"

"Matilda and Curtis Bromley own a fish camp up the river from the boat launch."

I connected the dots instantly. The boat that the Bromleys had reported—with what might have been a drugged or dead Eve wrapped in some kind of drop cloth or rug—had headed upriver, possibly toward their camp, which they'd failed to mention. And why had the Bromleys felt the need to come forward with the purse they'd found? Coincidence, or something darker?

"Meet me at the paper," Cece said. "I have to make sure the photos from Harold's party are laid out correctly. Then I'm taking the rest of the day off." She cleared her throat. "Bring your gun."

"What about Tinkie?"

"We can do this without involving her."

And now, not only was I going behind Coleman's back, I was leaving my partner in the dark. But I understood Cece's impulse. If things went bad, it would be best if Tinkie wasn't involved. Cece was worried that we'd find something tragic. Tinkie didn't need to see a dead pregnant woman and baby. That was a true fact. Then again, neither did Cece. Or me. It was pointless, though, to try to convince Cece to call Coleman in.

I fed the horses, took off their blankets because the day promised to be sunny, and fed Pluto and Sweetie Pie. While they ate, I drank my coffee and made some toast. I wasn't hungry, but I'd learned one great old saying Aunt Loulane had never taught me: "Alcohol dissipates in the flames of carbohydrates." I'd had enough to drink the night before that some carbs would set me to rights. I ate three pieces of buttered toast, then loaded up the pets and headed for the *Zinnia Dispatch*.

Cece was waiting on the sidewalk for me. Sweetie gave her the front seat and we were off to an address north of Fortis Landing. It was still part of the river community, and if I followed the Tallahatchie River south, I would come to the boat launch where we'd met the Bromleys.

I turned where Cece directed, but I wasn't surprised when the dirt road we followed went deep into a river brake. The woods crowded close and I knew in the summer we'd be dive-bombed by yellow and horseflies and a number of other bloodsucking little varmints. We were almost on top of the cabin before we realized it.

"Let me go look," Cece said. "Just wait here with the motor running. Maybe turn around for a quicker get-away."

All good instructions, but what if she peeped in the window and got her head blown off? "There's not a vehicle here." The Bromleys had been driving a navy-blue pickup.

"Doesn't mean the place is empty. I'll be careful." She opened the door and, before I could stop her, Sweetie Pie was out like a streak. She coursed through the under-brush and headed up the steps. The cabin, made of cypress, was up on pilings to prevent flooding when the river was up.

"Sweetie!" I loud-whispered her name. She ignored me and clawed at the door. If someone was in there, they'd know they had visitors.

Cece got out of the car and stalked toward the door. She was the most ladylike of women until she was mad.

Then she developed this angry way of walking—which let everyone who could see her know to beware. To add to the stomping, she was wearing clodhopper boots that could have been steel-toed. She didn't have a gun, but she wasn't helpless.

I turned the car around so we could leave in a hurry and then got out with Pluto. I retrieved my gun and checked to be sure it was fully loaded.

Cece was climbing the steps to the front door, where Sweetie frantically barked and clawed. I was halfway up the stairs when I heard the door crash open. Cece had kicked it in. When I got to the porch, Cece and my dog were already inside. From the high elevation, I could see the river only fifty yards away, a slow-moving current of brownish yellow. I also noticed a road that ran along the riverbank. While the river was low it was perfectly passable. Come spring, it would be underwater.

"No one is here." Cece stated the obvious. The cabin was one large living/kitchen/bedroom area, furnished like most fishing cabins. I checked the bathroom to be sure. Empty. Sweetie moved about the room, sniffing and snuffling until she came to a heavy recliner and began to dig at the rug beneath it.

I got on my stomach and felt beneath the furniture until my hands captured a large, empty prescription pill bottle. I examined the bottle and discovered it was for prenatal vitamins for Dara Peterson. The script had been written several months earlier.

"Who is Dara Peterson?" I asked Cece.

"No idea." She took the bottle. "Another pregnant woman? I'm feeling there are just too many coincidences here. Are aliens stealing pregnant women and babies? I can't take much more of this."

"I'm on the same page. This is a strange coincidence and we have to figure out what it means."

"We're going to find out," Cece vowed. "I don't think Eve is dead. I do believe she's been here in this cabin." She held out a pacifier she'd found on the kitchen countertop. "And there're toys under the bed. There was definitely a child here."

"But Eve's baby wouldn't be old enough to play with toys or use a pacifier," I reminded her.

"I can't explain it, but this is all connected to Eve's disappearance."

Sweetie howled softly and went to the now permanently open door. "Listen," I said. The sound of a boat coming up the river was clear. "We have to get out of here."

"Take the medicine bottle. We can check at the pharmacy."

"Let's go." Sweetie Pie and Pluto needed no urging. They scampered down the steps and onto the wooded trail that led to the car. We didn't have time to try to repair the door, and it would have been pointless. Cece had destroyed the wood frame that once held the hinges. Someone was going to be majorly pissed off. My concern, though, was getting out of Dodge before we were caught. I heard the boat motor cut off just as we tore down the driveway. I hoped the arriving boaters hadn't caught a glimpse of my car, but it was too late to worry. It was time to drive.

Mud whipped from the wheels of my antique roadster as I beat it out of the bushes and onto the paved road. Instead of going back by the river, I hooked a left, preferring to drive several miles out of my way and double back rather than risk being seen crossing the river bridge.

"That was close," Cece said. She released her death grip on the door handle.

"Okay, so who is Dara Peterson?" Every time we followed a lead, we ended up in a pool of new questions. I felt like I was in a maze with pregnant women hiding around every hedge wall. "What does she have to do with Eve? *If* she has anything at all to do with her."

"She does," Cece said so seriously that I knew she believed wholeheartedly she was telling the truth.

"How do you know?"

"I didn't have time to tell you, but I found something." She reached into her coat pocket and brought forth a photograph. It was the same photo I'd found in Eve's apartment—the two babies swaddled and held in someone's arms. The headless torso, wearing the hospital gown, was female, but that was all I could tell. The babies were newborn, still all squinched up and mottled.

"Who are these kids?" I asked.

"I don't know, but we have to find out."

"This still doesn't prove that Eve was in the Bromley's fishing camp." I had to be sure Cece understood that we had no real evidence tying Eve to the Bromleys.

"I know she was there, Sarah Booth. I could . . . sense it."

That wasn't good enough. I didn't doubt her, but we needed evidence. The photo showed a clear link between Eve and the Bromleys, and I had no doubt they'd lied to us. But what was the link? I didn't know, and they had seemed like good people. Could they be responsible for Eve's disappearance? Were they holding her hostage? For the money? "Why would Curtis and Matilda put themselves in the spotlight by telling us about the purse if they were involved in her abduction?" It didn't make sense.

"Maybe they wanted us to know she was alive so we'd be sure and get the money together."

"But we don't know she's alive. And you already told the kidnappers you would get the ransom together."

"Eve has to be alive." Cece's voice cracked. "She has to be."

"I think she is alive, but we're no closer to finding her. What purpose would that whole trip to the river and the purse serve, if the Bromleys are involved with the abduction? Think about it logically, not emotionally."

"Maybe they wanted to see if we'd bring the law with us. Maybe this was a test run for the money drop and return of Eve. To see if we could be trusted."

Now that made a little more sense. If we'd shown up with the law, Cece was correct, we'd likely never see Eve again. "Breaking into that fishing camp might not have been the smartest idea."

"Only if they saw us. Did they?"

"I don't know, Cece. I hope not. Let's see what we can find on Dara Peterson."

We drove back to Millie's Café for breakfast and to call Tinkie. I refused to continue without including my partner, and Cece reluctantly agreed. Tinkie was huffy at first, but when I explained where we'd been and what we'd done and why we hadn't called her at butt-crack-o-dawn, she forgave us.

We showed her the prenatal vitamin bottle and she rolled her eyes. "You don't need a prescription for this," she said. "It's an OTC vitamin. I wonder why this Dr. Warren wrote a script for it."

"Maybe to get insurance to pay for it," I said, looking at Cece's puzzled expression. "Some policies cover OTC drugs, but only if there's a prescription."

"Why would you know so much about prenatal vitamins?" Cece asked Tinkie.

"I know about poisonous plants, too." Tinkie popped a bite of biscuit in her mouth. "All the girls I went to college with—except you two—have kids. What do you think they talk about at club meetings? Babies, pregnancy, doctors, and how fast their little tulips are developing into genius babies."

I wouldn't know. I hadn't kept up with college friends other than Tinkie, and I certainly had refused to join the Delta social clubs, which involved fancy dressing, husband bragging, reproduction, gardening, and community service.

"What are we going to do about this Dara Peterson? There aren't any Petersons that I know of in Sunflower County. But she could be from up around Fortis Landing. There's a whole community back along that river. They keep to themselves."

"Coleman could help us." I realized I hadn't seen him in four hours and I was already missing him.

"Fortis Landing isn't in Sunflower County," Cece was quick to point out. "Coleman has no jurisdiction."

"But he has experience and legal connections." I said it as gently as I could. "Please, Cece."

"No." Her chin jutted out.

I shook my head at Tinkie. "Then let's do some investigating. Cece, why don't you go to work? Seriously. Tinkie and I can handle this better without you."

"I can't believe—"

Millie, who'd been hovering near our table, wrapped her arms around Cece and held her close. "Let them handle it," she said. "I heard enough to know what's going on, and I agree. I'm going to make a box of breakfast pastries for you to take to the newspaper, and then you go there and wait. Stay busy. Or you can come to the kitchen and help me with some pies."

Cece blinked back her tears. "I think I'll help you bake, if that's okay."

"God help the people of Sunflower County," Tinkie said drolly. "Cece baking is almost as bad as me."

"Wrong," I said. "Nothing is as bad as what you create in the kitchen. Trust me, I remember those doggie treats you tried to make. I don't know how you turned ground meat, vegetables, and mashed potatoes into lethal weapons, but you did. The stench was enough to kill."

"Go on, Sarah Booth." Tinkie snapped her fingers under my nose. "I haven't seen any Betty Crocker awards hanging on your walls."

"You two take your bickering on the road." Millie pointed at the door. "Cece, you come on back with me. I have an apron hanging on the back wall. You know, I'm putting together those special Christmas tarts with fresh cherries and apples. They're so pretty and perfect for the holidays. I hate to see you get that nice outfit all messed up, but . . ." They went to the kitchen, Millie murmuring all the way.

I picked up the go boxes I'd ordered for Pluto, Sweetie Pie, and Chablis, Tinkie's little dust-mop dog. We had to hit it before Cece came out from under Millie's motherly spell and tried to join us. We would be far more effective without her.

8

Our first stop was Marlon Drugs, where Dara Peterson had filled her vitamin prescription. There were still two refills left on the bottle, and I thought I'd give it a try to see if the pharmacy might have an address for Dara. The Tallahatchie County pharmacy was in an old building and exuded character. Tinkie decided I should try to get Dara's address for a delivery. Tinkie, as the daughter of Avery Bellcase and the wife of Oscar Richmond and the Queen Bee Daddy's Girl, was too well known.

I turned in the bottle to be refilled and then moseyed around the store, looking at nail polish and Christmas candy. I was ready for a dark chocolate-covered almond reindeer. Yum. I resisted and kept moving. When Dara's name was called, I went to pick it up.

"Birthdate, please," the clerk said.

"I'm a friend. I didn't get her birthday. Sorry." I smiled sincerely. "I'm just doing Dara a favor."

"Address and phone," she said.

Another smile. "Look, I work with Dara. I'm sorry, I just don't know this information. I'm going to take the prescription back to the office with me. She'll pick it up later. Like I said, I'm only doing a favor."

She looked me dead in the eye. "Ms. Peterson will have to pick up the prescription herself. I'm sorry."

"It's prenatal vitamins, not crack," I couldn't stop myself from snapping. "Call her."

The clerk had gone from uninterested to annoyed. She began tapping on her screen and reached for a telephone. From behind the orthotic aisle, Tinkie let out a horrific scream of pain. "Help! I've fallen and I can't get up."

I had to turn away to hide my smile. Tinkie was awful. She was playing her part way over the top, but it was working.

"Help! I'm going to sue this place. There was water on the floor. Help me!"

The clerk and the pharmacist raced out from behind their counters and ran to help Tinkie. I swiveled the computer screen so that I could see Dara's address and phone number. When I had it memorized, I sashayed to the front of the store and left. I was waiting in the car when Tinkie came outside, looking like the cat that ate the canary.

"I take it you were successful in getting an address for Dara, thanks to my great acting," Tinkie said.

"I've fallen and I can't get up? What are you, a hundred and twelve?"

Tinkie laughed with delight. "I've always wanted to say that."

"It's the little things that make life worth living." I put the car in drive and headed out for Bison Street.

The property listed as the address for Dara Peterson put a pall over us. The lot was beautiful and shady, but the little house seemed to slump in the middle, as if the foundation had given out. Rusted tools and toys were scattered around the yard that was barren of any color or attention. Debris had clogged the gutters of the house, and a front porch swing hung by one chain.

"This is one of the most depressing houses I've ever seen," Tinkie said. "It isn't the poverty, it's the neglect. I mean, look at the mess. It wouldn't take much just to pick up the trash."

I had a terrible sense that Dara Peterson didn't have a single ounce of energy to spare. She was drowning in her life. "Do you think anyone lives here now?" The place certainly seemed abandoned to me.

"Maybe not." She got out of the car and walked to the front door. Sweetie, Chablis, and Pluto were right behind her. I was the caboose, but I put it in high gear.

No one answered Tinkie's knock, but Sweetie nosed the door open and we all trooped inside. The interior was worse than the outside. Dirty clothes and dishes were scattered about the floor. Even in the bitter cold, the detritus had attracted a swarm of flies. I heard them buzzing in the kitchen with a loud drone.

"Someone should call the health department," Tinkie said as she started toward the kitchen. "Or else the fire department. It might be kinder to torch this place."

"I'll take the kitchen if you check the bathroom," I said. Either room could contain a plague. I headed for the sound of the flies. The minute I stepped into the kitchen, I stopped. Blood was all over the floor. Not a pool big enough to indicate a person had died, but a lot of blood.

"There's nothing in the bathroom," Tinkie said. "I'll help in the kitchen."

I backed out and closed the door. "Call Coleman."

"He doesn't have any jurisdiction in this county," Tinkie reminded me, puzzled by my behavior. "What's wrong?"

I didn't want her to see the blood. I didn't know if it belonged to Dara, Eve, the baby, or what. "Just call him and ask him to meet us here. Now."

"Okay." She whipped out her phone and made the call. "He wants to know why he should come here."

"Because someone's been hurt really bad."

She relayed the message and hung up. "He's on the way. What's in the kitchen?"

I couldn't keep her out, so I pushed the door open and we went in together. Sweetie, Chablis, and Pluto had taken a seat by the front door. They were smart enough not to step into a crime scene. Tinkie and I stopped two feet into the room.

Blood had been smeared over the cabinets and the sink was filled with bloody towels. Beneath a chair at the kitchen table the flies had begun to settle in the carnage.

"What the hell happened here?" Tinkie asked.

"I don't know." It looked like a lot of blood. "I don't think it was a fatal accident."

"We should call Cece." Tinkie said it but I knew she didn't want to. Not until we had no other option.

"Let's see what Coleman says. Cece is already going to be furious that I called him, but I don't know the sheriff here in Tallahatchie County. It's best to let Coleman handle it or we might end up in jail. We're the closest thing to a suspect the sheriff is going to have."

She handed me her phone. "Better call Cece."

"Coward." But I took the phone and dialed. When Cece answered, I got right to it. "We're at Dara Peterson's house." I gave the address. "Something terrible has happened here, Cece. There's a lot of blood. I've called Coleman. I'm sorry, but this is a crime scene."

I listened to Cece's reply and then gave the phone back to Tinkie. "She's on her way. She's not mad that we called Coleman. In fact, I think she was more than a little relieved."

"Yeah, I'm glad Cece wasn't angry."

We talked back and forth for a few minutes, trying to get past the shock of the scene and the terror of what might have happened. At last, Tinkie spoke of the elephant in the room.

"Do you think Eve started to have the baby and got into trouble?"

I'd been thinking the same thing. "No, of course not. Probably someone was chopping up food and cut themselves." Man, was that ever lame.

"Yeah, that's probably it. Should we go outside and wait for Coleman?"

"And think of why we entered this house without permission." We had some stories to fabricate and quick. "We can say we thought we heard a struggle."

"Okay." Tinkie backed up until she was well out of the kitchen. We both went out the front door with our pets following. "We can say that. He won't believe it, but we can say it."

"If you think of something better, let me know." I was

agreeable to a more digestible lie. "In fact, you handle Coleman. I'm going to search the grounds before he gets here." I took off for the backyard, ignoring Tinkie's pleas for me to wait. Coleman was going to be furious with the two of us. Tinkie could be the sacrifice this time.

"Coward!" Tinkie hurled after me, but I just kept going. Sweetie, Chablis, and Pluto were with me. Tinkie was on her own in dealing with an irate lawman.

The property sloped down the back toward what was a fast-running little creek. It had to be spring fed from some source, but I wasn't in the mood to play Lewis and Clark and track upstream. It was big enough for a small boat or canoe to navigate, but I gathered it was mostly used to drain storm water. My goal was to hang out in the canopy of trees until Tinkie had soothed Coleman's ruffled feathers. Sometimes it was smart to be spineless.

The water's light and airy babbling drew me down the slope. Weaving among the trunks and fallen limbs and leaves, I found my way to the water's edge and stopped. Farther upstream, Sweetie Pie had started barking relentlessly. It was the big hound-dog bark, with Chablis filling in with her squealing little bark that was like an ice pick in my ear.

"Give it a rest," I said as I moved along the bank until I came up on the dogs. Then I understood. Trapped among the limbs and branches was a pink baby blanket. It had hung on a root, and was bobbing in the water.

A dozen questions came at me all at once, but the most important one was, where was the baby? The blood in the house, the blanket here in the creek, it was too much. I grabbed a tree trunk to steady myself and turned back to the house at a run.

I blasted in the back door and found Coleman talking to Tinkie in the living room. The anger faded from his face when he saw me.

"What's wrong?"

"Baby blanket." I pointed the way I'd come. "In the creek."

Coleman looked at Tinkie. "Stay here. When the crime scene people arrive, tell them everything you and Sarah Booth touched. Sarah Booth, show me. Quickly."

I saw the pain in Tinkie's eyes, but there was nothing I could say to protect her from the truth. If a baby had been put in the freezing creek, we had to find it right away. If it was still alive, it wouldn't be for long.

"I'm afraid someone put a baby in the creek," I said to Coleman as we fought our way down the slope and to the water.

"Where?" Coleman asked.

I pointed to the pink blanket bobbing in the amber water. "There."

He started forward and stopped on the edge of the water. The day was sunny, but the water was very cold. Without hesitation, Sweetie Pie plunged into the current and swam across to grab the blanket in her teeth. In a moment she was back beside me, shaking off the cold water. Pluto and Chablis did their best to avoid getting soaked.

Coleman examined the blanket and faced me, his expression grim. "There's blood here, too. We'll have to see if it matches the blood in the kitchen."

"Do you think . . . ?" I couldn't finish the question. I didn't want to know what Coleman thought about all that blood.

"Let's not jump to conclusions," he said. "This isn't my jurisdiction, but I called Sheriff Cobbs. I'm sure he's up at the house by now. He's going to be aggravated by you and Tinkie messing up his crime scene."

"He wouldn't have found it if it weren't for me and Tinkie," I said.

"True. Be sure and remind him of that."

"And Sweetie and Chablis found that blanket."

"Another point to remind Sheriff Cobbs about."

I could see Coleman wasn't going to work very hard to get me and Tinkie off the hook of a possible trespassing charge. Maybe even breaking and entering, since we'd opened the door and entered. I glared at him. "I did call you."

"And now you're going to tell me exactly what's going on." He put a hand on my shoulder and stopped me in my tracks. "Now."

It was pointless to fight him—and I didn't really want to. "Cece's cousin, Eve Falcon, has been kidnapped and is being held for a one-hundred-and-fifty-thousand-dollar ransom. She's very pregnant and due to give birth sometime around Christmas Eve. Tinkie and I have been trying to find her. Last night we had to go with Cece when she got a call that someone had found Eve's purse in the mud at the boat launch in Fortis Landing. That's where we went. That's how we ended up here, at this house."

"All of this in twenty-four hours?" Coleman asked.

I nodded.

"When is the drop for the ransom?"

"We don't know. The person said they would call. Cece knows to ask for proof of life, but I don't think she will. The kidnapper said if she called the law Eve would be killed. Cece's terrified. And she asked Tinkie and me, as her friends, to honor her decision to handle things herself."

"I understand." He turned away. "Let's get Cece and see if we can find who made those ransom calls to her."

I almost told him she would be furious with me, but it didn't matter. "I should have told you immediately."

"Second-guessing won't change a thing, Sarah Booth. You did what you thought was right, and that's all anyone can do."

That he wasn't angry with me was completely terrifying. It was almost as if he knew something tragic had occurred and he was trying to hold back the self-blame that might kill me.

9

The Tallahatchie sheriff had some questions and a few pointed remarks to make to me and Tinkie, but when his deputies found no additional evidence in the small creek behind Dara Peterson's place, he let us go after Coleman vouched for us.

Earning my everlasting gratitude, Coleman kept quiet about Eve Falcon's abduction. Her case now stretched across Sunflower, Leflore, and Tallahatchie counties, if we could prove that Dara Peterson was somehow involved in Eve's disappearance. There was no sign of Dara and no one who seemed to know anything about who she was. The Tallahatchie sheriff revealed to Coleman that he knew almost everyone in his county, but not her.

The house where Dara supposedly lived had been vacant for months; the owner had moved to Arizona for health reasons. It looked as if Dara was a squatter.

"What about the blood?" I asked Coleman as he was pretty much strong-arming me and Tinkie out of the cottage and into our car.

"That's up to the Tallahatchie sheriff now. Get out before he decides to arrest you. He could, and I wouldn't blame him."

"But what if Eve is hurt?" Tinkie said. She looked back at the wooded cottage, but got in the car when Sheriff Cobb came to stand on the little front porch.

"You need to take your detecting somewhere else right now," Coleman said. "I'll find out what I can, but drive away from here."

"You bet." I made sure my critters were in the backseat and put the car in drive. "See you tonight," I called back to Coleman.

When we arrived at Dahlia House, Cece and Madame Tomeeka were waiting. They'd decorated the entire balustrade on the front porch with magnolia boughs, cedar branches, and red ribbon. It looked wonderful, but they looked stressed out.

"Has anyone called about making the money drop?" I asked as I walked up the steps.

"No." Cece was on the verge of tears. "We decided to decorate to kill time. I've always loved Christmas, until this year."

"It's beautiful." And it was, but also sad. "Cece, I think you should call Jaytee and tell him to come home."

"I did," she said. "I've faced so many hard things in my life alone. I don't want to do that now. Not at Christmas. He and the band cancelled the rest of the tour and they're coming home."

I put an arm around her and gave her a hug. "I know how hard this is," I whispered.

Madame Tomeeka joined us in a huddle. "That baby's still alive," she said. "I feel it in my bones. I had a dream about two babies. They were in little bassinets, side by side. They were both healthy."

Tinkie jumped on it. "Are you sure, Tammy?"

"It's Christmas." Tammy nodded sagely. "Miracles happen at this time of the year."

Madame was trying to put the best spin on Eve's disappearance, but it might backfire on us if Eve was harmed. False hope was worse than no hope.

We trooped into Dahlia House and Tinkie made drinks while I put on coffee for Tammy. When we all had a beverage, we told Cece and Tammy everything we'd learned. Even about the blood. Cece took it hard, but she didn't break. She was made of sterner stuff.

"Has the kidnapper called again?" I asked.

"No. I've kept my phone on me to make certain I didn't miss a call. What if I never hear from him?" Cece's eyes brimmed with unshed tears.

It was a bleak prospect, but one I couldn't protect her from. "Cece, make some calls to the Bank of the Deep South at their Memphis headquarters. As Eve's cousin, you can ask about her. See if you can find someone who knows anything that might help us. She hasn't lived in Cleveland all that long. Maybe the kidnapper is someone from her past. Maybe even someone who cares about her." I, too, was grasping at straws. "We're jumping to the worst possible conclusion and we have to stop it."

"People who love you don't hold you for ransom," Cece pointed out.

"Not normally. But nothing about this case is normal," I insisted.

"What are you going to do?" Tammy asked me, swiftly changing the subject.

"Tinkie and I are going back to the river. We'll take a photo of Eve with us and see if anyone at Fortis Landing has seen her." I also wanted to get some clothing from Dara's house. It might not be useful, but if we found something with her scent on it, Sweetie Pie and Chablis might be able to track her. We had nothing to lose by trying. And I intended to pay a visit to Dr. Warren, the obstetrician listed on Dara's vitamin prescription. He might not tell us much, but I intended to ask.

"Okay." Cece stood up and paced. "I can't sit still. Let's move on this. I left some pastries in the kitchen, Sarah Booth. They're really good. Millie baked them and I watched."

Tinkie and I rose also. "I think I'll have one for the road," I said.

Cece tried for a smile and failed miserably. "Call me as soon as you find anything."

"Of course." Tinkie and I spoke simultaneously.

"Would you mind making some small holly wreaths to put around the candles on the dining room table?" Keeping Cece busy was an act of kindness. "And there are twenty or so presents to wrap in the closet under the stairs. The gift paper is there, too. You know I'm all thumbs with that kind of thing. Thanks!" I waved brightly as I drove away.

"You didn't give her a chance to say no," Tinkie said.

"Which was the point."

Because the sheriff was still at Dara's house, we went to the ob-gyn clinic where Dr. Milford Warren worked. Tinkie intimidated his nurse into bringing him to speak to us in a small office. He was a middle-aged man who carried a stack of charts and scratched his neck in frustration at being interrupted in his office visits.

"Whatever you ladies are selling, I'm not interested."

He thought we were drug reps. I'd wondered why the nurse even let us speak with him. "Dara Peterson. We need to find her."

It took him a moment to connect the dots, but when he did, anger flared behind his glasses. "Get out. I'm not at liberty to discuss anything about my patients with you."

"We're private investigators," Tinkie said. "Dara might be involved in the abduction of a young pregnant woman. Or she might be in serious trouble herself. There's blood all over her house. When is she due to deliver?"

That blast of information set him back on his heels. "Dara had her baby two months ago." He frowned. "Is the child still alive?"

"What?"

He realized his mistake, then shrugged. "The baby had a genetic disorder. Dara and her husband didn't have insurance. I got them an appointment at a children's hospital in the hopes they'd qualify for financial help, but I don't know if they fell under the purview of the hospital's treatment."

"When was the last time you saw Dara?"

"When I delivered her baby, about two months ago. She didn't show up for her post-birth check." He sighed. "I should have had the nurse call her. I knew Dara had financial issues. I told her it didn't matter. I would help her. But her whole focus was the baby. Not her own health."

Then the blood in her kitchen wasn't part of a delivery—unless it was Eve's delivery. Had Eve and her child been abducted to replace Dara's sick baby? Oh, that was a really bad thought. Women who stole other women's babies seldom had a need to keep the birth mother alive once the baby was born.

"What was wrong with the baby?" Tinkie asked.

The doctor shook his head. "I've said more than I should have. But understand that Dara wouldn't harm a pregnant woman or her baby. I simply can't believe that. If she's involved in this, it isn't willingly."

"What about the husband?" I asked.

"Never met him. Which told me a lot. These men who aren't involved in the wife's pregnancy, it's not a good sign. Used to be that men weren't really allowed to participate. They were given orders to wait while the doctor took charge. Then once the baby was born, the child became the woman's province. But it's healthier for the husband to be involved throughout the pregnancy. When the child comes, he already has a connection."

"Dr. Warren, was Dara's life in any medical danger? There was so much blood . . ." Tinkie trailed off.

"She delivered without a hitch. Two months have passed. She should have been healed. There's nothing I could think of resulting from her pregnancy and delivery. That still leaves a lot of things that could have happened, but I won't speculate. Now, I have patients waiting and one in delivery at the hospital."

Tinkie nodded, and I could see the shimmer of tears in her eyes. She was so tenderhearted. "Thanks, Dr. Warren."

We took our leave, and I was glad to vacate the doctor's office. Even though I adored Doc Sawyer, who'd taken care of me and Tinkie since we were as big as butter-beans, I still got the heebie-jeebies in any medical facility.

"Back to Dara's house?" Tinkie asked.

"Yep."

We were in luck because the sheriff had gone by the time we arrived. The front door was blocked with crime scene tape, but I went in a window and returned with a baby onesie and a woman's blouse. Just for good measure, I also took a man's long-sleeve flannel shirt. Presumably, the shirt belonged to the missing husband of Dara Peterson. The caller wanting the ransom had probably been male. It was a scenario I could work with, as far as pinpointing a villain. But I had no proof Dara and Eve were connected in any way.

When I got back to the car, which Tinkie had turned around and kept running in case we needed to make a quick getaway, I tossed the clothing into the backseat and jumped in the passenger seat. Tinkie took off, giving me a smile. "I love your mama's car," she said. "It may be old, but it is the perfect car for you, Sarah Booth."

The old Mercedes Roadster was listed as an antique, but it ran like a top. "I know. Sometimes I dream about riding in the car with my mother driving, the wind blowing her hair, and her laugh." I'd loved those sunny afternoons when I had my mother to myself. We had all kinds of adventures in the woods and fields and creeks. She'd taken me for horseback riding lessons from an old farmer who had ridden in the US Cavalry. He took no sass, and he gave me confidence as a rider and a real understanding of the bond between human and equine.

"Good memories," Tinkie said. "My mother would never have a convertible because it mussed her hair."

Tinkie's mom wasn't nearly as much fun as mine, but

she loved Tinkie in her own way. Ever since Tinkie had married Oscar and he'd taken over the day-to-day operation of the bank, the Bellcases often traveled. They were in Rome at the moment. They loved the Italian sunshine in the winter, and I didn't blame them, but Tinkie had grown up feeling like the odd girl out in her parents' marriage. They were the couple, and she'd often been left with hired help. Excellent hired help, but not family.

"I remember the Christmas party your mother hosted for you when you were ten. It was a lovely tea, and I can still see all the decorations in your home. When your mother came down the stairs in the beautiful ball gown as the Wish Fairy, I was in awe. It was so magical."

"And you had ghost stories and a sleepover party." She smiled at the memory. "You had fun. I had . . . elegance."

"Love is love. We each give what we know how to give. Elegance was how your mom shared her love." I patted her shoulder. "Now you can have any kind of party you want. And a husband who's willing to bail your friends out of trouble. That's a lot, Tinkie."

"Yes, each gift we receive is precious." Her hands tightened on the steering wheel. "Sarah Booth, I have a special Christmas wish this year."

"Sounds like Oscar is a lucky man, but no, I won't videotape any of your bedroom hijinks." I wasn't sure where she was heading, but I wanted to keep it lighthearted if I could. Tinkie didn't whine, but I knew the one thing she wanted more than anything else was a baby. That's why this case troubled me so. It opened an old wound for Tinkie. In a most recent case she'd been certain that three witches who'd opened a boarding school in Sunflower County had worked a potion or spell or something that would allow her to overcome scarred Fallopian tubes to conceive. The months had passed without incident or pregnancy and I'd hoped she'd put that dream behind her. Now here we were, back at babies again. Almost as if the universe wanted to rub her nose in it.

"When we finish here, I want a nice drink. How about we stop at Odell's Roadhouse? They have a Christmas band. Maybe we'll karaoke."

"Sounds good." Tinkie's request was unexpected, but upbeat. I was in for a drink. Odell's had been a high school hangout down a tiny dirt road in the backwoods of Fortis Landing, but I hadn't been inside in years. It was naughty behavior to slip into the roadhouse when I was in high school and the laws for selling booze to minors were a lot more laxly enforced. None of my group really drank—maybe a beer or Jack and coke. Pretty much pantywaist drinking. But we'd thought we were bold and badass. "We'll call Cece and the gang to meet us. Until Jaytee gets home, she doesn't need to be alone."

"Good thinking." A snuffling noise in the backseat made me turn around. Sweetie Pie and Chablis were sniffing and snorting at the flannel shirt I'd taken from Dara's house. "What's with them?" I asked.

Tinkie checked them out in the rearview mirror. "If only they could talk. They must like the way Dara smells."

I called the Tallahatchie hospital to check on any accident victims or pregnant women being admitted and came up empty. The new laws dictating patient privacy were hard to get around, but I had a good story prepared—I was looking for my niece and I feared she was in an automobile accident. I believed the receptionist when she said that no accidents had been reported. Wherever the blood had come from, neither Dara nor Eve had been taken to the hospital.

We breezed into Fortis Landing as the early winter dusk was falling. The community itself was several miles from the actual boat landing, and it was a one-block village more than a town. Main Street was fronted with buildings that gave the silhouette of an old west town. I could visualize the place with mule teams and well-tired horses tied to the hitch rail in front of the handful of stores. The old general merchandise store was now a pawn shop, and the locals shopped at the Get and Go for milk, bread, cigarettes, and beer. There was a beauty parlor and a chiropractic office, two insurance offices, propane gas, and an electric power office. The big chain grocery and the strip malls were twenty miles down the road.

In the gloaming, the street was empty. Sadness seemed to steal over the little community as the emptiness became acute. As we slowed to take in the stillness of the night, the Christmas lights popped on. Little Fortis Landing had the old lights that had been strung along power lines with silver tinsel. I hadn't seen them in years. The bigger cities had gone to the easier pole lights or even lighted shrubbery planted around town. I loved the old tinsel and lights and because I was a passenger, I could tilt my head back and let the lights pass in a blur as Tinkie drove the convertible.

"Most of the houses are along the river," Tinkie said. "It's another ten minutes."

"Hit it!" This wasn't a lead likely to turn up any new information, but it was one that had to be marked off the list. And we didn't have much time. We needed to be home and dressed for the Christmas Pageant. I had a lot of worries, but I didn't want to share them with Tinkie, who looked depressed enough on her own. "I really like being driven." It was a true fact.

"Don't get comfy. We're at the river."

The road abruptly ended in the Tallahatchie River. "What did Billie Joe McAllister throw off the Tallahatchie Bridge?" I asked in a terrible imitation of Bobbie Gentry's famous song.

"I sure as hell hope it wasn't a baby, and let me just add that if you're going to sing a cappella, I need earplugs."

"Clever, Tinkie. Really clever." But even Sweetie Pie was shaking her head and flapping her ears as if they hurt her. "Let's do a door-to-door and get this over with."

We parked at the end of the paved road where the river flowed swiftly by. A pig trail veered right along the riverbank. We set off on foot with the dogs leading the way and Pluto bringing up the rear.

The river lapped gently against the banks, shushing into the tallgrass that grew in the shallows. It was a cold winter night, almost Christmas, and we had two missing mothers and two missing babies and a room that had too much blood spread around in it. I tried to beat those thoughts back as Tinkie and I trudged along.

"These boots aren't really made for walking," Tinkie said as she stopped to kick some clots of river mud from the bottom of her high-dollar dress boots. "If we're going to stomp around the river bottoms, I need some paddock boots like yours."

"Maybe we should go shopping. I could get you boots for Christmas." I knew Tinkie would view my offer more as threat than treat. No one trusted my shopping skills.

"Uh, some coffee beans would be a lovely gift." Tinkie sidestepped a puddle with a dainty leap. "Or just your company."

I'd already found the perfect Tinkie gift—a sequined

scarf from a little shop on Rodeo Drive. I did have my upscale gift sources when I needed them. But I liked to torment her. "I saw some cowgirl boots that would be perfect for you, Tinkie. You could get a little denim miniskirt with studs and bedazzling all over the butt and we could go dancing."

She hurried ahead of me. "No, I don't think dancing is a good idea. Let's stop in at this cabin."

The place she indicated was up on stilts, as were all the homes along the river. Lights burned in the front room, and we could hear the soft twang of a guitar as we climbed the steps. The dogs dropped back and let Tinkie lead. She knocked on the door. When it opened, she took a step back so she could fully take in the nearly seven-foot-tall young man who answered.

"May I help you?" he asked.

"We're searching for a missing young woman," Tinkie said. "Have you seen her?" She offered the photo of Eve that Cece had obtained from an internet search.

The young man frowned. "Maybe."

"Maybe you've seen her or maybe you haven't?" Tinkie asked.

"Maybe." He grinned. "Why are you looking for her?"

"She's missing." Tinkie was about to lose patience. "Her relative is worried about her. She's very pregnant."

The grin left his face. "I'm sorry. Didn't mean to step on your worry. I haven't seen the young woman. At least I can't be certain. There was a young woman here a couple of days ago. Staying down the river, I think. She was pregnant, but I didn't get a good look at her."

"Do you know who she was staying with?" I asked.

"Look, there're a lot of people here who don't want

folks prying into their business. I try hard to keep my nose on my side of the property line."

"It's a simple question," Tinkie said. "Have you seen her?" Her voice broke at the end, and I think that was what brought the tall man around.

"I'm pretty sure it was her. She left in a boat with a couple. Headed upriver. I don't know who they were or where they were going. I was on my way to the bar for a burger and beer."

"But you saw her!" Tinkie was so relieved.

"I'm pretty sure I did. It was dark."

"She was walking on her own?"

"She was sitting in the boat." He stepped out on the porch and pointed to the boat landing, which was a good fifty yards away. "I came out here a couple of nights ago and stopped to smoke a cigarette. That's when I looked down at the pier. A middle-aged couple was getting in the boat with a younger woman. She looked big, like bundled up but also pregnant. They headed toward me, and I looked closer when they passed me as I was walking to the bar. She looked at me for a moment, then away. I think it was that girl you're looking for."

It wasn't the best identification I'd ever heard, and eyewitnesses were often unreliable, but it gave Tinkie hope.

"Did you know the couple she was with?"

He inhaled. "If I see her again, how about I call you?"

He wasn't going to answer Tinkie's question, which told me he likely knew the people. Societies that sprang up around rivers were often closed to outsiders. They looked after their own, and they didn't like rats or snitches. I pulled out a business card and handed it to him. "We only care if Eve is okay. Eve Falcon, that's her name. No one wants to make any trouble. Her cousin, Cece Falcon, is worried about her. She has no intention of involving the law or anything. We just want to know she's safe."

"She looked safe to me," he said, somewhat reluctantly.

"Thank you." Tinkie reached up and tapped his chest where his heart would be found. "Thank you. That helps more than you'll ever know."

I was a little shocked at my friend. She normally wasn't touchy-feely with strangers. We headed down the steps and back to the road. I was ready to go to the car and call Cece, but Tinkie put a hand on my arm. "He's lying through his teeth."

"What?" I'd bought her whole gratitude routine completely.

"He's lying."

"About what?"

"I don't know, but I know he's not telling the truth. He may have seen her, but he knows more than he's saying. He just wanted to get rid of us. Move the car and I'll stay here and watch. I'm wondering if he won't get in touch with someone or maybe even go to them."

Tinkie was brilliant, which made me even more brilliant to have taken her on as my partner. "Good thinking!"

"Go," she said. "Move the car up to the bar and then come back."

"Should I call Cece to join us?"

"No. Let's see how this plays out. We can call her later."

"Good plan."

10

I left Sweetie Pie, Chablis, and Pluto with Tinkie—she needed someone to keep an eye on her—while I drove my car up to Odell's and left it in the lot with thirty other vehicles. I found what I hoped was a secluded place where most people wouldn't see the old Roadster. Tinkie and I needed less conspicuous vehicles when we were working.

As I left the car, I heard Garth Brooks on the jukebox inside. "Friends in Low Places" was the tune. I was fortunate in my friends, and that was the best Christmas miracle ever. The next song up was Burl Ives singing "Holly Jolly Christmas." Whoever was feeding quarters into the jukebox needed to be physically restrained.

The gravel crunched beneath my sensible boots as I made my way back to the river and down the dirt road to the place where I'd left Tinkie. Which was completely empty. No Tinkie. No dogs. No cat. Just the flashing red and green lights on the house set back from the road.

"Tinkie!" I whisper-hissed her name. "Tinkie! Where are you?"

The night had no answers for me. Not even the dogs made a sound. I moved down the road, glad I'd been smart enough to bring a flashlight and my gun, though I was reluctant to turn the torch on for fear of alerting folks to my presence. Lights pricked the total darkness through the thick growth of trees. This was a river community, and many people would not welcome a stranger knocking at their door. So where was Tinkie? Had something happened to her?

"Tinkie!" I called a bit louder. "Sweetie Pie! Pluto!" Calling the pets was a long shot because they often ignored me in the best of circumstances. To my shock, Pluto came out of the trees and joined me on the road. He curled around my ankles and bit at my knees.

"Where the hell is Tinkie?"

He started into the woods. Trusting his ability to navigate the darkness better than I could, I followed. As we wound our way through the trees, I grew more and more concerned. Tinkie wasn't the kind of woman to take off through the underbrush in the dead of a winter night. She was wearing dress boots, not real boots. She didn't have a weapon or a light. And why would she willingly fumble into a place where tree limbs poked at my eyes and tore at my clothes and hair? Tinkie was not a fan of the windswept or twig-swept look.

I stopped to get my bearings. The trees were so thick I lost sight of the dim lights that had marked a few of the houses down the road. Even the sound of the river water gently lapping the bank was gone. It was as if I'd stepped under a glass bowl where I was disconnected from everything except my immediate surroundings.

Using my flashlight as little as possible, I eased forward. Where in the world were Tinkie and the pets? Now even Pluto was AWOL.

Far in the distance I heard the sound of music. I recognized the Christmas ballet I'd always loved. What was going on? Where was my friend? I felt the pressure of panic pushing at me. I stepped forward in the darkness and came to an abrupt stop. Someone was in my path. I clicked on the flashlight to reveal an older man, who I knew instantly as Uncle Drosselmeyer. The man with the magic in *The Nutcracker* ballet.

All around me, the beautiful melody of the ballet came from the trees and limbs and branches, and Uncle Drosselmeyer began to dance. The leaves of the trees reflected a soft, diffused light that illuminated the woodland clearing in a mystical glowing orb of light. From behind the tree trunks, animated toys came into view. They joined in the dance with the great magician of the ballet. I thought back over my day to be sure I hadn't ingested any hallucinogens. What I saw right in front of me wasn't possible, yet I was seeing it. The toys and snowflakes danced to the lovely music, and Drosselmeyer, who was a fine figure of a muscular and lithe man, danced and leaped and whirled with such grace I was breathless just watching.

Drosselmeyer danced toward me and unveiled the nutcracker toy. He jetéed around a large oak tree and then rested the nutcracker in a nook of roots. I was transfixed with the agility of the dancer. At last I thought to pull out my phone and record what was happening. Just as I did so, Uncle Drosselmeyer began to change. Slowly, the dancer turned into someone I was far more familiar with, even if it was almost as impossible. Jitty, disguised as a beloved member of the ballet troupe, had followed me into the woods of Tallahatchie County.

With one magnificent grand jeté, Jitty twirled and faced me. Unsurprisingly, my phone camera had captured only blank darkness.

"What are you doing here in the woods?" I whispered because, in my heart of hearts, I hoped Tinkie was close by.

"You have to believe, Sarah Booth." Jitty unbuttoned the top of her suit coat. "That's your problem. You really don't believe. Christmas is all about believing."

"I have to believe in Santa Claus to find my friend and my pets?" Annoyance was clear in my tone.

"You have to believe in yourself, and in the power of the season."

"Bull crap." I had a missing pregnant woman and another missing mother and child. I was in the middle of the bitter-cold woods, unable to find my partner or critters. This wasn't a time to lecture me on believing in magic or Christmas characters. Next she'd be after me to find Rudolph to light my way home with his red nose.

"Do you believe the nutcracker came to life?" Jitty asked. Her costume had begun to disappear and she was no longer the dancer, but Jitty, the haint of Dahlia House wearing my favorite jeans and green Christmas sweater.

"It's a ballet. It's fantastic and wonderful, but it is a stage production."

"Am I real?" Jitty asked.

I had the good sense to stop the first answer that bubbled to my lips. "You're very real to me." I'd almost said she wasn't, and a deep vein of fear opened up at what might have happened if I'd said that. Would she have disappeared? Would I be left at Dahlia House without Jitty, my friend, protector, and connection to the Great Beyond, where most of my family resided?

"And if you tried to tell someone about me, would they believe you?"

That was a tougher question. "They would want to believe me." But I knew Tinkie would think I'd fabricated a means of communicating with my dead parents. And Cece would think that I'd opened the door to a subconscious desire made manifest. Madame Tomeeka is the only one who might believe me. She was hooked into the spirit world in a way that was much stronger than I was. But could she believe that I lived with the ghost of my great-great-great-grandmother's dead nanny who'd been a slave and best friend? I couldn't answer that.

"But would they believe?" Jitty pressed.

"They would try. And each one might come to believe in his or her own way."

"The ability to believe in the unbelievable is what makes life magical," Jitty said. "Without belief, your Granny Alice and I would have opted for a suicide pact. We had to believe that the sweet potatoes would make, and the okra, and that somehow, the two of us could scratch out enough food to feed the chil'ren and ourselves through the winter."

"She couldn't have made it without you, Jitty." I'd thought many times that I didn't have the grit of my Grandmother Alice or Jitty, or even of my parents, who'd stood up to injustice in a very public way.

"She couldn't have made it without believing that the future would be kinder than the present. That we could somehow figure it out and manage to keep body and soul together. We believed, Sarah Booth. Else we would have given up."

"You believed in your own abilities to do whatever was necessary. That's different than believing in Santa Claus or the tooth fairy."

"Is it?" Jitty did a quick and deft plié, letting me know that even in my jeans she could cut a fine figure on a stage.

I thought about her question. Really thought. Was it so different? Was self-sufficiency a more solid belief than in a mythical figure? "I don't know," I answered honestly. "Believing in magic is very powerful."

"And you just made my point, girlfriend!" Jitty held up a hand to high-five. She was done with classical ballet and rational thought. She'd one-upped me in the logic department and she wasn't interested in further debate.

"Make-believe won't keep Eve and her baby safe or help me find Tinkie."

Jitty sighed. "Call her."

"What?"

"Whip out that cell phone you love so much and call Tinkie. And, just so you know, twenty years ago few folks on the planet would have believed you could carry a phone in your pocket and dial a friend from almost anywhere in the U.S. of A. Now I have work to do."

Leaps and twirls took her to the edge of the woods, where she turned. "You'll come around, Sarah Booth. I know it." There was a burst of giggling from the animated mice and toys, a flash of the soft lights from the fluttering tree leaves, and then Jitty was gone.

The cell phone in my pocket rang.

"Where the hell are you?" Tinkie asked, more than a little annoyed.

"I could ask you the same. I've been trudging through the woods looking for you."

"I'm standing in the road right where I've been for the last half hour, waiting for you. Not a single car has passed and the tall man hasn't left his home. Good thing one of us is doing our jobs!"

I noted her sarcasm and chose to ignore it. The sequence of events didn't make any sense at all. Tinkie hadn't been on the road. She'd disappeared into the woods first, which was why Pluto had followed her in, and I'd followed Pluto. "I'll be right there." I backtracked and found myself on the rutted road in front of the cabin where the tall man lived. The dim lights of houses scattered down the road were easily viewed. The woods were not as thick as the grove I'd just left. I walked fifty yards down the road and found Tinkie standing with the dogs and Pluto. "Did you ever leave the road?" I asked.

"Are you a fool? There could be alligators in those woods," she said.

"Or worse. Ballet dancers."

She looked at me like I'd lost my mind, which I likely had. "So are we going on down the road to interview people or have you decided to play Hansel and Gretel in the woods?"

Her question gave me pause. "I'm going to find Eve and her baby. I believe they're okay."

Tinkie put a hand on my forehead to check for a fever. "Are you okay?"

"I'm better than I've been in several days. We're going to find her, Tinkie. I know we are. Christmas is the season of miracles, and we're overdue."

Tinkie knelt down by Sweetie Pie and Chablis. "I don't know what's going on with Sarah Booth, but let's roll with it, okay? She's so much pleasanter when she's in a positive mood."

Sweetie Pie barked twice, as if agreeing. My own hound dog was betraying me.

"Let's head down the road." I started walking fast, knowing the pace would prevent Tinkie from talking too much. "Here." I handed her the gun. She was a better shot.

"You think I'll need to plug someone?"

"You sound like you'd like that." Sometimes Tinkie's bloody streak surprised me.

"I would, if it's the person who abducted Eve."

"Just as long as we have a plan," I said sarcastically.

"Tomorrow is Christmas Eve," Tinkie said.

She was correct, but that was the date set for Eve's delivery. "We need to find her." I couldn't help the feeling that time was running out for us. It was harder to believe in Christmas miracles when the stakes were so high.

We knocked on the doors of several more houses and ended up with no information to help us. Some of the homes were empty—the occupants out for the evening.

"Let's head back to that roadhouse," I said. "This is getting us nowhere fast."

"I agree," Tinkie said. "You need a drink."

I pulled out the phone and called Cece to join us.

"I have news," she said. "I'll tell you when I see you."

Before I could respond, she hung up. I relayed the information to Tinkie. "Is it good news or bad news?" Tinkie asked.

"We'll know soon enough."

11

Tinkie and I bellied up to the bar at the roadhouse and I ordered Jack Daniel's on the rocks. Tinkie opted for the same. Best to keep the drink orders easy and simple. We'd left the pups and cat in the car, snuggled into a warm comforter. We wouldn't be long in Odell's, but we needed to meet with Cece.

Tinkie was what a lot of men considered "fun sized" because she was petite, so I kept a wary eye out for anyone who might give us trouble. Normally no one had an interest in us, but we were strangers in this bar, and it was a lively place with pool tables, loud music on the jukebox, and more single men than women. We sipped our drinks and huddled together, talking about the case.

"Where did you go, Sarah Booth?" Tinkie asked. "You acted like you were lost."

How I wanted to tell her about Jitty and Uncle Drosselmeyer. But I couldn't. Jitty's lecture on believing in my own abilities had given me renewed hope that I desperately wanted to share with Tinkie, but how to explain that I was haunted by a woman dead for one hundred and fifty years who'd appeared as a fictional character from a Russian ballet. It was impossible to explain. So I told a half truth. "I thought I heard something in the woods and I got turned around."

"That strip of woods is only about forty yards wide." Tinkie didn't believe a word of what I was saying.

I shrugged. "I don't know how it happened. I'm just glad we're back in civilization."

"That's a questionable assertion." Tinkie tucked in closer to me as a big guy stopped at her elbow.

"Care to dance, ma'am?" he asked.

I nudged her. "Go on and dance. It'll help pass the time."

She cast a murderous glare at me and headed to the dance floor. It was a quick two-step and the man was a fine dancer. In a moment, Tinkie's reservations had blown out the front door and she was having the time of her life. Any woman knows a strong lead makes dancing fun. This guy was good at leading and Tinkie was light on her feet. He had her spinning, whirling, and moving from the dancer's frame to side-by-side and back. They were fun to watch.

"Ma'am, would you like to dance?" I looked up to find a green-eyed cowboy holding out his hand.

"Sure. I'm not as good a dancer as my friend, but I do like to dance."

We hit the floor and in a moment the fast pace of the song had all of my concentration on not stomping his feet. At the end of the tune, our partners returned us to the bar with a gentlemanly "thank you."

We danced three songs before the door of the bar swung open and a face I recognized entered the establishment. Two faces. Curtis and Matilda Bromley took one look at us and froze like 'possums in the headlights of a car. It wasn't just that they hadn't expected to see us—it was something else. They reeked of guilt.

I waved them over to the bar. "Let's get a table," I said, ignoring the obvious signs that they preferred not to talk to us.

Tinkie cleared up our bar tab as we found a table in a corner. "This is perfect. We can talk. My partner and I have some questions." Suddenly the Bromleys were not the innocent good Samaritans that I'd first thought them to be. They'd found Eve's purse and called Cece—what I'd assumed to be an act of compassion. Now I had a far darker motivation assigned to their actions.

"What are you doing at Odell's?" Curtis asked, trying not to make it sound accusatory and failing completely.

"Oh, we're looking for someone," I said.

"Yeah, that Falcon girl," Matilda said. "We haven't seen her."

"Have you seen Dara Peterson?" Tinkie asked, a quick thrust of her interrogation skills.

"Wh-who?" Matilda asked. The color left her face.

"We know all about it," I said. "In fact, we were just about to call the law."

"For what?" Curtis quickly grew belligerent. "We haven't done anything wrong except try to keep Ms. Falcon from worrying about her relative."

"Where is Eve?" I asked.

"If I knew that, I'd take you there." Matilda kept her gaze leveled at mine. "I mean it. I don't know where she is."

"But you do know something." It wasn't a question.

"She was alive when we saw her," Matilda said. "We should have just come out and said it instead of planting the purse and trying to pretend we didn't know. She was perfectly fine. She got in the boat and went upriver."

"Who was she with?" Tinkie almost jumped across the table.

"I didn't know the people. Honestly." Matilda was still holding my gaze.

"Did you speak to her?" I asked.

She nodded. "She was very pregnant and I didn't think it was a good idea for her to be getting into a small boat. I asked her if she needed help and she said no, she was fine. There was nothing else I could do. She dropped that purse and it wasn't an accident. I did what I thought she wanted—got in touch with her kin."

"You can tell us who has her." Tinkie cut to the chase. "If anything happens to her or that baby, you're going to be charged as an accessory."

For the first time, Matilda's gaze faltered, and my heart sank. Did she know that something terrible had already happened to Eve? She'd never tell me, no matter how long I questioned her. "All we want is to find Eve and know she's safe."

"I don't know where she is, but I do believe she's safe." Matilda punched Curtis on the shoulder when he tried to stop her from speaking. "They know we know." She turned back to me. "She's okay. Pay the money and get this over with."

"Has she had the baby? It's due tomorrow." Tinkie grasped Matilda's hand. "Just tell us."

"No. She hasn't delivered and she isn't in labor. But she wants to get back to her life. Just pay the ransom and put an end to it."

"Cece has the money," I said. "We're waiting for instructions to make the drop. If you want to wait here, Cece is on the way. She can bring the money right now. We just want this to be over." I wondered how deep they were in this.

"We aren't touching any money," Curtis said. "None. We don't have anything to do with any of this. We only wanted to try to let you know Eve was safe. We wanted to do a good thing and now you're threatening us."

"A good thing would have been to send Eve home. You can't hold a woman hostage for a ransom and call it a good thing." I spoke as calmly as I could.

"You call it what you want to call it." Matilda's eyes narrowed. "I call it doing a good deed. Now we're leaving, unless you want to call the police, and I don't think you want to do that."

There was a clear warning in her words. "No, we aren't calling the law," Tinkie said sharply. "We won't jeopardize Eve or her baby. But if anything happens to either of them, understand that I'll be looking for you. And I will find you."

"When this is over, you can stop by and apologize," Matilda said stiffly. "Let's go, Curtis." They both stood up and walked out the door and into the night.

"We should stop them," I said, but I didn't make a move.

"We could follow them. See if they lead us to Eve."

But we both knew they were smarter than that. We'd

made our decision when we let them leave the bar without calling Coleman. They would never lead us to Eve. This was a dead end—except that we now knew Eve was alive and well.

The bar door opened and Cece came in, searching the dimly lit interior until she saw us in the corner. She signaled a waitress as she headed to join us. When she sat down, the lighting emphasized the furrow between her eyebrows. She looked tired and unhappy.

"We have reason to believe Eve is perfectly fine," Tinkie said.

"What?" Cece almost stood up, but I signaled her back into her chair. "How do you know? What did you find?"

"Hold your horses, Cece." Tinkie put a hand on her hand. "The waitress is here for our order. We'd like another round, and she'll have a tequila and grapefruit juice." Cece looked like tequila was exactly what she needed.

When we were alone again, we leaned in closer so we could whisper. Tinkie told Cece all about our meeting with the Bromleys and what we'd learned.

"You should have detained them." Cece glared at us.

"Honey, they weren't going to tell us anything, and I truly believe they don't know where Eve is. They do know she's okay."

"How do they know that?" Cece asked.

"Because I believe they know the kidnapper," Tinkie said. We'd come to the exact same conclusion. "Eve is with someone they know and care about. And to be honest, Tinkie, if we'd detained the Bromleys, it could have gone badly for Eve. It was clear to me they knew about the threat of going to the police. They pretty much dared us to call the law. We could have forced them to stay here, but . . ."

"No, you did the right thing." Cece's entire body slumped. "I'm not second-guessing you. It's just that I want her back so much. I have such guilt that I let her slip out of my life and I didn't fight to keep her in it."

I remembered when Cece was going through her surgeries and the changes that had taken such courage. She'd been part of the Delta elite families and heir apparent to the Falcon land and money. When she'd decided to transition, she'd lost everything, including her family. "You had all you could manage just to get through each day, Cece. You can't blame yourself for this."

"But I do."

There it was, the guilt we all shouldered even when we shouldn't.

"Cece Dee Falcon, you stop this right now." Tinkie was hot under the collar. Her face was beet red, and she was almost hyperventilating she was so angry. "Eve made her choices. She was in a bad place with those scoundrels she calls her parents. They're about as loving as cornered honey badgers. But that wasn't your fault. And it wasn't Eve's fault that she lost touch with you because her parents disapproved. It's just a fact. And she moved on with her life the best she could—just as you did. No one is to blame. The important thing is that we are all here, right this minute, doing everything we can to see that Eve and her baby are safe. That's the only thing that matters. The past is done and gone."

I wanted to applaud, but I settled for holding up my glass for a toast. I took a swallow of the fresh drink and stopped. "This is tea," I said. "It isn't Jack."

"I know," Tinkie said calmly, reaching over and taking

it from my hand. "I'm driving, remember? I've been in enough hot water with Oscar. If he has a clue I'm drinking and driving he'll have a conniption fit."

I couldn't argue with her logic, so I kept my lip zipped and took a long swallow of Jack from my actual glass that burned nicely going down. I was glad Tinkie was a responsible driver. "Cece, you had some news," I said. "Spill it?"

She looked so miserable, I wondered what could have gone so wrong.

"I got the ransom call. They want me to deliver the goods tomorrow at ten o'clock in the evening."

"Coleman, Oscar, and Harold will all be busy at the church Christmas pageant," Tinkie reminded us and gave Cece a big smile. "See, it's going to work out. We'll deliver the money and get Eve and go straight to the hospital. I'll have Doc on call for us."

Doc always had our physical health in the forefront, but I doubted he would be so agreeable to being manipulated. I blew out a breath of air. "Where's the drop?" I asked.

"Upriver from here," Cece said. "I used Google Earth to find it and it's pretty isolated. We won't be able to pull any tricks. It's a narrow road in and only one way out."

"Which shows the kidnappers know this area like the back of their hands. They'll have the advantage. What we have in our favor is that if we get Eve back we don't care about the money," Tinkie said. "They can have it. We just want her and the baby to be okay."

"It's a lot of money." Cece was clearly upset. "A lot. How will I ever repay Oscar?"

"Some things aren't worth worrying about right now, so let's not worry. Will they call you with instructions tomorrow?"

Cece nodded slowly. "How can I be sure Eve is even still alive? I know to ask for proof of life, but what would that be?"

"A photo holding today's paper," I suggested. "Or her saying something that happened in the news this morning on the phone. Or if they let you talk to her, have her answer a question only she would know the answer to. They couldn't fake that. She'd have to be alive."

"She is alive," Tinkie said with such certainty. "Look, the Bromleys went to a lot of trouble to try to alleviate your worries. The whole purse thing was a ruse to let you know she was still alive. I know this may sound radical, but they seemed to be following a good impulse. They didn't have to call you about the purse, but they did, to let you know Eve was okay."

What she said was true, but assigning noble motives to kidnapping conspirators seemed like a risky business. Those who abducted people for ransom were not good people. The goal here, though, was to reassure Cece. "Tinkie could very well be right. So the money drop is tomorrow. How are we going to manage that without alerting Oscar, Coleman, and Harold? The only reason they're playing a part in the production is because we pushed them into it and insisted. If we aren't at the church for the Christmas pageant, they're going to know we're up to something."

"Good point," Tinkie said. "But we can't let Cece make the drop by herself."

That was out of the question. "Anyone have a plan?" I asked.

12

Silence settled over the table and I heard an old classic country song I'd loved for years. "Put your sweet lips . . ." Jim Reeves sang. "We'll Have to Go" was the title. It brought back a lot of memories of winter nights when Cece was Cecil and we'd gathered in the enormous third-floor ballroom of the big Falcon home for get-togethers and high school gossip fests. Even then, Cecil had been one of the girls, a friend who had real elegance in helping us dress and do our hair. No one knew what to call his difference—or cared to call it anything. He was Cecil Falcon, a little eccentric but so smart and always kind. He was merely our friend. While his mother made pizzas or coke floats, we'd raided his father's record collection for those golden oldies. Good memories.

"Earth to Sarah Booth!" Tinkie waved a hand in front of my face. "Are you formulating a plan or tripping through a daydream."

"Memory Lane," I said. I reached across the table and grasped both their hands. "We've been through a lot and survived. All of us. We can't forget that or let despair stop us. Together we can make this right."

"What memory are you visiting?" Cece asked. "The time you and Coleman blew up the high school chemistry lab with some wild ass concoction you'd made? Everyone knew it was you but the teachers didn't want to believe Coleman was involved with it. Funny how no one really came to your defense." She grinned wickedly. "You were trouble from the get-go."

"We didn't blow up the chemistry lab," I corrected. "There was only a slight explosion. Yes, some beakers were broken, there was a small fire, and Mr. Bryant evacuated the entire school because he thought the mix of chemicals and flames would blow everyone to Mars." I had to defend myself, and Coleman, though it had been his idea to make sure we got out of school a few days early for Christmas holidays. "No one was injured."

"Not true! Not true!" Tinkie crowed. "Mrs. Bradley, the Spanish teacher, had heart palpitations and had to be rushed by ambulance to the hospital. The principal called all the students that took chemistry into his office, one by one, and gave them a spanking." She skewered me with a look. "And not a one of them tattled on you and Coleman."

That school year I was on my last chance. If I'd been reported, I would've been expelled. My friends had stepped up for me. "It wasn't that bad. It was a minor explosion."

"You singed Betty Sue Olty's hair completely off. She was bald for weeks." Tinkie was trying not to laugh. "Who knew Coleman would grow up to be the sheriff and you a private investigator?"

"The explosion was an accident. We honestly didn't plan it." They all teased me about deliberately blowing up the lab, but in truth, that hadn't been my intention. I'd meant only to generate a lot of smoke so that we could rush out of the building like in a fire drill. The ultimate goal was to avoid a test just before the holidays and to start the holidays a few days early. For the last day of school before Christmas holidays and before I was expelled, I'd been a high school hero. Then I'd been caught. Expulsion loomed, and worse than that Aunt Loulane would have been heartbroken. Luckily I'd negotiated a deal for leniency before I admitted my sins.

"You never let on that Coleman was involved," Cece said. "You loved him even then. You took the whole rap for him."

I smiled. "I don't know that I loved him. His father would have hurt him. I knew Aunt Loulane would be 'disappointed' but not violent. I'd survive with little cost. The same couldn't be said for Coleman."

Tinkie looked dreamy eyed. "Cece is right. Even then you had a thing for Coleman and everyone knew it but you two. I remember that Christmas. Squatty Mayfield had that big Christmas party and her friends smuggled in a lot of liquor. Folks got really drunk. She'd set her cap for Coleman, but he escaped with his honor." Tinkie laughed. "She offered to pay me to get you drunk and out of the way."

"Coleman wasn't . . ." I didn't finish. The truth was, I'd shared a slow dance with him that left me tingling and disturbed. I was innocent and hadn't known what to make of my reaction. And he'd lurked in the background after that dance. He watched me, but he didn't ask for another dance. He didn't try to talk to me. I'd flirted with some of the other boys because I didn't understand why he was so stand-offish.

"And remember that night we all went caroling." Cece grinned wickedly. "Coleman was your shadow, and you didn't even notice. He followed you everywhere you went, like he was guarding you."

"It was a long wait, but now she's making his Christmas bells jingle!" Tinkie cleared her throat. "Fa-la-la-la-la, la-la-la-la!" She hit the last la with a high note that stopped all conversation in the bar. "Sorry, my friend was remembering a Christmas encounter with the man of her dreams," she said to a lot of cheering and clapping. "She's really learned how to ring her boyfriend's holiday bells."

Cece stood up and lifted her glass. "To good friends and hot sex."

As much as I wanted to throttle them, I couldn't help laughing along with them. It was the first time I'd seen Cece happy since Eve had gone missing. There were possibly some hard days ahead, so it was good enough to just let them have their fun.

We'd strayed far afield from a plan to go with Cece to make the money drop. And I motioned them back to their chairs. "Okay, here's the plan. Cece, if you're determined to do this without Coleman's help, which I advise against, here's what we can do."

They both drew closer, and I lowered my voice. "We'll meet at the Christmas pageant, and we'll each leave to go to the ladies' room about ten minutes before it begins.

The men will be busy with makeup and costuming, and that'll be our best chance to leave without them. They're going to dim the house lights while the pageant is being performed. The men won't know we're gone until the show is over and the lights come up. By then we'll have Eve."

"They're going to be very angry." Tinkie was solemn. Oscar put up with a lot from her, but this was a straw that would weigh very heavy on the camel's back.

"I know." Cece's features had fallen back into the lines of worry that had drawn harsh furrows between her brows and at the corners of her mouth. "I'm so sorry to put you in this place. I am."

Tinkie shook her head. "This is part and parcel of friendship. Don't be sorry. You'd do the same for me or Sarah Booth. The men would do it for their friends. It'll just take a little while for them to see that."

I wasn't so certain Coleman would forgive me, but as Tinkie noted, it wasn't a choice for us. Love was a peculiar beast, and life tested it all the time. I didn't want to deceive Coleman. My fondest wish would be to spend the evening at the Christmas pageant watching the three most important men in my life pretend to be wise men in the telling of the birth of baby Jesus. But my friend Cece was in a desperate place, and the least I could do was be with her. Torn between two loyalties was a truly unpleasant spot to be in. We left Odell's with the outside Christmas lights pulsing red, green, and white to Brenda Lee's rendition of "Rocking Around the Christmas Tree."

On the way home, I called Coleman to let him know I was headed to Dahlia House and to invite him for a sleepover. I couldn't stop the excitement that swept over me when he agreed. After my breakup with Graf, I'd really thought I'd be alone. If not for the rest of my life, at least for a good long time. Now, I would celebrate Christmas with a man who was as deeply rooted in the Delta soil as I was. My mother had never really talked to me about true love or marriage. I was only twelve when she died. But she had shown me about the things in life that were real and how even when she was mad at James Franklin, as she called my daddy, that she always respected him. "Respect is what lives through the hard times," she'd said. I'd always respected Coleman because he had no bluster, no need to be the big man in anyone's eyes. He owned the ground he stood on. I wanted him to view me the same way.

In half an hour, I pulled into Dahlia House with Sweetie Pie and Pluto. The night was crisp and my breath fogged when I exhaled, but it wasn't a bitter night. The damp had stayed behind near the river. Instead of going in the house with Pluto, Sweetie bayed her long, mournful howl and set out around the house. Slightly concerned, I followed.

The light in the barn was on.

The hair all over my body stood on end. Who the hell was in my barn with my horses? I slipped back to my car and got my gun out of the trunk. I'd started carrying it only a few cases back—after I'd come close to death. I wasn't a terrific shot, but I was good enough to protect myself. If I had to.

I eased from shadow to shadow, edging closer to the barn. I heard nothing from inside except the snuffling of the horses and the stamping of their feet. They should have been out in the pasture, though. Not in the barn. They only came in to eat unless it was raining or snowing. I moved to the crack in the doors and peeped into the interior. All three horses were in stalls munching hay.

I hesitated, trying to decide how to handle this. Before I could do anything, an arm slipped around my waist from behind and a hand went over my mouth. "Be very still," a man whispered in my ear in a strange raspy voice.

I wanted to ask him what he wanted, but I couldn't force words past his palm. And he held me very tight. Too tight. So tight that I felt something quite alarming pressing against my hips. I tried to turn around, but he wouldn't release me.

"Be still," he whispered.

Not a chance. I stomped his foot as hard as I could. Because I was wearing my paddock boots, I could put a lot of force into that maneuver.

"Hey," he sputtered, turning me loose.

I whipped around, gun drawn, ready to plug the deviant. "Coleman!" I was surprised. "You were disguising your voice!"

"Just a little fun," he said, hopping on the foot I hadn't stomped. "Damn, I didn't think you'd cripple me."

"You molested me!" I saw the humor in our peccadillo, but I wanted to keep him on the hook a little longer.

"No, I merely apprehended you. It's not my fault you're a sexy beast. Your body communicated with my body, and . . . well . . . nature took its course."

"What are you doing out here in the barn?" Coleman was an accomplished equestrian, but he didn't hang out in the barn on dark winter nights.

"I thought we might go for a midnight ride. Maybe go to some nearby houses and carol."

"You have heard me sing, right?" No one ever wanted me to carol. Even humming was forbidden by my crew.

"It's the thought that counts, Sarah Booth. You don't claim to be Judy Garland."

That was an odd choice of singers. She'd been one of my father's favorites. "Over the Rainbow" was a song he often sang walking around the farm. I looked at the horses. Reveler and Lucifer were already saddled and waiting. Coleman wasn't playing around.

I whistled up my hound. Sweetie Pie would be devastated if I left her behind. "Let's ride!"

The moon was full and bright as we led the horses out into the yard. I climbed up on Reveler while Coleman mounted Lucifer. The fiery Andalusian was a perfect match for the wicked glint in Coleman's eye.

The farm fields were fallow. Away from the pastures I'd cut out for my horses, the land was wide open, without fencing. There were trails around the fields that farm vehicles traveled when the lease holder, Billy Watson, plowed and planted. The heavy equipment had packed the earth so that the trails were solid footing for the horses, and the moon gave plenty of light—enough to cast shadows. As we set off at a trot, our black silhouettes followed, giving me a sense of how so many things in my life were like shades that followed behind me.

As Coleman leaned into Lucifer's mane, giving the signal to gallop, I had no time to worry about the past tagging after me. I embraced the moment, leaning forward in two-point and giving Reveler his head. He surged forward, taking the lead from Lucifer and Coleman. And the race was on. As Lucifer drew abreast of me, Reveler shortened his stride.

The wind bit my ears with a nasty snap, and my hands

were frozen on the reins since I'd failed to grab riding gloves, but I didn't care. Coleman rode beside me so close our knees were almost touching. Our horses were matched stride for stride, and the need to win fell away from both of us. We rode as one, a rhythm that wasn't lost on me—or Coleman if the look he shot me was any indication. I went from cold to hot in a nanosecond.

We rode through the night, covered at least five miles, before Coleman motioned me into a small brake where the thick growth of trees served as both a windbreak and an indicator that a small stream cut through. As we stepped into the secluded area, I stopped in amazement. Twinkle lights had been strung in the trees. In a small clearing, wood had been stacked for a fire. Nearby was a bale of alfalfa hay for the horses—a treat for them over their normal Bermuda grass hay. And there were pillows and blankets and champagne chilling in a bucket of ice, which was possibly unnecessary on the cold night.

"What is this?" I asked, though I knew full well.

"You've been so busy, I thought I'd plan a little Christmas celebration. Tomorrow night is the pageant, and we'll be busy with friends all evening. I wanted to have some time alone."

My heart pounded as I slipped from the saddle. Coleman had thought to leave halters for the horses so we could take their bridles off and allow them to eat the hay freely. He'd thought of everything. Even a big, meaty bone for Sweetie Pie, who'd found it and started gnawing beside the fire Coleman lit.

In the center of the blankets was a beautifully wrapped gift. "I didn't bring a present for you." How could I have known?

"It's okay. This is a present for both of us."

It was a very flat box to hold a present for two. "Summons to court?" I guessed. "Wanted poster of the two of us? What could it be?"

"Let's have a glass of champagne and then open it."

"You're a master with a party agenda." I eased under some of the soft blankets that smelled of cedar and pine. Coleman really had thought of everything, even the scent of the season. I accepted the glass of bubbly Coleman filled for me. When he had his glass, he eased down beside me under the blankets and I curled into him. This was magic, a moment of absolute pleasure—my favorite things—created for me by Coleman. And the best of all was the solidness of his body against mine, the feel of him, so real and there.

He handed me the present and I pulled the bow loose and opened the paper and box. It took a moment for the tickets to register. Two tickets for Ireland. "Budgie is doing some research on the Delaney family, Sarah Booth. We're going to the Emerald Isle to find some relatives for you. If it works out, next Christmas maybe you'll have family to celebrate with, too."

Emotion stopped me from answering. I clutched the box and kissed his cheek. "Thank you." Inadequate words to convey what I felt. It seemed my heart had expanded inside my ribs. "Do you think we'll find someone I'm related to?"

He kissed my forehead. "We will. Even if I have to pay them to accept you into the family."

It was the perfect answer. I laughed and felt the pressing emotion pass, leaving only wild joy and anticipation. I was going to Ireland with Coleman!

The fire crackled and cast a warm glow on us as we snuggled, sipping the champagne and letting the night sounds of a hoot owl echo over the field. This was a moment to hold tight. I would remember it forever. A few clinging dead leaves rustled in a soft nature musical. I had a terrible thought! What if Jitty showed up dancing through the night in some nutcracker costume?

"What's wrong?" Coleman was incredibly intuitive.

"I was thinking of a dead relative," I said, opting not to lie completely.

"Someone you love?"

"Oh, yes. More than she'll ever know." I did love Jitty.

He leaned down and kissed me, a tender kiss that built quickly to something quite different. We broke apart, tossed back the champagne, and then free of the glasses, engaged in a searing kiss. The blankets and fire had chased the chill away and so when Coleman began to remove my clothes, I was already battling an internal flame that demanded his attention.

I unzipped his jacket and worked the buttons on his shirt. We took our time, letting the firelight play over bare flesh. The thing I loved best about Coleman—one of the many—was his ease in his own skin. He never gave a thought to his appearance as long as he was neat and clean. I never saw him look in a mirror to check his reflection. He prepared for the day and went about his work. The firelight caught the hairs on his chest and gave them a reddish gold burnish, and I ran my hands over them, marveling at the sculpted muscles of his chest and torso. He wasn't a man who worked out in a gym— he worked out in real life. He'd chopped a winter's worth of firewood for Dahlia House. He'd taken to showing up to fix a fence or sweep out the hayloft for the new winter supply. He did the things that all Delta boys and men knew to do to prepare for the coming season.

"You've traveled far away, Sarah Booth," he said.

I was finally aware he was watching me. "Not so far. I was just thinking of your thoughtfulness in helping me at the farm."

"It's my pleasure."

"I know you do the same for some of the older people." He did. DeWayne, his deputy, told me about Coleman's good deeds.

"When I can."

"All that hard work sure looks good on you." My hands moved over his bare chest and upper arms. "You're a fine specimen of a man."

His hands circled my waist and lifted me astride him. "We're lucky, Sarah Booth. We have everything, including good health. Now I suggest we take advantage of it."

I didn't answer. I bent and kissed him, letting our passion rekindle in that flash flame of desire that swept everything else away. For a time it was just our breathing, our bodies, and the devouring passion that consumed us.

13

I awoke to frosty toes and the stamping of my horses' feet. Coleman was still asleep, a man with a completely innocent conscience. With his tousled hair and resting features, he looked like the teenage Coleman that was forever imprinted in my mind. Sleep had erased his cares. And frozen my nose. Worse, I had to find my clothes and climb in them without moving from beneath the covers. It was too cold to dress.

"Coleman." I nudged him awake. "We have to go home." We'd been asleep only half an hour. The night spoke to me in quiet rustlings and the flutter of bird's wings as I went in for one last snuggle. "Hey, we have to go home. It's two in the morning."

"We shouldn't have killed that champagne." He

stretched and shivered as the cold hit his arms. Before I could stop him, he threw the covers off us. "Let's shake a leg."

I considered biting him really hard on the butt. "You are a jackass."

"True. And you love being with me. You know what my grandmother used to say, 'For every jenny there's a jack.'"

I couldn't help but laugh. Coleman's grandmother was an endless source of great country sayings. My aunt Loulane was legend for her repetition of axioms and sage wisdom like "a stitch in time saves nine." But Coleman's granny came up with wild sayings that mocked conventional wisdom and often dealt with sexual proclivities in a humorous way. Needless to say, I'd adored her before she passed on. She'd made hot cocoa and pimento cheese sandwiches for many a high school gathering at her house.

"Roll out." Coleman snatched the rest of the blankets off me and I had no choice but to levitate to my feet pulling on my jeans and sweater. It was going to be a cold ride home, no way around it.

"We didn't make it to caroling," I reminded him as I laced my boots clumsily in the dark.

"I have to confess, Sarah Booth. It's the first pay-off I've taken but the locals gave me a nice donation for my re-election fund if I stopped you from singing."

"You're certainly a frisky biscuit," I said. This night, for all of its many pleasures, had also left me with a desire for payback. I would not forget Coleman's devilish tricks.

"Mount up and save your thoughts of revenge for a later time." He lifted me onto Reveler's back. While I'd been boot lacing, he'd bridled the horses. He kicked the fire to be sure it was dead, and then he mounted.

The horses were eager for the barn and we let them gallop all the way to the driveway before we pulled them back and walked home. They had to be cooled before we untacked them and set them free. Coleman reached across and caught my knee for a warm pat. "These last few weeks have been the happiest of my life, Sarah Booth. I know I almost ruined it for us when I didn't leave Connie."

Coleman's ex-wife, Connie, was a manipulative witch and not all that smart. She'd lied and used duplicity to hold Coleman to her, but he finally caught on and divorced her with a clear conscience. By then I'd been involved with another man, someone else from my past. That hadn't ended well either.

"I try not to think about the fact we're finally together without anyone standing in our way," I confessed. "I'm afraid of jinxing us."

"My parents didn't have a happy marriage," Coleman said. "But you had the opposite experience. Your mom and dad loved each other. It was clear to every kid in the county who saw them. You have no idea the envy kids had for your family and home." He shook his head. "I wonder what kind of man I'd be if I'd had that in my life."

"You'd be the same man, only with better memories." I knew that to be true, but I realized listening to him that he was as afraid of ruining what we had as I was. We weren't old fogeys, but we were cautious adults. As Aunt Loulane would tell me, "Everyone goes over fools' hill. Best to do it when you're young and your bones aren't brittle."

"I think about your loss, Sarah Booth. To have had that kind of parental love and then lose it, that's a blow. And you were a child. I think about the car accident that killed them. I'd give a lot to know what made your dad lose control on a flat, straightaway with no traffic. Most likely a deer jumped out or something."

That he understood the incident that defined who I was made me realize how lucky I was to know him. People survived tragedy all the time, but we were always marked. Always. "It did change who I am." Understatement of the universe. "I learned I can stand alone, whether I like it or not."

"I can hear your aunt Loulane right now. She'd say, 'The hardest things in life we always do alone.'"

"'And she'd be right.'" As I'd learned the hard way. Loss, death, illness, those things could be shared only so much. The darkest paths, we walked alone. While some few could keep us company a piece down that road, the long journey was primarily a solitary one.

"I love the way Cece and Madame Tomeeka decorated the front porch." Coleman adeptly changed the subject, realizing that sometimes the past is a bog that can sink a person.

"They did a great job." Dahlia House was festive in her holiday finery. And even walking by on the horses I caught a whiff of the delightful cedar and pine.

"And why was it they were decorating your house?" he asked.

He was far too clever and slick. "Because they're good friends. Sometimes friends go out on a limb for each other." It was a coded message that was completely clear if he chose to get it.

"I don't know what you and Cece and Tinkie are planning, Sarah Booth, but I know you're up to something. I can help you find Eve or at least make the money drop. Don't shut me out. The guilt will kill y'all if this goes south."

He was right about that, but wrong about my ability to share with him. "I would tell you everything, Coleman. I trust you and love you." The "l" word came out so easily. "But it isn't mine to share. Trust me with that. I have you on speed dial if a crisis arises. That young woman is due to give birth and there's no sign of her, no indication that she's getting medical care. I'm heartsick."

"She disappeared in Bolivar County. The only crime scene I've seen is in Tallahatchie County. I don't have jurisdiction, but I do have a world of experience. A kidnapper is no one to play with. Once he has the money, Eve becomes a liability. She most likely can identify him. Or her. Or them. The thing is, it may be more expedient to kill Eve than release her, no matter what promises are made."

We'd reached the barn and I slid from the saddle and quickly began untacking. I was freezing, and now my black little heart was a sad lump of frozen coal. Because I knew Coleman was right. "I can only promise that the minute I can, I'll let you know everything."

"Just let me know you're safe. And Cece and Tinkie, too. I hope that young woman is okay. Now let's untack and get inside. I need to sleep a little. Tomorrow is Christmas Eve and I have to lead the city parade at eleven. Santa is throwing candy and toys."

Zinnia still followed the tradition of a big parade with the high school bands and dancing cheerleaders and majorettes and floats from all the local businesses. It was a lovely part of my childhood that still continued. So many local traditions had been lost.

"Can I ride in the patrol car with you?" I asked.

Coleman gave me a wicked grin. "Only if you're wearing handcuffs."

"You don't need handcuffs for me. I'm a prisoner of your heart." I tried to play it demure and sincere.

"Want to try that line again?" Coleman asked.

"I'm not afraid of you," I said boldly. "You wouldn't dare put handcuffs on me."

There was a glint in his eye that was downright dangerous. "Maybe not. Then again, do you really want to test it?"

I turned Reveler loose and he shot out of the barn snorting and bucking, glad to be back with his lady love, Miss Scrapiron. Lucifer followed him out when Coleman set him free. Hoof beats on solid ground pounded away. The horses whinnied wildly as they ran around the big pasture, loving the crisp weather and the freedom. I loved that I could give the three horses as natural a life as a horse could have in captivity. They were not free on the range, but they also never went hungry or faced predators. They had a farrier every six weeks, their teeth checked at least once a year, wormers, vaccinations, hay and feed, and a regular veterinarian visiting.

"Now, what was that about handcuffs?" Coleman asked.

I was five feet from him and about ten feet from the barn door. I knew he was raring for a confrontation. I broke and ran as fast as I could, thrusting the barn door open and screaming as I ran into the night.

"You can run but you can't hide. I'm gonna getcha!"

Coleman was right behind me, which only spurred me

to run faster. I aimed for the front door with the wide porch that had multiple paths of escape, if I needed them. The back door was a death trap. Steep steps to the door and no way out if I wasn't quick enough. Coleman was gaining on me.

I pushed at the front door and screamed again as he captured me crossing the threshold. "Kings! Kings!" I held up my crossed fingers in the age-old sign of safety. When we'd played as children, we'd always honored the call. Coleman totally ignored it.

"A little late with that," he said. "I think my prisoner is trying to escape." He was trying hard not to laugh. He swept me into his arms and carried me into the foyer, kicking the door closed behind him after he made sure Sweetie Pie was inside. He stared into my eyes, somehow reading my intentions with that police officer's sixth sense. He knew my one goal was to reach the ice bucket in the parlor. My game plan was to dump the ice down his pants. "What wicked plans you lay," he said. "Too bad they'll never come to fruition."

"I just want to get warm," I lied. "You've captured me and proven you're the faster runner. What more do you want?"

That was the wrong question to ask. He didn't put me down. Instead, he bent his head down so that his scruff teased my cheek. Then he took it one step further and nibbled on my ear—sending chill bumps over me—as he said, "I have my own plans for you, my dear."

Though I wanted to kiss him, I couldn't yield without a fight. "Hey, Cro-Magnon. Let me go. I can walk." I couldn't let him melt me like a pat of butter in a hot skillet. He'd always have the upper hand if I didn't put some starch in my spine. I wiggled with force, which only made me more aware that Coleman's intentions were amorous. So were mine—but I couldn't be too easy. A girl had a reputation to uphold.

"I'm not putting you down. You're a sly fox, Sarah Booth. I'm weighing my options."

Before I could protest, he tossed me over his shoulder like a sack of potatoes and started up the stairs.

"Coleman!" I beat his butt with my hands. "Put me down."

"In due time," he answered.

"I'm going to vomit on the backs of your legs," I warned him.

"Not a chance. When you were a kid, you'd rather explode than vomit. I doubt that's changed."

Oh, he was taking full advantage of our long friendship. He took me into the bedroom and tossed me on the bed. Before I could scramble up, he pinned me with his body weight, holding my wrists in each of his hands.

"Let me up." I tried bucking him off, but he was solid muscle, even though he was weakened by laughter.

"You should see your face. You look exactly like you did when you were ten years old and Andy Calhoun accidentally knocked you down when you both went out for the same pass.

It had been an accident during a game of touch football in the schoolyard before the bell rang. "Andy apologized. I doubt you'll do that."

"Nope. But I have my ways of making it up to you."

"Don't you dare! Don't you dare manipulate me into having sex with you after you've treated me like produce!"

"Not produce. My captive."

He shifted my wrists to a one-handed hold over my

head. His fingers lightly traced my rib cage. He was going to tickle me. Oh, he would pay for this. It might take me years, but he would pay.

"Don't you tickle me." I spoke the words even though I knew better.

"What would you prefer to a good tickling?" His fingers lightly traced across my stomach. I tried not to flinch but couldn't control it. I wasn't normally super ticklish, but he'd hit the button. Now anything he did would tickle. He kissed my ear and nuzzled my neck. "Like this better?"

In fact I did. A whole lot. But I wouldn't give him the satisfaction of saying so.

"Okay, then back to a little tickle."

"Stop! I want a kiss." He rolled over and pulled me atop him. "You're a devil, Coleman. You're bigger and stronger and I'm no match."

He laughed so hard I began to worry. "No match! Oh, right. Who was the last man you pulled that on and it worked?"

I thought about it. "No one." I leaned down and kissed his earlobe—before I bit it hard enough to make him jump. "That's for tormenting me."

"Is that it?" he taunted.

"My mind has turned to romance," I whispered. "Payback can wait until you least expect it."

"If I'm good at my job, you won't remember I need to be paid back." He drew me to him and we kissed. It was as if we were both starved for a passionate connection. Though we'd made love for an hour in the woods and fallen asleep, we were on fire.

* * *

By the time I finally staggered out of bed, the sun was up and my cell phone was ringing. It was Christmas Eve. A lot of things would happen today and I felt like I'd been run over by a truck. Coleman wasn't a lot spryer. He groaned as he grabbed his clothes and pulled them on. "I'll shower at home and find a clean uniform," he said.

"Coffee?" I asked.

"A cup might help a lot."

We went downstairs and I put on the coffeepot before I called Tinkie back. "Coleman is just leaving. Give me fifteen minutes," I told her.

"I'll be at your door in twenty. We have work to do."

Before I could ask another question, she'd hung up.

14

"Sarah Booth, I have to tell you that Dahlia House looks lovely. I didn't realize you were such a fan of *The Nutcracker*. I love the dance where the sugar plum fairy is center stage." Tinkie held a cup of coffee in one hand and moved around the parlor in a gentle glide as the beautiful music swelled around us. I didn't have the heart to tell her that I hadn't turned the radio on. Jitty had found the obscure FM station playing the ballet—a station I'd never heard of and suspected could be found only in the Great Beyond, not in Memphis. Jitty was driving her message home—if only I could figure out what her message was. The lovely ballet obviously was symbolic to her, but of what?

I'd said goodbye to Coleman and parting was indeed

sweet sorrow. I'd also managed to knock back two cups of coffee and take a steaming hot shower, all within the allotted time of twenty minutes that Tinkie had set. She'd arrived right on time, wearing a forest green tunic and pale green leggings. "You need some little shoes with the toes turned up and a pointy hat. You could be a forest elf. One of Santa's helpers."

"You need to go to bed at a reasonable hour instead of having sex all night and looking like clotted sawmill gravy the next morning." She grinned.

I instinctively put my hands to my cheeks. I did look rough, no way around it. "What's the work we have to do?" Best to move on to new topics. I'd learned the art of distracting and deflecting since I'd moved home.

"The money drop is tonight." Tinkie walked to the kitchen to refill her coffee cup and I followed. "We have to stick to Cece like glue. She's going to try to ditch us, but one of us has to be with her at all times. Do you want the first shift or should I take it?" She laughed. "Never mind. Grab a couple of hours of sleep. I'll go sit on her like a hen hatching an egg."

I nodded my agreement. I really did need at least two hours of sleep or I'd be a worthless zombie. "Text me and keep me abreast."

Tinkie nodded. "Think of a way to keep Cece safe tonight. I'm worried."

"Me, too." My gut instinct told me to include Coleman even if the location was out of his jurisdiction and even if Cece got mad. Yet I couldn't make myself take that action.

"Go to bed," Tinkie directed gently. "You act like you're in a fog."

"Thanks, maybe some sleep will help me think more clearly."

I stood at the front door and watched Tinkie and Chablis cross the front porch and get into her new car. They tore down the driveway. Tinkie always drove at top speed, and it was one of the many things I loved about her.

Honoring my word, I trudged up the stairs to return to my warm bed, but even as I climbed beneath the covers, I knew it was pointless. My brain was racing and my conscience was engaged in a terrible tug-of-war. Acting as Cece's friend, what should I do about Coleman? Each passing moment put me closer and closer to telling him— and possibly putting Eve in more and more danger. I pulled the covers over my head and tried to sleep.

A low howling started at the foot of the bed and I peeked from beneath the quilt to stare at Sweetie Pie Delaney. I swear the dog was giving me the evil eye. I felt something in my hair and realized Pluto was playing with my curls. The critters wanted me up. It was pointless to resist. Next Jitty would be prancing around as a character from a ballet. It was time to get up and get busy.

I dressed in warm clothes and went down to the kitchen. When I picked up my jacket to slip into it, the photograph of the two babies fell onto the floor. Who were these infants and what role did they play in Eve's abduction? This image had to be the key to figuring out everything else. I just didn't know how it applied. There was one place to start asking.

When the horses were fed, my coffee-to-go was in the insulated cup, and I had a toasted bagel in a napkin, I called my pets. "Load up," I told them. "We're on a mission." I resisted the temptation to call Tinkie and Cece and headed out to the farm where Carla and Will Falcon lived. They were going to speak with me—and give me the truth—before my friend was hurt beyond repair. And before my relationship with Coleman was irrevocably damaged. The Falcons might not recognize the babies in the photo, but they might. Carla and Will would give nothing up voluntarily, but if I caught them unawares, they might give away information that would help us find Eve.

The drive was pleasant; the day was overcast, the large gray clouds forming on the horizon. They moved in massive fronts, like the mist of giants warring with each other. I'd laughed at the weatherman's prediction of snow for Christmas Eve night, but looking at the pregnant sky, it was a real possibility. Snow made the whole world new again, and we never had a white Christmas in the Delta. This would be an occasion to celebrate.

When I pulled up at the Falcon farm, Carla was staring out the window at me. I stopped by the front gate and got out. I wanted to speak to them one at a time so I hoped Will was busy or gone. Sweetie and Pluto ran to inspect the yard and generally snoop. I went to the front door. Before I stepped onto the porch, Carla banged out the door, her face pinched with fury. "I told you to leave this property once. Now I'm telling you to leave and don't come back or I'll be pressing charges against you."

"Go ahead." As I spoke Pluto slipped past Carla and into the house. There would really be hell to pay now. Sweetie sauntered up to the edge of the porch, watching with that innocent hound dog expression that belied her great intelligence.

"What do you want?" Carla asked.

"Do you know who these babies are?" I held the photo out to her, but she wouldn't step close enough to take it.

"No. I don't know and don't care." She looked down when she spoke.

I assessed her reaction—her refusal to even look. She'd treated Eve abominably. What mother could do that to her child? To my amusement, I saw Sweetie Pie slink behind Carla, cutting off access to the front door. From inside the house Pluto pushed the heavy door closed with a big slam. Carla froze. She'd been outmaneuvered by a dog and cat.

"You'd better not hurt me." She actually looked afraid.

"Why would I hurt you?" I asked softly. I stepped onto the porch, closing the distance between us. "Cruelty to a helpless child might be a reason, don't you think? Good thing my partner isn't here. She was very angry when we learned of the way you treated your own daughter. See, my partner would give anything to have a child, and you had one and did everything in your power to make her life a misery. You can see how that might piss Tinkie off."

"You have no proof about anything you say. You can't even prove Eve is really missing. Maybe she just moved, like she did when she was sixteen. She's always done exactly what she wanted." She lifted her head on her scrawny neck and I realized I could probably wring her neck like an old chicken. It was a very tempting visual.

"Who are these children?" I pushed the photo at her again.

"Not mine, and that's all that matters." She edged backward but stopped when Sweetie gave a low growl deep in her throat.

"You know these babies, and somehow they relate to Eve. I'm going to figure it out, Carla. In the meantime, if anything bad befalls Eve, I promise you I'll make you pay."

"You think you know so much, but you don't know anything. Now get off my property." She shook a finger in my face and Sweetie Pie obliged with a serious growl.

"I wouldn't tempt my dog, Carla. She can sniff out a child abuser from a mile away." It was a harsh judgment but one Carla had earned, as far as I was concerned. I had one chance to pressure the truth out of her and I didn't intend to squander it, even if I had to play hardball with her.

"I'll have that mutt put to sleep," she warned.

"Not if you're dead." I really disliked her. A lot. "You know these children and you're going to tell me who they are and why they matter to Eve." She was like a cornered rat—dangerous and vicious. I had to squeeze the truth out of her and quick. Any minute Will would come out or she'd rush into the house. Sweetie Pie might trip her, but my dog wouldn't bite. It was now or never. "Who are these babies?" I jammed the photo in her face.

She knocked my arm down. "All that matters to me is that they're not my blood. And not my responsibility." She regained her composure. "You get off my property or you're going to be sorry." Carla opened the door to go inside, but cast a look back to make sure I was leaving.

I'd seen the truth. She did know the babies in the photo. She knew them and something about them scared her. "Sweetie Pie! Pluto!" I called my pets as I slammed through the gate and to the car. Sweetie was right beside me and Pluto shot out the front door before Carla could slam it shut. She hadn't told me what I needed to know, but now I knew where to look. Carla had given me more than she'd ever dreamed. Her selfish, cold heart had betrayed her.

I drove straight to the Sunflower County courthouse. Sure enough a crane was removing the statue of Johnny Reb. I took a minute to register the thud to my heart. More than an emblem of any war or cause to me, Johnny Reb was a part of my childhood. He'd been there, a landmark to my childhood, when my daddy worked in the courthouse.

Before I continued into the building, I bid the statue a sad goodbye. The chancery clerk's office was my destination. I resisted the temptation to duck into the sheriff's office to see Coleman. Now wasn't the time. I went back to the record room and began my math calculations. I needed adoption records from twenty years ago.

With the help from a clerk, I went to work. An hour later, I finally found what I was looking for. Will and Carla Falcon were approved to adopt a little girl.

Eve was not their natural child. That's why Carla hated her so much. She wasn't blood—therefore she was an intruder, an outsider, someone who somehow threatened Carla's place in the family. Which meant that Eve was likely Will's child from an affair.

How had no one told us this? And if the photograph was indeed a picture of Eve, who was the other baby?

I called Cece, glad to know she and Tinkie were putting the last-minute touches on the costumes for the three wise men for the Christmas pageant. "Thank goodness you called. We've been gluing and sewing for the last three hours. If I go to the bathroom, Tinkie follows me like I'm going to flush myself down the toilet and escape through the sewers. God save me, Tinkie has me making up the beards for the wise men. They're going to look like something off *Duck Dynasty*. What's up?" Cece asked.

"Why didn't you tell us Eve was adopted?"

There was a slight pause. "What?"

"Eve isn't Carla's child. She may be Will's, but not Carla's."

"I have to sit down. This explains so much." She clicked the phone to speaker and brought Tinkie into the conversation.

"Do you ever remember hearing family discussions of Will having an affair?" I asked.

"No," Cece said slowly. "Will was my father's brother, but they were estranged, for the most part. No one liked Carla. My mother detested her. We saw them on holidays but there was never any real interaction other than those duty visits."

"So you never saw Carla pregnant?" I asked.

"Carla stayed on the farm," Cece said. "She didn't belong to any of the social clubs. She was from that rigorous religious background where social events or fun were looked upon as the devil's temptation." She cleared her throat. "Are you saying Will had an affair that produced Eve, then forced Carla to take her in as her own child?"

"Looks that way."

"I remember some gossip," Tinkie chimed in. "Back when we were just starting high school, I was up at the bank with my daddy. Will Falcon came in and went into my father's office. Of course, I didn't know anything about him then, but I've always been a snoop. The door was cracked and I heard Will ask about taking out a loan for a child, one that he couldn't personally take care of but who needed support. It never occurred to me until this minute that he was looking to provide for an illegitimate baby."

I looked down at the photo I held. "That picture we found in Eve's house. If she is one baby, who is the other one?"

"A sibling? A baby born at the same time. That looks like a hospital gown the woman is wearing, but there's not enough of her torso showing."

"If Eve has a brother or sister, that could be big. We have to resolve this."

"What if Will somehow convinced Carla to adopt the one baby, but not the other one? That's so horrible." Cece's voice registered her distress. "Carla never loved Eve. She resented her from the get-go and over the years as Eve grew more beautiful, Carla just grew more and more bitter and meaner and meaner. This explains a lot."

"It's a likely supposition you've put together," Tinkie said, "but we have to prove it. We have to have solid proof. If there's a sibling still alive, we need to find that person, too."

"How does this help us find Eve?" Cece asked.

"I'm not sure, but what if her birth family has abducted her? What if the man stalking her in Cleveland is a relative?"

"I need to speak with Uncle Will." Cece's voice was tight with anger. I could imagine her jaw so clenched she was at risk of cracking her teeth.

"It may not do any good to talk to Will." Tinkie was gentle but upfront. "He seems to have bought into Carla's worldview."

"I have to try." Cece rustled the telephone and I could tell she was gathering her things to leave. "Now you two listen to me. I'm going to talk to Will, and I have to do this alone. He's a proud man and if Eve is the offspring of an affair, he's not going to want to admit it in front of you." There was a pause. "Especially not if he cared for one child but not the other. Tinkie, could you help Mrs. Ethel with that headdress for Mary? Then we can leave."

"I'll be right back," Tinkie said.

When I knew she was away from the phone, I continued. "Cece, promise me you'll be careful and no matter what you learn, you won't do anything rash."

"Will has always been a coward, but to be bullied into abandoning his own child. That just takes it too far. The Falcon family once had pride and integrity. I'm not the son my father wanted, but at least I know right from wrong and have enough starch to stand up for the ethical thing."

"You're a good person. Never lose sight of that. And none of us are responsible for our relatives. We can't help the family we're born into."

"Thank you, Sarah Booth."

"Please bring Tinkie to the courthouse," I suggested. "I could use her help looking up some old records. And be sure to drop her at the back door. She'll be upset at what's happening out front."

"Sure thing. What's happening out front?"

"The statue is coming down."

"Oh, dear. It has to be done, but a lot of people are going to be hurt by this. I'll get a photo for the paper while I'm there. We must own the truth of our past or forever live in the shadow of it," Cece said. "I'll drop her off." And Cece was gone, the phone call ended.

* * *

"Sarah Booth!" Tinkie called to me as she entered the vault-like room where old records were kept. Newer records were on the computer, but the older ones remained in large books that weighed a ton.

"Here!" I raised a hand over the stacks of bound volumes and other records and caught her attention.

"Have you found out who Eve's birth mother is?" Tinkie asked.

"There wasn't a mention of her in the files. Eve was born in the Tishomingo County hospital. Her birthday is June 21. Why don't you give the hospital a call and see if they can tell you the birth records from that time."

"They probably won't tell me. HIPAA and all of that. But they'd tell Coleman."

She was right about that. "That's a good point, but you're preaching to the choir. We need Coleman's help, in my opinion." I sighed. "I wish Cece wasn't so bull-headed."

Tinkie's grin was a hundred watts. "Why don't I sashay down to the sheriff's office and see if Coleman or DeWayne or Budgie can help me track down Eve's birth mother? As a favor."

She was gleefully tormenting me. She knew I was itching to have a reason to go to the sheriff's office. I was behaving like a teenager, and she could read it all over me. "Sure. That's a good plan. When Cece chops your head off for bringing the law into this, I'll make sure Oscar buries you all together." But she had raised an interesting point. There was a way around this dilemma and I would still get to spend a few minutes with Coleman. "I have a Plan B. Why don't I lure Coleman and the deputies out of the office, then you can sneak in there, pretend to be the dispatcher, and call the hospital from their phones? It'll show up on caller ID as the Sunflower County SO and the hospital will be more likely to share info."

"Okay."

I looked up in shock. Tinkie never gave in that easily. "That's it? Okay?"

"It's a good plan. How are you going to distract them?"

"I don't know yet." I hadn't anticipated her capitulation. "Do you have any ideas?"

"Sex always works with men." Her grin widened. "Then again, that may be old hat for Coleman now. Or maybe you broke it."

I gave her my best Darth Vader death stare, but she only laughed out loud. "You are so much fun to tease."

She was right. I was an easy target. "Okay, now help me think. What about coffee at Millie's? I could invite them for coffee and pie."

"They might want to go but they wouldn't leave the SO unattended for coffee. No, it needs to be an emergency of some kind. One that requires all of them. And one that isn't very far away." She was right about all of the parameters.

"Okay, I hate to do it but I can."

"What?" Tinkie was wary.

"I'm going to get into a brawl with Mrs. Hedgepeth about Sweetie Pie."

"She really does hate you. On sight." Tinkie frowned. "Why is that?"

"No clue; don't care. She hated me when I was a child. She was always calling my parents to claim I was up to some horrible behavior."

"She's had it in for Sweetie Pie for a long time, too."

"True. You can call Coleman and tell him I'm about to slug her and that he'll need help to break up the fight. Tell him to bring all forces before we tie up like lady wrestlers."

"How do you know Mrs. Hedgepeth will rise to the bait?" She rolled her eyes. "Okay, I know she always rises to the bait when it's your dog. She hates Sweetie Pie."

"No, she hates all dogs and cats. She's a mean old woman and all the Zinnia children avoid her like the plague. I'll head over to her house with Sweetie Pie and you please call Coleman. Once they leave the courthouse, you can slip in and call the Tishomingo County Hospital and find those birth records."

It wasn't a sophisticated or even very clever plan, but I hoped it would work.

15

Sweetie and Pluto had evacuated the car and were watching the removal of the statue. The day was gray and brisk, perfect from the critters' perspective. They had no attachment to Johnny Reb so they plopped on the court house lawn and rolled in the grass. I called Sweetie Pie to me and we headed off to Mrs. Hedgepeth's house with Pluto following behind like a bad toddler.

Mrs. Hedgepeth had been gunning for me since I was nine years old and would ride my bike down her street and pick up the pears that fell from her tree onto the sidewalk and verge. She didn't really want the pears, she just didn't want anyone else to have them. And she took every opportunity to call my parents and report my "stealing" as she called it. My father had waited a few days and then gone down the street and busily picked up the fallen sand pears. When she came out the door, pleasant as could be imagined, he told her he was retrieving them for me. She'd never forgiven him or me. And that had begun a series of her attempts to try to get me in trouble. For the next three years, she called at least once a week, claiming that I looked at her wrong. I tried to hit her with my bicycle. I was rude and uppity. Even when I crossed the street from her house and rode on the other side, she still had it in for me.

Since I'd returned home from New York and adopted Sweetie Pie, she'd been after my dog every chance she could get. So far, Sweetie Pie had escaped her many attempts at entrapment, and there was only one good thing about the situation: Coleman would believe I'd kicked the hornets' nest with Mrs. Hedgepeth. He would come to rescue me.

I hustled Sweetie Pie and Pluto down the street and made a beeline for the older woman's yard. She was decorated to the gills for Christmas. Inflatable Santas bobbed about the front lawn beside lighted wicker reindeer and tree silhouettes created by strings of glowing lights and flashing icicles. One of the machines that cast moving light shows on the walls of her house was hidden in her shrubbery. When it came on, the effect would be dizzying and annoying. It was like Christmas on steroids about to go into a 'roid rage. I looked at Sweetie Pie and I looked at the decorations. It would be very easy to go to the dark side here. After all the accusations she'd made against me—for things I hadn't done—maybe it was time to do something a little bad.

As if she could read my mind, Mrs. Hedgepeth blasted out her front door and came rolling into the yard in some sort of muslin sack dress with a sash and head gear that looked like a dishtowel with a braided rope around the forehead. "What the hell?" I said before I could snap my lips shut.

"I'm Mary, the mother of Jesus," she said.

I gave her a cool look. She'd left herself wide open for a real set-to. "More like Mia Farrow and the mother of the antichrist."

"How dare you?" She was easy to rile.

"Oh, I dare to do that and a lot more. Tell me you're not in the church Christmas pageant tonight?"

"I have the starring role. I'm Mary, who gives birth to the baby Jesus." She reached into the voluminous folds of her robe-slash-tent and brought forth a bald-headed baby doll circa 1950. The little plastic face was molded into a smudged, permanent frown, the Kewpie doll lips swollen and angry. It was the ugliest baby doll I'd ever seen.

"You're playing Mary? As old as you are that would be a miracle birth." I drew first blood. I'd have her angry enough to start something physical in a short time.

"You are a rude and obnoxious adult, just like you were a terrible little brat."

"What was it about those pears?" I asked. "Did you really care that a child picked up two or three? You left them to rot on the sidewalk."

"You should have asked permission."

I couldn't believe it. "I was nine. I didn't know you, and the pears were all over the sidewalk. No one wanted them. A lot of them had rotted."

"You should have asked."

"My mother would have skinned me if I'd gone around knocking on a stranger's door. The pears were on the sidewalk. They didn't belong to anyone."

"That's how you young people think. That everything is just yours for the taking. You don't have to ask, you don't have to work for anything. You just take."

"Why are you so angry?" I was suddenly more interested in learning the truth than in picking a fight to entertain Coleman. "What happened to you that made you so horrid?" I looked around at the Christmas decorations. They were so over the top that I was suddenly struck by the answer. "You never had children but you really wanted them. Why didn't you just adopt?"

"You don't know anything." She dropped the plastic baby doll onto the ground and stepped back from me. In the distance I heard sirens. Tinkie must have scared Coleman good. There were two patrol cars singing their way toward me.

"I never meant to take anything you wanted. I was a kid. I thought the pears were there for anyone to take. I'm sorry if I took something you valued."

She had the grace to look ashamed. "Your father apologized for you."

I never knew that. "He shouldn't have. It was my place, not his."

"That's what I told him, but he said that you were innocent in your thoughts and actions and he would protect that innocence with everything he had."

And that had made her envious of me. It wasn't children she'd longed for, but someone to protect her. "My father was a smart man, but this time he was wrong. He should have told me and let me make amends."

Mrs. Hedgepeth loosened the belt around her costume and let it fall to the ground around her, revealing her normal slacks and a sweater. "I shouldn't play Mary."

Coleman, Budgie, and DeWayne jumped out of the

patrol cars as if I were forcing Mrs. Hedgepeth to strip in her front yard. I didn't know what to do so I just stood there.

"What's going on?" Coleman asked as he approached.

"Mrs. Hedgepeth needs a costume adjustment before tonight's pageant," I said. I'd gone there to torment her, but now I felt sorry for her. I'd lost my zest for wicked repartee.

"I'm not going to play Mary," she said.

"Now, Martha." Coleman gave her his arm and assisted her toward her house. She was not disabled or ill, but she leaned on his arm as if she were exhausted. "Let's get you inside and figure out what's wrong."

DeWayne scooped up the fallen costume and tried to hand it to me, but I backed away. "The one person she doesn't want inside her house is me. You two take her the costume."

Sweetie Pie, Pluto, and I stood under the bare branches of the pear tree that had been the bone of contention between this woman and myself—for reasons neither of us understood at the time. Now it all seemed like such a waste of energy. She'd disliked me, a kid, because I had a loving father. And I'd tormented her because I'd viewed her as mean and crotchety instead of broken. Big waste on both of our parts.

DeWayne shook the dead grass out of the costume and handed it off to Budgie, who'd backed up to stand beside the patrol car.

"Convince her that she has to be in the pageant tonight. The show can't go on without her." I gave them both a thumbs-up.

"Why me?" Budgie looked just like a kid being assigned to re-shelve books during study hall.

"Because you're a man of the law." I punched him lightly on the arm. "You do all the community things that are necessary to keep the citizens of Zinnia safe. If Mrs. Hedgepeth wakes up in the morning and realizes she passed on her chance to be the star of the Christmas pageant, the world will not be safe." I picked up Pluto. "And she needs cheering up. The holidays are tough for a lot of solitary people."

I instantly saw my chance to torment Budgie. Since he'd become a deputy, he had really blossomed. He was smart and helpful and had taken a load off Coleman in the research department. But he had also been a substitute high school teacher, and as a former student, I couldn't resist messing with him. "She's only fifteen or so years older than you. Why don't you take her to dinner? Make this holiday special for her."

He cast me a sidelong look and considered my suggestion. "You're a devil, Sarah Booth. I may just do it because it's the kind thing to do. You know she lost her husband and son in a terrible accident back when you were an infant. She probably is lonely."

I felt my prankster mojo wilt. "I didn't know that."

"Her husband, Ronald Hedgepeth, was a great guy. He worked with the sheriff's department repairing toys for children who often did without. Their son was the kind of kid who went around town mowing lawns for single ladies and helping older gentlemen with gardens and such."

I felt lower than a heel. The idea that Mrs. Hedgepeth had lost a husband and a son was bad enough, but they sounded like wonderful people. "My parents never told me that. They never mentioned what happened to Mr. Hedgepeth and I never knew about the son."

"His name was Randy. He was the pitcher on the softball team and was going to be valedictorian. He was about to graduate when he and his dad were killed in a terrible accident."

"What kind of accident?" I was wallowing in guilt now.

"Oh, it was a tragedy. They were driving home late one night from delivering meals on wheels when they came up on this steep hill slick with ice. They went over it and that was it for them."

"What hill? The Delta is flat. There aren't any hills."

He grinned wide, and I realized DeWayne was also way too amused. "Fool's hill, just like you." He stepped back in case I took a swing at him.

"Dammit, Budgie." He'd reeled me in like a hooked fish. "When did you become such an accomplished liar?"

"I had a lot of great teachers, but mostly this clutch of high school girls who could tell a lie and look as innocent as angels. Shall I name them?"

"No, that won't be necessary."

"I'll take Mrs. Hedgepeth her costume and tell her how much we're looking forward to the play."

"Wait a minute, please. What did happen to Mr. Hedgepeth?"

"He ran off with his secretary because Mrs. Hedgepeth was having an affair with the insurance salesman. He caught her parked in the woods when she put her high heel through the ragtop of the insurance salesman's car and got her shoe stuck."

Budgie was still laughing when he left to take the costume in the house. I owed him one, big-time.

16

Tinkie was waiting for me on the front steps of the courthouse. She looked mighty forlorn, looking at the pedestal where the statue had once stood. Sweetie Pie and Pluto sat at her feet while her pup, Chablis, cuddled in her arms. The critters were good at giving comfort.

"I'm sorry you saw this," I said.

"The good news is that they're going to create a park where cities and counties from all across the state can bring their statues. The Mississippi Artistic Council is going to commission many additional statues to tell the whole story of the history of Mississippi. The end creation will be a natural history trail of personalities and historic markers, coupled with a nature trail that tells the story of how the land here once was, how it was cleared, how the environment is changing because of humans, and how we need to protect it." Her smile was sad but not desolate. "The Harrington sisters are in charge of the nature trail. Imagine that. The Wiccans have gotten a state grant. I hear the plan is for the schoolchildren to help identify all the native plants. Things are changing in Mississippi."

She was right about that, and while change always hurt, it also brought hope. Things could be better—for everyone.

"What did you find out?" I asked, eager to hear what she'd unearthed. "Did you have any trouble posing as Coleman's deputy?"

"Not a bit of trouble. I sold it completely, and I did find the birth records, but I don't know how much it will help us. The birth mother was a woman named Joanne Woodcock. She gave birth to two babies, twins. A girl and a boy. She abandoned them at the hospital, where they were taken in by the state and put up for adoption."

I found it hard to understand how a woman could simply walk off and leave her newborn babies, but I'd never faced the circumstances some women had to live with. "What happened to the babies?"

"The girl was claimed by a relative. The other baby, the boy, went into the system. He was taken in by the state orphanage."

"Did the hospital have any records showing who might have adopted the little girl? Did she list the name of the father?"

"No and no."

"It's going to be hard to trace that baby."

"Yes, but the big news is that I think you're right about

Ms. Woodcock and Will Falcon. We just can't prove it. But it's possible Eve has a brother."

"And one who may have a long-burning resentment that Eve found a home and he didn't."

Tinkie nodded. "The description of the young man stalking Eve could easily fit her brother in age. If this is about blood and abandonment, I'm not certain that paying a ransom will help get Eve home."

"That's damning with slim evidence, but my gut tells me we're on the right track."

"I agree, but we have to remember that this is a hunch unsupported with real evidence. The bad news is that I'm not finding a lot of other people who would think to kidnap a pregnant bank employee and ask for that kind of ransom. This is someone who knows Eve and wants to cash in on what they know."

That I couldn't argue. "Did you get an address on Woodcock?"

"She's deceased. Or at least that's what the person in records at the hospital said."

"Well, damn." That was a dead end when we really needed a live lead.

"Onaria, the records clerk, was a friend of Joanne. And she had some interesting things to say."

Tinkie was dribbling her information. "Spill it, Tinkie, before I have to hurt you."

"Onaria said she believed the babies' father was Will Falcon. She said he and Joanne were courting. He led Joanne to believe he was leaving Carla and was going to marry her. He said he wanted to take care of her and both babies. Then something happened and it was over. He said he couldn't divorce Carla and that he couldn't see Joanne or the children. Joanne couldn't take care of herself much less twins. After the babies were born, Carla agreed to take one child. She made Will choose which."

Now that was a hellish way to punish a man for infidelity—to make him choose between his own children.

Tinkie couldn't keep the emotion out of her voice. "He picked the little girl because he thought the boy would be better able to take care of himself."

"Yeah and the way it turned out, picking Eve may not have been much of a blessing for her. Carla hated her and showed it every day."

"I know. Carla was mean, but she was particularly awful about anything Eve might enjoy. Imagine hating a child enough to ban the celebration of Christmas in a house."

"How did Joanne die?" I asked. "And when?"

"Suicide. Almost twenty years ago. Onaria said Joanne was so depressed at leaving her babies in the hospital that she just lost all hope and didn't want to continue on. I couldn't live if I had to give up a baby." Tinkie put a hand on her flat stomach and I knew how much she longed to have a child.

I decided right then and there I would talk to Oscar about adoption. It wasn't my business, true enough, except that Tinkie's happiness was always my business. There were plenty of babies who needed a home. Oscar had rejected adoption long ago, but that was before he'd fallen in love with little Libby when Tinkie cared for the infant. All Oscar needed was a push in the right direction to give his heart to another child. After this case was solved, that would be my number one mission. Tinkie deserved to be a mother. Now, though, we had to resolve the baby brother issue and find Eve. "Tinkie, what about the baby boy?"

"Just gone. The hospital records indicate he was sent to an orphanage north of Jackson, but I called the adoption agency there and couldn't find any files that a male infant had been brought in on the dates associated with Joanne giving birth. It's been almost twenty years and the state was keeping paper records back then. They've closed the old orphanage north of Jackson and if I'm not mistaken, the building is razed. I'm afraid a lot of the records were also destroyed. And there's always the chance there was never an adoption. Back in those days, a family member could step forward and take on the responsibility for a child. As you know, some of the relatives really weren't related. Convenient uncles and such."

"Then there's no way to track those children now," I said. It was a depressing reality.

Tears rimmed Tinkie's eyes. "It breaks my heart to think of children lost in the system—or worse. I hope a loving family adopted him. Every child deserves a chance at love."

"That's a hot button for you, Tinkie. When this case is over, you're going to have to tell me why. Right now, I have an idea. I know who might be able to turn over some new facts."

Tinkie looked at me and her blue eyes lit. "Budgie! He's a dynamite researcher!"

"Yep. And a very smooth liar. I fell for some of his alternative facts hook, line, and sinker."

"We could ask Budgie to research for us and maybe he wouldn't tell Coleman."

It was possible. If Tinkie asked. She had a way with men and getting them to do her bidding because it made them feel manly and good. "We can try. Or rather you can try."

"I'll handle Budgie." She looked once more at the empty statue pedestal and then at the two patrol cars pulling into the parking lot. "The boys are back, Sarah Booth. You should leave before Coleman decides to arrest you. I know he's dying to exert his authority over you. Maybe a little discipline? You sort of bring out that need in people, you know."

She was teasing me, which meant I could pay her back when I found the proper venue. "Fine. I'll see if I can run Cece down and see what happened between her and Will Falcon. She needs to know that Eve has a brother, too." I paused for a moment, considering the fact I had no relatives. "Cece has a cousin she doesn't know a thing about, if the child survived and grew up. I wouldn't mind finding some long-lost relatives."

"They might not want to be found," Tinkie teased gently. "We need to make our plans for the money drop and escaping the men."

"Good idea." That was going to take some major manipulation.

Before I went back to Dahlia House, I needed to pick up another gift for Coleman. I'd never match his present, but I had something special for him, too. Because of the Christmas pageant, we'd planned to open presents early Christmas Day—and if Coleman was still speaking to me. I'd bought several things I thought he'd enjoy, but there was something special I'd had made for him. Gift giving was not one of my natural talents, but what was Christmas without that one present that came from another's most special place to yours.

The thing I loved with all of my heart was Dahlia House, the land, Jitty, the horses, the critters, my private eye agency, my friends, Coleman—not in any particular order. It changed from day to day. But I wanted to share my passion for some of these things with Coleman, and so I'd ordered him some handmade riding boots. He was a fine rider, and he didn't need special gear to make him more accomplished or more exciting to see astride Lucifer or Reveler or Miss Scrapiron. But good boots were always such a pleasure, and these were an open invitation to the world I loved so much.

There was a local boot repair shop in Zinnia. The owner, Luther Lee, also made a few pairs every year. He did it for pleasure, and he put his heart into the job. I'd opted for a plain design—Coleman was not a fussy man. He went out of his way to avoid calling attention to himself. With that in mind, I'd gone for a stitched design that was crafted with the skill only Luther could bring to the job. The bootmaker had said the boots would be ready by lunchtime.

The boot shop was close by the bail bond shop that my friend Junior ran, and I stopped in to say hello. Junior looked like a tired old hound dog with wrinkles that sloped from his scalp in toward his nose. His skin seemed to hang in folds of weariness, but he was an active man for his age. He'd been a friend of my father—an integral part of the justice system my father believed in so strongly. Junior offered the accused a chance to get out of jail and work or prove their innocence. My father had been opposed to holding the poor in jail because they couldn't pay a bond. Junior did his best to make bail affordable for those he deemed were not a risk.

I hurried toward Junior's establishment as fast as I could walk. The entire city of Zinnia had a door decorating contest for local businesses. Some shops brought in the local teens to decorate, putting up foil and wreaths, evergreen boughs, and strings of lights. It made the town a showplace.

For his Christmas decorations Junior had gone minimalist. Glued to his office door was a pecan, a package of saltine crackers, and a gumdrop—all in a row. I stood outside his shop staring at the puzzle. He was a big one for puzzles and loved to keep everyone guessing.

I saw him get up from behind his desk and walk to the window watching me. He was grinning to beat the band.

I pushed open the door. "What the heck is this, Junior?"

"It's about Christmas."

"Really? Pecan, crackers, and gumdrop?"

"Think about it, Sarah Booth. It should have special meaning to you. Your mother loved this particular . . . Christmas ditty."

I hadn't heard the word ditty in a long time. Heck, it was probably Jitty who'd last used it. Jitty! Damn! I got it. Junior had created a rebus on his door. Pecan—nut. Saltines—cracker. And finally the gumdrop—Sweet. Nutcracker Suite. Jitty had invaded poor Junior's brain to give me another indecipherable message.

"Your mother would be proud," Junior said. "Your daddy would think you're wasting your brain power. You know, he figured you'd be a journalist or a lawyer."

"Do you think he would have been upset at my desire to act?" I'd often wondered what my parents would really make of the decisions I'd made in life so far.

"Naw, he would have been perfectly comfortable with your choices. He knew you inside and out, Sarah Booth. You ended up back here where you belong and you're working for justice in your own way. Both James Franklin and Libby would be proud. That little brain fever of a sojourn in New York City notwithstanding."

Junior always made me feel good and connected to the past. He and my father often drank coffee together at a little café that had long gone out of business. In my mind's eye, I could still see them sitting on the orange stools at the Three Sisters lunch counter, sipping coffee as they talked over politics, justice, and how to keep the Zinnia Chamber of Commerce under control. My father hadn't been a fan of development for the sake of growth and had fought many a battle over it.

"Are you going to the Christmas pageant tonight?" I asked.

"Wouldn't miss it for the world. Tell me, after last year's fiasco they aren't going to use live animals again, are they?"

I honestly didn't know. But there had been a terrible pig episode at the last Christmas pageant where two juvenile delinquent young boys had tried to ride a pig toward the manger and nearly trampled several of the children in the pageant. Hence this year the adults were playing the major roles.

"I don't think they're using live animals. I've discouraged it. The animals hate it and that pig incident, and the spitting llamas, were the last straw, I think. I'll see you there. And Merry Christmas, Junior."

"You, too, Sarah Booth. I hope Santa brings you everything you desire."

"I already have it," I said. Not everything, but the other wishes on my list couldn't be purchased or tracked down by even the best living sleuth. That was Jitty's department.

I blew him a kiss and headed over to Luther's Boot Repair to pick up Coleman's boots. With the beautifully tooled boots in a box under my arm, I went on to the newspaper to look for Cece. She'd just arrived back from talking with her uncle Will, and she looked like she was ready to explode.

"He is the biggest jackass. He is a spineless cockroach. He is a jelly-root booger. He is green pond scum. He is pig shit between my toes. Aaarrrrgh!" She actually grabbed fistfuls of her hair and for a moment I thought she would pull herself bald.

"Cece! Stop it!" I gathered her in my arms and held her—or she might say restrained her. She struggled but finally stopped when she realized she couldn't easily shake me off. She stood in the circle of my embrace, heaving and sobbing.

I was surprised that Will had come clean with her about his illegitimate children, but I was glad I didn't have to tell her. "I'm so sorry. Tinkie has been trying to find the second baby, the little boy. We haven't given up, but there aren't any records and I don't know how to trace what happened to him."

"So I have a male cousin, and that infant was abandoned by his father. He's disappeared without a trace. We don't even know if he's still alive." Cece's loud anger had turned into cold fire.

"Will and Carla took in one baby and left the other?" The blood had drained from her face except for two spots of bright pink in her cheeks. She was furious. I hadn't seen her this mad since seventh grade when hormones kicked in full force and she'd beaten up a bully at school who was three times her size. She had made him beg for mercy. If she got away from me and made it to Will and Carla's, she would pound them into the dirt.

"I don't know what happened for a fact. We're still looking into it."

"What do you know?" Her eyes were completely steel gray, like a shark's. "Tell me."

I told her what we'd found about the babies being born and left at the hospital for adoption. How Will and Carla had taken Eve but left the baby boy. How Joanne Woodcock had taken her own life, and the male infant had disappeared into the system.

"I'm going to kill them." She said it and meant it. "I'll figure out how to do it so I don't get caught. Will fathered two children and abandoned one of them! He let that bitch Carla abuse Eve and he doesn't have a clue what happened to his son. I used to feel sorry for him, but not anymore. He and Carla deserve each other. I'm glad my father isn't alive to see what Will has become. I am truly going to kill him."

Her big talk was all bluff, merely an indication of how badly she was hurting. Cece wouldn't really kill anyone. Or so I hoped. "Tinkie and I think the person who took Eve may be her brother, this missing baby."

"Because she was adopted and he was rejected?" She scoffed. "If he knew what hell Eve lived in with my shit-for-brains uncle and that rabid witch who is his wife, he would be dancing at the idea he was left behind."

I knew, and she knew, that such rational thought would be completely overridden by the rejection, loss, and humiliation that any child would feel at being un-wanted. At having a sibling chosen, while he was left behind. That would bite with cruel teeth.

"How can we find this . . . man?" Cece asked.

"I don't know. You're a relative, maybe you could go down to the adoption agency north of Jackson and ask. Tinkie called, but they said they didn't have any records. It was probably the truth, but sometimes folks aren't properly motivated to look for old paperwork and the truth is, there probably aren't any records."

"That's at least a five-hour drive." Cece did the cal-culations in her head. "What if the kidnapper calls and demands the ransom sooner. I'm afraid to be too far away."

She was right about that. I had a solution, but she wasn't going to like it. "We could send Budgie. He's the best at research. He knows all the current computer pro-grams and how to use them. He can do in an hour what would take me a week. And we don't have a week."

"What if he gets Coleman involved?"

"That might happen. I can't ask Budgie to lie to Cole-man. That would be wrong, especially since Coleman knows about the kidnapping but you won't let him help with the money drop."

"Ask Budgie," she said begrudgingly. "Ask him to go now and please hurry."

I nodded. It was a step in the right direction. Because we didn't have another single lead—except for the Brom-leys. I had a terrible suspicion they might know a lot more about Eve, her brother, and the whole mess than they'd let on. I had to get my partner and head to the river to talk to them.

"Cece, what are you going to do?" Cece at loose ends was unacceptable. She'd end up in jail because she'd drive right back to Will and Carla's farm and pulp them.

"I have to cover a Christmas party for the Delta Women's Society. Trust me, if I could get out of it, I would."

One thing about Cece, she took her job seriously. The Delta Women's Society Christmas party was their biggest fundraiser of the year. All of the high society dames would be there dressed to the nines. Cece photographed it every year—and she couldn't miss this time. She would be safely tied up with work.

"Okay, I'll talk to Budgie." I pretended I didn't want to do it knowing full well Tinkie, in all probability, already had Budgie corralled into doing her bidding. If baby boy Falcon could be found, Budgie would do it.

"Thanks, Sarah Booth. I don't know what I'd do without you and Tinkie."

"Me either." I said it and felt only a twinge at my tiny deception. "Now I'd better make tracks."

Before she could ask more questions, I beat it back to my car and called Tinkie. "Plans have changed. I'll pick you up in front of the courthouse."

"Where are we going?"

"To pay a visit to the Bromleys."

"Again?"

"Oh, yes. Third time's the charm, or haven't you heard?"

"What's up?"

"We have to make them tell us the truth."

"I agree. But how?"

"Just be ready."

"Sarah Booth, time is running out. If we deliver the money and Eve is released, that's all well and good. But if we meddle in this and something happens . . ."

She didn't have to finish. "Look, we each have to do what we believe is best. Cece thinks we shouldn't involve the law. I've honored her wishes, even though it goes against my gut instincts. We can't guarantee the outcome." I was talking to myself as well as her. If this went bad and Eve or her baby were harmed, it wouldn't matter whether Cece forgave me because I could never forgive myself. I also knew assuming that guilt wasn't fair to me but I would do it anyway. I was well and truly in a pickle.

"What do you expect the Bromleys to tell us?" she asked.

"What happened to Eve's brother. They know. I'm positive they do. They've been involved in this up to their ears. And they don't want the money. In fact, I believe they only want Eve to be returned safely. But they are linked to this someway. They have a responsibility in this, and I believe it's because they know the kidnapper."

"And you believe it's Eve's brother?"

"I do. I wish I didn't, but I do. I think maybe the Bromleys adopted him or took him in or somehow got involved in his life and now they're neck deep in this mess. All they want is for Eve to go home safely and have her baby."

"And what about Dara Peterson? And her baby? Where are they in this whole snarl?"

"I don't know." This was the most troubling aspect of the case, aside from Eve's safety. We had a new mother, a sick infant, a blanket in a freezing creek, and a kitchen covered in blood. If there was danger to Eve and her child, it centered around Dara Peterson and her baby, but I couldn't see how the pieces fit.

"There are an awful lot of babies mixed up in this case." Tinkie sounded a little woebegone.

She was echoing my thoughts, but I saw no reason to encourage her fears. "And all of them are going to be fine. We'll make it so."

"Sarah Booth, do you think you and Coleman will have a child?"

Her question stopped me cold. I hadn't given it conscious thought, but if I were honest, I'd have to admit that I'd had little flashes of Christmas with a toddler in the house. Would he, or she, be able to see Jitty? Oh, if the baby could see her, then Jitty would well have met her match. She'd be reduced to the role of imaginary friend—the thought made me smile. I was still smiling as I pulled to the front of the courthouse where Tinkie waited.

"You look like the cat who ate the canary." She was still talking to me via her telephone.

I ended the call and turned to her. "I don't know about a child. Both Coleman and I have dangerous jobs. Is that fair? I know what it's like to lose my parents."

"That was an accident," Tinkie said. "There's no guaranteed way to prevent tragedy. It can and does happen to everyone all around us. That's an excuse because you're afraid to care that much about a child."

"Maybe." I wasn't going to argue. "I don't know what Coleman wants, or if we'll even be together long enough to consider a child. How about we put that on the back burner for a year or two?"

"You don't have much longer than that. I mean those eggs are viable for only so long."

She eyed me and I felt like a horse being judged by its teeth. Its very long teeth. "Thanks, Suzy Sunshine." Before she could insult me further, I stepped on the gas and shot out into traffic. It was Christmas Eve, a very busy time in Zinnia proper. Last-minute shoppers clotted the roadway and I drove carefully. I didn't want to bump off a pedestrian.

"Sarah Booth?"

I didn't like the winsome tone in her voice. "What?"

"They're performing *The Nutcracker* in Memphis. Want to go? We could double date, like back when we were in high school."

I thought of Jitty. "Sure. I'd like that a lot, if Coleman is game."

She whipped out her phone. "I'll get the tickets. It'll be a wonderful new Christmas tradition, just the four of us."

I liked that thought.

17

We were prepared for an unwelcome reception when we pulled up at the Bromley's river cabin. It was so well hidden from the road that had I not been there before, I might have missed it. Tinkie and I parked on the road and walked down the rutted driveway. As we drew closer, we could hear arguing. A young woman's raised voice came to us.

"This is the stupidest thing I've ever heard. You're going to jail. All of you will. And it isn't going to help. Don't you know that the bastard can go back on his word and refuse at any time?"

We crept up the stairs but before we could hear more, the front door was jerked open and a young woman stepped out on the landing, her face streaked with tears.

"Who the hell are you?" she asked, unwittingly stepping back to let Tinkie and the critters into the cabin. Before we could get into the house I heard the back door slam. Someone had made a quick exit. I waited a moment to see if I could catch a glimpse of who it was coming around the house, but the person never appeared. He or she could have cut around the house in the other direction or through the woods.

"Friends of the family," I said as I followed behind my crew and stepped into a room I was already familiar with. Someone had gotten the holiday spirit. Now there was a Christmas tree, decorated to the hilt. The young woman closed the door, and I noticed she wore a warm flannel shirt and leggings. She held a plastic container of cereal in her hand. Two toddlers, one a boy about two and the other a younger child of indeterminate gender, played on the floor.

"I'm Tinkie Richmond, and this is Sarah Booth Delaney. We're looking for Dara Peterson." I didn't say it, but I thought I'd found her.

The woman rattled the a plastic container of Cherrios, calling the children over to her. "Why are you looking for Dara?"

"We've been concerned for her."

She eyed us, summing us up. I wondered what she saw when she looked at Tinkie in her beautiful red and black outfit and me in my jeans and a warm jacket. "No one has been concerned about her up to now. Her fairy godmothers have been few and far between. Why the sudden wave of alarm from two women who aren't her friends?"

"How do you know we aren't her friends?" Tinkie asked.

"Dara doesn't have friends like you. People with money. Besides, Mom and Dad would have mentioned you were dropping by. I'm Mariam Bromley Akins."

I was disappointed that I wasn't already talking to Dara, but I pressed on. "Where is Dara?" I asked, ignoring her reference to us as unfriends.

"Bite me." She pointed at the door. "Get out. Now. I don't know who you are or what you're up to, but you can leave on your own or I'll call my husband back in here to throw you out. He hasn't gone far and he's already aggravated."

Tinkie looked at me and shrugged. "Let's go, Sarah Booth."

I wasn't ready to give up so easily, and I was legitimately worried about the young woman. I couldn't get that bloody kitchen out of my mind. "Is Dara okay? At least tell us that much. We know she was having medical problems, and we're concerned." That statement caught the young woman off-guard.

"Dara is fine. What makes you think otherwise?"

"We're private investigators. There was a lot of blood in the kitchen at her house."

"We know she just had a baby and there were health problems," Tinkie said. "I promise you, we only want to help."

The girl's eyes filled with tears but she was too angry to cry. "How do you know all of this about my sister? Are you spying on her?"

"We're actually trying to help her. For real," Tinkie said, and she stepped closer and put a hand on the young woman's shoulder. "I don't know what's going on, but I know someone is desperate. We can help, if you'll let us."

Tinkie's gesture was sincerely meant in kindness, but

I wasn't certain the young mother would recognize it as such. Somehow, I didn't think a lot of kindness had fallen to her lot in life. But we did have a firm connection now between the Bromleys and Dara Peterson. That much we'd gained.

The woman sniffled and then turned away to give the Cheerios to the older little boy. "Here, Jeremy, give your sister a snack." She sobbed quietly before she gathered herself. "No one understands the miracle of a healthy child until they have a sick one."

As if the child sensed her mother's distress, the baby toddled toward the young woman, who I could see was near exhaustion. The little girl dragged a very ugly little doll by one leg, its head beating a rhythm on the floor with each step she took. One eye was sightless, but the other was blue glass. Exceedingly creepy. And familiar. Probably from some horror movie.

"First, is Dara okay? There was a lot of blood in her kitchen." Tinkie spoke softly.

"I know. The sheriff talked to me. Dara is fine. She cut herself on a broken glass. It was her blood. She had to have stitches, but she's okay."

I wasn't certain I was buying her story, but I didn't interrupt. She seemed more willing to talk than anyone we'd encountered along the river. "Mariam, we're looking for a missing person. A young pregnant woman about your age. Her name is Eve Falcon."

She went very still, but only for a second. "I can't help you."

"Are you sure?" I tried to be as gentle as Tinkie, but I didn't have her touch—or her patience.

"Please leave. Now."

"Mariam, I promise you, we want to help. I don't

know what you know about Eve and her disappearance, but she's due to give birth any day now. Her cousin Cece is sick with worry. We just want to get her home safely." Tinkie glanced at me, her brow furrowed. "I heard something outside. Like someone calling out?"

I hadn't heard anything out of the ordinary. "No."

"Are you sure?"

The kitchen opened off the living room and Tinkie hurried to the sink, where a window looked out over the woods that grew right up to the back steps. We both scanned the dense greenery below us.

"I don't see anything," I said. A back door offered an exit with a small porch and a steep flight of stairs to the ground.

"No one is here except me and my kids. My husband took off out the back door when you arrived," Mariam said. "You have to leave. Now."

I joined Tinkie at the window, aware that the height of the cabin gave us a better view into the woods than we'd ever have from ground level. What looked to be a deer trail ran from the back stairs into a dense growth of cypress and scrub oaks.

"Is that a building back in the woods?" Tinkie asked. She was standing on tiptoe.

"Yes, it's an old woodshed," Mariam said. "It's rotting into the ground. Go check it out if you want. It's filled with spiders, snakes, and cobwebs, not to mention old mattresses and things I wouldn't touch on a dare. Go right out there and look. Just go." She pushed us toward the back door. "Please just get out of here." She opened the back door and Sweetie Pie, Chablis, and Pluto took off down the stairs at breakneck speed.

Tinkie balked. "Look, Mariam, no one cares about

the ransom money. Cece is completely willing to pay the ransom, as long as Eve is okay. No one is going to press charges or try to involve the police, if Eve is returned unhurt. I swear that to you. If you know where she is, just tell us. We'll take her and Cece will still pay the money. She has all of it. The whole hundred and fifty thousand. She won't bat an eye."

The color drained from Mariam's face. "Stupid idjits," she said under her breath. "Now you have to leave. Right now. My folks will be back any minute and I don't want them upset. They let me and my kids come here, and we don't have anywhere else to go, so you have to leave." She all but pushed us out the back door.

"If you know who has Eve, tell them the money is irrelevant. We just want her returned safely." Tinkie pressed her point before the door closed in our faces. "Dammit," Tinkie said, "that Mariam knows where Eve is. I know it."

"We can't force her to tell anything. What we know is that she's Dara Peterson's sister, and that Dara has a newborn. This is all connected, and when we figure it out, we'll be able to find Eve."

My partner looked at me. "What do Eve and her sibling have to do with Mariam and Dara?" The pieces were there—we just couldn't put them together.

"We didn't get anything out of the Bromleys because they weren't here," Tinkie said. "And I don't have a clue how to run them down."

"We're here. We need to check out that woodshed. I doubt there's anything there, but it won't hurt to look." I was headed in that direction when my cell phone rang. It was Cece.

"You have to get back here," Cece said. "Coleman is

here at the paper, and he's asking questions. I know he only wants to help, but if someone sees him here, it won't matter what I did and didn't tell him. Please, can you do something?"

She was right. If someone was watching Cece, all they had to see was that Coleman was at her workplace. I checked my watch. Time was running out on us. "Okay, I'll think of something." I turned to Tinkie. "Aren't you helping with the wise men's costumes? Can you call Coleman right now and tell him to meet you at the church for a fitting or something?"

"Sure."

"Let me check out that woodshed. Then I'll take you to the church." I ran around back and plowed through the underbrush until I came to a clearing. The woodshed was as Mariam had described it. Part of the roof was caving in. There was no sign of life, and no electric lines ran to the shed. Without power to heat the interior, it was uninhabitable. The only thing that gave me pause was Sweetie Pie sniffing around and giving that strange yodeling bark-howl that meant she'd caught a scent—likely of a nest of rats or some raccoons. Chablis ran back and forth barking. I shoved my way through heavy growth up to a window and looked inside. Cobwebs, spiders, and possibly snakes for sure. No sign of a prisoner. Wherever Eve or Dara might be, it wasn't the shed. There wasn't time for further investigation—I hurried back to where Tinkie waited, forcing the dogs to come with me.

"Oh, crap. I'm late to help with the costumes anyway," Tinkie said, picking up a hissing Pluto in her arms. "The men will be at the church waiting. I called Coleman and he was suspicious, but he said he'd be there."

"Will it take you long to fix the costumes?" I was wondering if she could keep tabs on Cece for the rest of the day.

"It's just a matter of tacking those robes together here and there. The hard things are the headpieces. They're a bit awkward. If I glued them to their heads, do you think they'd forgive me?"

"Sure, you try that glue thing. That will keep the men busy while we make the drop. And then they'll kill us both."

"You are tragically overdramatic, Sarah Booth." Tinkie winked at me.

"I'll take Chablis to Dahlia House with my crew. I want to do some research on the Peterson family and the Bromleys. They have to be connected." Nothing else made sense. And somehow, Eve had been pulled into their sphere. I'd considered that Eve and Dara might have been childhood friends, but nothing I'd found confirmed that. Eve had gone to a small high school near the farm she grew up on, and when she was sixteen she disappeared from the area completely. "I know there's a link, I just don't know how it's all connected. If I find anything, I'll call, and I'll be sure and get with Cece."

We loaded up in the car and headed back to Zinnia. Something niggled at the back of my mind. Some connection I was missing. Some question I should have asked.

It didn't take long to get back to town, and I let Tinkie off at the church, where cars were beginning to fill the parking lot. A lot of people were involved in preparing for the pageant, and the annual Christmas eating frenzy that was a big part of it. The social before the pageant brought out Zinnia's best cooks. Everyone who had a claim-to-fame dish would bring it to share with the congregation. Ella Prine would have her sweet potato salad, and Velma Brown's coconut cake would take center stage. That cake never lasted longer than ten minutes. Although I wasn't hungry at all, my mouth was watering.

"See you in a bit," Tinkie said as she got out of the car.

"If you can put a slice of Mrs. Velma's cake back for me, I'd really appreciate it." I watched her walk inside the church and then I started toward Dahlia House. I drove on automatic pilot. The critters in the backseat were snuggled up and comfy. Sweetie Pie let out a soft doggy sigh and eased into the passenger seat. She loved to ride with her head out the window, and though it was cold, I rolled the window halfway down for her. The cold air would liven me up, maybe kick my sluggish brain cells into gear.

I was halfway home when a deer leaped out of a pile of brush on the verge. I hit the brakes and swerved, sending Sweetie Pie off balance. She clawed at the dash to regain her footing and popped the glove box open. My gun and some paperwork scattered onto the floorboard. Rattled, I pulled over to check the animals and to put the gun away. Also to compose myself. I was a fast but careful driver, but that deer had caught me unaware.

With the car stopped, I checked Chablis and Pluto in the backseat. Pluto yawned wide, telling me he was bored with my fit of anxiety. Chablis jumped into my lap and licked my face. Like Tinkie, she doled out the comfort. I leaned down and grabbed the gun, returning it to the glove compartment. The papers were old receipts, car maintenance records, and the photo I'd taken from Eve's cottage. I'd kept it in the car in case I found someone to ask about it.

I took a moment to examine it again, letting the small details stand out. The headless woman holding the babies wore red nail polish. Bright red. It was the nail polish of a young woman with hopes and dreams. She'd painted her nails before going into labor, an observation that hit me right in the heart.

Her hands were lean and young, the fingers slender and tapered. Ringless. What had her expectations been when she carried those children? That Will Falcon would divorce Carla and make a family with her? I couldn't help but believe Will's life would have been much happier. It was just a supposition, because I couldn't know. But Carla Falcon was a dried-up prune with a plum pit for a heart.

I looked at the babies. They looked alike, but then all babies looked alike to me. They all bore a marked resemblance to Winston Churchill. On a bad day. These two were wrapped in white blankets, which didn't indicate gender, and both were asleep. There wasn't much to discern from studying them except they looked healthy.

I took a deep breath. I had to get moving. I was tucking the photo away when I caught sight of the ugly doll mixed in with the other baby paraphernalia. I froze. I'd seen that very same doll. There couldn't be two dolls that ugly. And then I remembered where I'd seen that toy. Mariam's child had been dragging it behind her on the floor.

If the babies in the photo were Eve and her brother, then somehow Eve was connected to Mariam, and now I had physical evidence to prove my theory. Mariam and Dara had to be the key.

Nearly twenty years had passed from the time the photo of the woman's torso and the babies was taken and

Mariam's child was dragging a sad doll around the floor. It wasn't evidence I could take to the law to have Mariam apprehended—not that I would do such a thing anyway. But it linked Eve, the Bromleys, Mariam, and Dara Peterson. The children were what tied it all together. They connected the families to the past and that gave me hope that I had found the leverage I needed to make the Bromleys tell me what they knew. And the place to start was that photograph. If I had a solid ID on the babies, the other dominoes would line up.

I blew through an empty intersection. I really didn't want to take the pets with me. With the coming of night, the temperature had turned bitter, and I didn't think the Bromleys would invite two dogs and a cat into their home. Well, probably the pets would be more welcome than a private investigator. This was going to be confrontational.

I gunned it home, put the animals in the house and closed the doggy door so they couldn't get out, and headed toward Fortis Landing. As I drove I called Cece. "Did you get the final details?" I asked.

"Not yet. I can't take much more of this, Sarah Booth. Why don't they call?"

She was fidgety and scared, and I didn't blame her. "When will Jaytee get back?" I asked.

"Any minute. They flew into Atlanta earlier. They had to get their instruments through customs and load up the van. It's what, about a six-hour drive?"

"Yeah. Remember, though, it's Christmas Eve. Traffic may be really bad."

"Right." She sounded totally defeated.

"I have to drop Sweetie Pie and Pluto off at home, then I'm going back to Fortis Landing. I may have found something and I want to check again to be sure. Tinkie is helping sew the wise men into their costumes. Text me the minute you get the drop information. I'll be fairly close to the location and I might be able to get there before anyone else. It's always smart to have someone on the scene long before the drop." I was torn between a desire to follow my lead or to force myself on Cece and stick to her like a second skin. The problem was that I didn't totally believe she'd get a call to retrieve her cousin. I'd chewed and gnawed on the big why—why would the Bromleys or Mariam or Dara Peterson be involved in holding Eve for ransom? We'd told them to just ask for the money and they could have it. Using a pregnant woman as a bargaining chip was sheer madness. Besides, they just didn't strike me as kidnappers. "Promise you'll call me."

"You know they'll likely change the drop location, Sarah Booth, and I will call. But whatever happens, do not tell Coleman."

"I haven't, but I still think we should."

"I only want Eve back safely."

"Cece, I think this has something to do with Eve's brother. If Tinkie and I are right in our supposition that the brother has kidnapped Eve, it might not be about money but about revenge. He wasn't wanted. She was. He could be very angry, and not completely rational." I didn't want to scare her but we had to face the truth. "We need to be prepared for that, Cece. We need someone who will take action if necessary. What if this young man is not right mentally? We need Coleman on the scene."

"Are you asking if I can shoot my kin?" she asked.

"I guess I am."

"To save Eve, yes. I can do whatever I need to."

"This is Eve's brother, which makes him your cousin, too. Eve may never forgive you. You may not be able to forgive yourself."

"Yet Eve will be alive. Isn't that what's important?" Cece had gone from sad to defiant.

"Yes, that's the bottom line. But I'd like to achieve that with a minimum of collateral damage if we can."

"I'll text you when I know more."

There was one more possibility I had to bring up. "Cece, what if Eve is working with these people? Are you willing to confront that if it's necessary?"

"I'll do whatever I have to. If Eve is trying to squeeze money out of me, she'll be sorry. I'd give her the shirt off my back, but I won't be played. Not even by someone I love."

Cece meant it, too. She'd fought too long and too hard to be who she was to take crap off a blackmailer.

"Okay. Text me as soon as you hear. I'll be in Fortis Landing trying to get the Bromleys to tell me their role in this."

"Good luck with that," Cece said.

"Okay."

"And thank you, Sarah Booth. Thank you for everything."

I drove along the narrow highway watching the last light fade from the sky. It was an early dusk because the night was overcast. The huge, heavy clouds collided on the horizon, making me think of the weatherman's hopeful forecast of snow. It wasn't impossible, but snow in December surely wasn't an ordinary event. The winter was a time for cold, clear nights. Normally, no place I'd ever been had a winter night's view like the Mississippi Delta, with the stars unobscured by any lights. This night, though, had a sense of foreboding. The weather played a role in my mood, but there was more to it. I'd partially figured out what was going on, but I didn't have the most important answers. Where was Eve? Had she had her baby? Was she okay?

I pulled into the back of the parking lot at Bullwinkle's. A thicket of sweet olive offered a perfect hiding place. Leaving the car there would mean a trek through the wooded area, but it would also give me the advantage of approaching the cabin from an unexpected direction. I'd have time to surveil the area thoroughly. While I expected to find the Bromleys or Mariam and force them to talk, in my heart of hearts I hoped for even more. My gut told me that Eve played a big role in everything that was happening. Possibly a willing role. If I was lucky, I'd find Eve inside.

The rowdy lyrics of "You Don't Have to Call Me Darlin'" came through the night, along with the stomping of cowboy boots and cat whistles. It was Christmas Eve at Bullwinkle's and folks were partying down.

Christmas Eve had always been a family time in my home. My years in New York, I'd gone to parties and theater gatherings, but it had never really felt like Christmas Eve. Now, all I wanted was to watch the Christmas pageant at the church and then go home with Coleman. Or barring that, I hoped by midnight I would be at the Sunflower County Hospital with Eve and that she would be giving birth to a happy baby.

Using my phone as an occasional light, I stepped into the darkness of the woods. I had to get back to the Bromley cabin. My best bet would be if I found Mariam alone so I could talk to her. She knew more than she'd let on, and I believed I could persuade her to talk. I believed she held the key to Eve's location. The ugly baby doll was proof. I felt sorry for her, but I also needed to resolve the matter of Eve's safety. I was on a mission.

A stick cracked to my right and I stopped, holding myself completely still. The woods were silent except for the scurrying of small animals looking for a warm nest. As aggravating as Jitty could be, I'd welcome her company at this moment. Another limb cracked as some creature moved a little closer to me.

The music in the bar, now a faraway echo, shifted to a Christmas carol. "Oh, holy night, the stars are brightly shining. It is the night of our dear Savior's birth." I listened to the lyrics that the choir at the church would soon be singing for the Christmas pageant—that I was going to miss. There was no help for it, though. Coleman and I would, hopefully, have many Christmases in the future to share.

Moving with great care, I left the music behind and edged in the direction of the Bromley's cabin. I wanted to come up on it from behind. As I crept forward, I tried to think of all the possibilities I might confront. I had to be mentally prepared. What if I saw Eve? What if she was truly being held captive? If she was in danger, could I shoot someone? More troubling were other questions. What if she wasn't in danger and was playing my friend? What would I do?

The blow came out of nowhere and landed on the side of my head. I dropped to one knee, struggling to remain upright. For some reason it was very important that I didn't fall over. I had to see who'd hit me.

"Girl, you should have minded your own business."

I recognized the voice. It was Curtis Bromley. I staggered to my feet and caught my balance against a tree.

"This would have all been over by morning, but you just couldn't stay out of it. Now you've forced me to do something I sure didn't want to do."

"Where is Eve?" I demanded.

"You're going to get that girl killed," Curtis said as he grabbed my arm when I started to teeter over. He frisked me and took my gun. "Now come with me and don't make any noise. If they know you're poking around here, I don't know what they'll do."

I couldn't follow exactly what he was saying. It didn't make sense. He was the one who'd struck me, but he was acting like he was protecting Eve. "Where is she?"

"She's in labor. That's a kink in our plan," Curtis said, and he was clearly worried. "Now you have to be quiet. I'm serious. You'll get her killed along with the rest of us. Matilda told me I should have tied you up this afternoon when you were at the house and poking around my shed, but I didn't want to do that. I didn't want to do any of this."

"Take me to Eve." My dizziness was clearing.

"Not happening. You're going to stay right here, trussed up like Tom Turkey, until this is done and the money has changed hands. Once that's finished, I'll come let you go. You just keep in mind that if they have a clue you're on to them, they'll kill you and maybe Eve, too."

"They, who is they? Her brother?"

He snorted. "Mitch wouldn't harm a fly."

"But he kidnapped Eve." Curtis helped me to sit at the base of a tree, which was a relief because my head was still spinning a little and my legs were tired.

"Mitch did no such thing. He would never harm Eve. That boy was so excited when he found out he had a sister. The chance that Eve might help him—that was more than he'd ever expected. You should know he's worried sick about her baby. If Eve's baby has the same medical problem that his son has, it's going to be bad if she delivers out here without medical attention. He tried to talk her out of this crazy scheme, but she wouldn't listen to reason. She and Dara. They said it was the only way."

I was completely lost. "What medical problem?"

"Something about how the blood doesn't clot properly and the liver isn't cleaning it. It's a genetic thing. That's why Mitch was so desperate to get to Eve. He meant to help her, and then it turned into another whole thing."

"You said it's genetic?" My brain fog was clearing up quickly, and I remembered the blood all over the kitchen of the little cottage. "We have to get Eve to a hospital if she's in labor."

"You think I don't know that? And you've just killed any chance of doing that. Now you stay here." He grabbed my hands and tied them behind the tree. "I'll let you go as soon as we have the money and Eve is free. I won't be gone long but I can't have you meddling. I'll be back as soon as I can. It's cold, I know, but not cold enough to harm you."

"What is Eve to you?" I asked him.

"Doesn't matter. All that matters is that we get through this night and get her to the hospital."

He sighed as he pulled duct tape from his pants pocket. "Good thing I always travel prepared." In another few seconds, he had me properly gagged.

18

I was in a fine pickle, stuck out in the woods, unable to move or even call out for help. Curtis Bromley hadn't bothered to take my phone, but tucked in my pocket, it was useless to me. What a miscalculation that I'd left the critters at home with Jitty. Help wasn't coming from that quarter. I hadn't told Tinkie where I was going because I knew she'd be mad and try to blow off her work with the costumes. I'd hidden my car so well, no one would notice it until the morning. I'd managed to put myself in a bad situation without any hope of rescue.

When I thought it couldn't get any worse, it started to snow. Big, fat, wet white flakes of Christmas magic that began to melt on my legs and face. Soon I would be nothing but a mound of slushy snow.

How many Christmas Eves had I wished and wished for snow? I'd seen a few winter wonderlands in New York City—and felt like I'd been brushed by a miracle. A white Christmas was the picture postcard of all holidays. I was about to get one, too. Only I was sitting on the damp ground, tied to a tree. My hands were already freezing. I'd read horror stories of people left out in the snow who had to have their fingers, toes, and noses removed due to frostbite. Crapola! That would not be a good look to sport on Christmas day.

As I started to shake violently from the cold, I tried to entertain myself with pleasant memories or foolishness. I began to make a list of foods I would never eat again if I got free of my situation. No more Cheetos or cheesecake no matter how bad the craving. No more sucking chocolate syrup out of the squeeze container in the refrigerator. I would toss out the frozen pumpkin custard muffins I'd been hoarding for an emergency. There were so many little things I'd always meant to get around to doing. Like maybe my taxes before the very last minute. At least I wouldn't have to deal with those if I froze to death.

From out of nowhere came the beautiful music of "The Waltz of the Snowflakes." It seemed to well up from the very ground I sat on. Of course I knew I was freezing to death. Auditory hallucination. Any minute, Jitty would appear and I'd know my end was imminent.

Just as I feared, a troupe of snowflakes from *The Nutcracker* danced onto the scene. I'd seen productions of the ballet, but I'd never imagined I'd see the waltz of the snowflakes while it was actually snowing. The magnificent dancers in their white tulle skirts frosted with silver glitter twirled and danced through the increasing snowfall. It was a beautiful vision to die with.

"Sarah Booth Delaney! Don't you dare quit!"

My eyelids weighed a hundred pounds, but I forced them up to confront a lovely mocha snowflake. While all the others looked to have been poured from milk with uniform blond hair, this snowflake, my Jitty, reminded me of hot coffee with a dollop of cream and glossy black hair. The other snowflakes were serene and ethereal. My Jitty was red hot with anger.

"Wake up, Sarah Booth. Don't make me do something you'll regret." She glared at me as the other dancers moved around us, leaping and whirling like an actual snowstorm.

"I'm tired, Jitty."

"And cold, no doubt."

"Not so cold." I smiled. "No, I'm not cold any longer."

"That is not a good sign," Jitty said, more agitated than ever. "If you go to sleep, you won't wake up in this world ever again."

The siren song of paradise called to me. "Will I be with my parents?"

"What about Coleman?" Jitty asked. She was the very devil.

"Coleman?" If I died, Coleman would never forgive himself. Nor would my friends.

"What about Dahlia House?" Jitty asked. "You're so busy regretting dietary choices, you never thought to regret that you didn't make a will. You got no heirs, 'cept for me, and no one is going to believe I should inherit Dahlia House. I'll be homeless and that will be your fault, too."

Damn. Jitty was going to blame me for everything. Any minute now I'd be responsible for world hunger and Twitter.

"Cut me some slack. I'm tied to a tree. I can't be responsible if I freeze to death. It's not like I sat down and quit." Amazingly I could talk clearly around the duct tape that clamped my mouth shut.

"What are you doing to free yourself?"

"What can I do? I'm not magic. I don't have a fairy godmother to call on. I don't have a grandmother or a mother. Or even Aunt Loulane."

"Sarah Booth!" My mother's voice came to me and she walked through the dancers to come to my side. She wore a favorite golden brown sweater exactly the shade of her hair, and her red lips were in a straight, thin line. "Get up right this instant."

"I'm tied to a tree." Did the dead have some serious issue with seeing the obvious?

"And what are you doing to remedy that?" My mother knelt down so that I could more easily see her face. Snowflakes clung to her long curls. Her gray-green eyes stared into mine, infusing my body with a kind of heat that started from my solar plexus.

"Where's Daddy?" I tried to look behind her, but the world was luminous. I couldn't see what was in the glow.

"I'm here, Sarah Booth." And he was. Right at my mother's shoulder. He put a hand on her and I realized they were both dressed for a party. She was wearing a beautiful green cocktail dress with the bodice trimmed in glittering lights. Battery operated—never. Mama had tapped into some angelic power source. My dad looked handsome in a tux with a dusting of snowflakes on his shoulders and in his hair. All around me the ground had turned white. For the first time in—ever—the weatherman had been right about snow. It was really coming down now. More than two inches had accumulated. Too bad I hadn't pranced into the woods after the snowfall. At least then I would have left tracks. Now the ground stretched white, pure, and untouched.

"Sarah Booth!" My father cupped my face in his hand. "Wake up! Now!"

I shook myself awake and drank in the sight of them in their party finery. I had a party to go to tomorrow. After celebrating with Coleman tonight. "I love that dress, Mom. Where are you guys going?"

"There's a gathering in the Great Beyond we need to attend. And you have a Christmas pageant, which is already going strong. Mrs. Hedgepeth is not exactly who I would have cast as Mary, but she does quite a bit of tithing."

"You mean those parts were for sale?" I was outrageously outraged. "How is that right?"

"Much in life isn't fair. Like the fact you're tied to a tree for the first Mississippi Delta snowfall of your adult life. But it's almost over. Sarah Booth, hang on. Just for a little while longer. You can do it."

I sighed softly. "No, I don't think I can." Maybe I didn't want to. If I could be with them . . .

"It doesn't work that way," Daddy said. "You can't quit and expect to reap the rewards of hard effort. I taught you better."

He was always the one who dictated the more difficult path. The easy path was not for a Delaney. "I just want to sleep."

"You can sleep in the grave." Jitty was back. "Now

perk up and tell your Mama and Daddy how much you love them. They can't stay much longer. There are rules in the Great Beyond, as you well know."

The glow behind my parents had become fiercer, and all of the dancing snowflakes settled into a tableau. "Sarah Booth, you have to fight."

It was my mother's voice, but it was also Jitty.

"Free yourself."

I wanted to complain and point out that if it was so easy, I would have been freed a long time ago. But I tugged at my bonds again and rubbed against the bark of the tree. The wet snow had given the rope a little bit of stretch, and I frantically began to tug.

"That's it." My parents approved of my actions. "You can do it."

"Mama, Daddy, did you think I was stupid to go to New York and try to be an actress?" It was a question I needed an answer to.

"Stupid, never." My mom touched the top of my head and it felt like the brush of an angel's wing.

"We think it was very brave, Sarah Booth. You went looking for happiness, and you were willing to take risks. You didn't find what you sought in New York, but at least you looked."

"Is Coleman what I seek?" If only I had their reassurance, it would allow me to leap past all of my doubts and insecurities.

"You know the answer in your heart. Never turn your back on a miracle. That's all we can tell you."

They started to fade, and the illumination went with them, along with the snowflake dancers and Jitty. I was alone in the woods, and I'd been there for a long time. But I was awake and fighting now. Fighting for my life and my dream. I felt the rope that tied my hands slip a little. I dug down into the snow and wet my hands and the rope again, using the wet slickness to my advantage. Real concern compelled me to act quickly. Curtis Bromley wasn't a killer. He hadn't intended to leave me tied to a tree in the snow. Heck, he'd never anticipated the snow. No one could have, not really. He said he'd come back, and I believed that was his intention. Something unexpected had happened, and that didn't bode well for Eve Falcon or her baby.

My cell phone vibrated in my pocket. I knew it was Cece calling with the drop instructions, and I couldn't answer as long as my hands were tied. But I could try. Using the heel of my boot, I kicked across my body at the pocket of my jacket where my cell phone was. If I could just turn it on. If I could somehow manage to answer the call before it stopped. With my last reserve, I wrenched my hip, knee, and ankle and slammed my heel into my pocket. "Help!" I said weakly.

"Sarah Booth?" Cece's voice was muffled and far away, distorted by the pocket of my coat.

"Cece, I'm tied to a tree close to Bullwinkle's in Fortis Landing. I know where Eve is, I think. Get Coleman and hurry. Things are way, way out of control."

"I have to make the drop."

"Don't go alone, Cece. Don't. It's too dangerous. Come and get me. You can't go alone." I had so much to tell her. "I know who's behind all of this. It's Dara Peterson and her husband. Her husband is Mitch, Eve's twin brother. There's something wrong with Mitch's and Dara's baby. It may be genetic. Eve may be in real danger." I remembered the ob-gyn's question when I first asked about Dara. *Is the baby still alive?* "Whatever is wrong, they need Eve's baby to fix it. It's so much worse than we thought."

I'd rushed to get the information out so Cece could be prepared. "Cece? Did you hear me?"

There was a garbled response and then I heard ". . . on the way."

I clung to those words as I collapsed against the tree. Was she on her way to me or to the drop? Cece was in a place without any good options.

Twenty minutes later, I freed myself of the rope. The hope of being rescued had given me the determination to save myself. That and the snow. My arms were tired and strained but I had no time to waste. I pushed up on my feet and staggered back toward the road and my car, all the while calling Cece back.

When she answered, I wanted to weep with joy. "Where are you?"

"I'm going to the drop, Sarah Booth. He gave me half an hour to get there and I didn't have time to re-direct and stop by for you. I'm sorry."

"I'm fine. I got free. I'll join you. Where is the drop? They changed the location, didn't they?"

Her hesitation told me everything.

"Please, Cece. You need someone there to have your back. You heard what I said about Dara and Mitch Peterson. Eve and her child may be in real danger. This is all connected to Carla and Will's illegitimate children."

"I've been giving that a lot of thought and so much makes sense now. Carla's ruthless and relentless cruelty, her lack of joy, her anger that burned away even the tiniest pleasure for Will or Eve or even for herself. She punished everyone around her every minute of every day."

"Did you find anything about Eve's brother?" I hadn't had a chance. I'd been, literally, tied up. "Where does he live? What does he do? What's wrong with his baby?"

"I only have a minute, Sarah Booth. I'll tell you what I know about Eve's brother. You say his name is Mitch, well he was taken to the state orphanage, just like we supposed. I tracked down an employee of the orphanage who remembered a male infant that was brought to the state institution, but before his records were transferred, someone came to claim him. Somehow the paperwork with the infant was lost, and no one asked any questions anyway. The only thing she remembered was that the couple who came for him seemed to be nice."

"And?"

"She said they were from Mississippi and talked about growing up on the river and what a good life he'd have."

"Oh, my." Now I fully understood the role of Curtis and Matilda. "It was the Bromleys who adopted him?"

"I don't think so," Cece said. "Dara is the Bromley's daughter. And she's Mitch's wife. Mitch is their son-in-law."

"What do they intend to do with Eve?"

"I don't know. Not yet."

"I don't think the Bromleys would harm her." I had to believe that. Parents desperate to save their child or grandchild might do many things, but I couldn't see Curtis and Matilda harming a pregnant woman. "There's something else going on. Something dangerous. It's more than just wanting money. I can't put my finger on it, Cece, but this is directed at you and Eve. This smacks of something personal. This is about hurting you."

"Why?" Cece sounded anguished. "Who could hate me so much?"

I knew the answer, but I couldn't tell her without proof. "Tell me where you're making the drop. I think they may have set a trap for you."

"It's not far from where you are. If you go past the road to the boat landing and take the next right, I'm supposed to be one mile down that road by an abandoned boat on a trailer. There's a loop of the river that cuts back that way to make a big lake. I'm already there."

"I'll be there." I hung up and called Coleman's cell. My watch told me he was likely standing at the manger with his gift of myrrh or frankincense, but I didn't care. I left a voice message. "Coleman, meet me on old Gunter road. One mile down it. Cece is making the drop for Eve and the baby at ten o'clock. I think whoever has Eve intends to hurt her and Cece. I think it's Cece's aunt, Carla Falcon. She hates Cece and Eve and possibly her husband. I haven't figured out all the details, but I think I've hit on the truth. I know this isn't your jurisdiction, but please, please come."

I didn't have time to wait for him. I hobbled back through the woods until the feeling returned to my extremities. Then I trudged to my car, crippled by the cold and being tied up but determined. When I got in it, I didn't drive to the money drop. Instead I drove to the Bromleys' cabin. They weren't home, which is exactly what I suspected. But I went to the woodshed in the back. Mariam had bluffed us good, and my cursory inspection of the shed was shameful. The exterior was a mess, but once I made my way around it, I saw that the interior had been carefully renovated. A gas fire burned brightly.

There was heat and power—it was an underground gas line.

When I went inside I found all the necessities for a pregnant woman, including some equipment I'd never seen. But there were no indications that Eve—if this was indeed where Eve had been staying—had been restrained or held there against her will. But I absolutely believed she'd been there. A quick check of the space showed the prescription for prenatal vitamins in Dara Peterson's name, books on parenting, and also a book on blood clotting disorders and organ transplanting.

What? The darkest, most awful thought hit me with the force of a train. Were they planning on harvesting Eve and/or her baby's organs? That couldn't be possible—except it could. And the specific amount of money demanded for the ransom was in the right range to buy a kidney or liver or heart on the black market.

I thought back to my encounters with Carla and Will. She was pinched up like an old corpse, but I hadn't detected bad color or anything that might indicate a medical condition that would require an organ. Will had looked unhealthy—and unhappy. And Eve was his blood. My god, was that at the root of this whole thing? If Cece didn't come through with the money then Carla and Will would harvest an organ from Eve or the baby?

And then an even more dire possibility came to me. Cece was an organ donor. It was listed on her driver's license. Maybe this whole thing was just an opportunity to get her into a place where they could shoot her enough to make her brain dead but keep her alive long enough to be a donor.

I dialed Coleman's phone again. "Answer! You have to

hurry. This is dangerous. They might shoot Cece and I know she's an organ donor. Coleman, please stop everything and come!"

He still didn't answer so as I stumbled through the woods I called Cece, who also didn't answer, and then Tinkie, who picked up. "Sarah Booth, you never showed up at the pageant. Coleman was looking for you. He's not happy."

"This is bad, Tinkie. Call Cece. Keep calling until she answers. Stop her from making the drop if you can. Stop her with any means you have."

"I thought you were going to be with Cece." Tinkie's voice was tight with fear. "Where are you? Where is she?"

I gave her directions to the drop point, and luckily, she was already driving in that direction to find me and was almost there. When I hadn't answered her calls, she'd left the pageant and started toward the original drop point. "Take a gun, Tinkie. I think this has to do with someone needing an organ, and they intend to take it by force if they have to."

"Holy Christmas," Tinkie said. "Call Coleman right now."

"I've already left messages. Call Oscar. We may need back up and Oscar is a good shot. If you can get him to answer, tell him to get Coleman to check his messages and hurry."

"They're all in the middle of the Christmas pageant. I slipped out as soon as it started."

"I don't care if he's negotiating for his soul with St. Peter. We need him. Tell him to bring a gun."

"I'll call Harold, too. Might as well get all the wise men there."

"Be careful. See if you can Google Earth the area and make sure there are no other exit routes, especially via the river. This is something we've overlooked. The Bromleys know the waterways like the back of their hand. There was that creek that cut up by Dara Peterson's house, and it was big enough for a small skiff. We've been on Eve's trail the whole time, and we were pretty close. I believe she was in that old shed behind the Bromley's cabin. I don't know what Eve's role is in this. She may be unwittingly assisting them and it could cost her her life if they intend to harvest her organs." I knew I sounded crazy. This was like something in a thriller or a medical horror novel. This kind of thing didn't happen to people I knew, yet it had. And at Christmas! With a pregnant woman! In the snow!

I finally made it to my car and when I got inside, I put the heat on full blast and tore out toward the drop location. I wasn't far. I wanted to beat Tinkie there so we could join up and go in together. More than anything, I wanted Coleman to check his phone and get there fast.

As I tore through the night I wished Sweetie Pie and Pluto were with me, but another part of me was glad they wouldn't be in danger. I worried that Cece would trust Eve too much. I had no clue what role Eve had played in all of this—victim or participant. If Cece viewed her as an innocent and took action on that belief, she might leave herself open to injury. So many things were up in the air—and I was driving into what could be an ambush or worse.

I called Doc Sawyer and at last got to speak with someone. When I told him where I was and what I believed was happening, he didn't bother hiding his worry. "I'll head out that way."

"Get Coleman," I begged him. "Please. Don't come out without Coleman or one of the deputies."

"You have my word. We'll be there as quickly as we can. Meanwhile, I'll see what I can find out about bleeding disorders and pregnancies. I'll give Dr. Milford Warren, that obstetrician, a call. He was Dara Peterson's ob-gyn and he may speak with me about what's going on medically. I need to be prepared."

"Thank you, Doc." Before I finished, I'd have half of Zinnia out in the woods hunting for Eve and her baby.

The icy white crystals continued to fall from the sky, and I worried that soon the roads would be slick and dangerous. This was Christmas Eve, a time for celebrating family and the birth of the baby Jesus, not out in the cold driving over slick roads into deadly situations. The need for speed only made it more treacherous. I took a breath and eased off the gas pedal. One of the old sayings Aunt Loulane had been so fond of—Arrive Alive—came back to me. If I wrecked, I'd be useless to Cece.

At last I came to the turnoff that led to the money drop. I continued past it and pulled into a byway that led into a field. I went in deep enough to hide my car, then walked back to the road. I hoped I was ahead of Tinkie, but I didn't know. When I called, her phone went to voice mail, which did not make me feel better.

It was only a mile to the drop, and I started walking, picking my way down the road in the dark. I had gloves that I'd found in the trunk while I was looking for Tinkie's gun, hoping she might have left it there on our last case. No gun, but I found an old blanket I kept there for pet emergencies. The good news was that tire tracks gave me a great idea where to walk. If the snow kept falling, the tracks would be covered up, but right now, they were my lifeline in the cold night.

My aunt Loulane had once told me something that I'd reflected on many times through my life. When I'd been scared or upset about something I faced and I wanted my parents to be there for me, Aunt Loulane had pulled me aside and told me, "You're a Delaney, Sarah Booth. You've had the advantage of being greatly loved. Your parents will always be on your side no matter what, but only you can face this challenge."

I thought of that wisdom now as I trudged into danger I couldn't see. Aunt Loulane had also told me another bit of wisdom that I clung to. "Remember that there is no limit on miracles. They happen every day, and especially at Christmas." She'd been a true believer in the season.

Tonight, I needed a miracle to keep my friends safe. Holding tight to that hope, I pushed on through the snow.

19

I'd been walking about twenty minutes when I heard voices. I stopped, aware that the snow crunched beneath my boots, which might tip someone off. I couldn't see because of the snow falling, but they were at the same disadvantage. I was afraid to step off the road—the land on either side was spongy and wet. I couldn't be certain, but it felt as if I'd been headed downhill at a gentle angle. It was entirely possible a dangerous slough could be only feet from the road. Just because it was snowing didn't mean alligators might not be active. Did they hibernate? I didn't have a clue and didn't want to personally find out.

Somehow, I had to get close enough to figure out what was happening without giving my location away.

"Eve, get up. You can make it to my car. It's just over there about twenty yards. You're in labor and you don't have time to waste."

That was Tinkie talking. She'd disregarded my warnings and driven right into danger.

"Keep your mouth shut. Make a move, Eve, and see what happens."

And that was Carla, which was more terrifying than if I'd been incorrect in my assumptions. The only thing that could bring Carla out in the snow was money or something even more valuable. A human organ.

I crept closer. Who else was there? Had Cece made it? A tap on my shoulder made me nearly jump out of my skin.

"Take it easy, Sarah Booth," Cece whispered in my ear. "I stopped to get something we'll need." She pressed a shotgun into my hand. She also had one. "I know you have a pistol but the scatter range on the shotgun gives us an advantage."

She was wrong about the pistol because Curtis had taken it, but she was right about the shotgun being a better weapon for this job. Close only counted in horseshoes and with a shotgun. We didn't have to be perfect shots. We just had to be close enough. "Tinkie's in there and Eve's alive, but she's in labor. Carla is there, too."

"And Will?"

"I don't know. I don't know who else. Listen a few minutes."

"I don't have time." She strode past me, raising her voice. "Carla, I'm armed and I intend to blow your guts all over the woods. Consider yourself warned."

I tried to grab her and pull her back but she was gone.

The shotgun discharged, a sudden, harsh sound that made me cringe. I had no clue what she was shooting at, and she couldn't see any better than I could. Damn! I didn't have a choice—I went right after her.

"Hey, hold up there," Curtis Bromley called out. I recognized his voice. "You're gonna hit someone you don't mean to hurt."

"I'm going to kill that bitch Carla." Cece was taking no prisoners. She pumped in another round and fired again. I was close enough to see the flare from the barrel. I didn't call out, though, because while they knew Cece and Tinkie were there, they had no clue I was. Moving to the left of Cece, I intended to flank where I thought Carla's voice had come from.

"Cece, Carla is here, and the Bromleys, and Eve and her brother Mitch. Eve is in labor. We have to go to the hospital." Tinkie wanted to be sure Cece knew her location and she was singing out.

"I've got you located," Cece said. "Where is that bitch Carla? Is Will here?"

"Don't hurt Will!" The voice was that of a young woman in great distress. "Please don't hurt him," Eve said. "He's my father."

"Bully for him." Cece pumped another round in the chamber. She'd found a gun that held a number of shells. I didn't even know she knew how to operate a shotgun. I should have, though. Dove hunting was the great sport of the landed gentry, and Cece had once belonged in that elite crowd.

"We need Will," Tinkie said. "Remember all the blood in the kitchen in that house. It wasn't Dara's blood. It was her son's. The little boy is Eve's nephew. He's really sick. Mitch's little boy needs a liver transplant. Will is a perfect match. You can't kill him. We need his liver."

"So what are we doing out here in the woods?" Cece asked.

"Carla was extorting Eve and Mitch to get the transplant. And she was going to sell part of Will's liver for a profit." Tinkie coated her words in contempt.

"I see," Cece said. "I'm going to remedy this problem right now. Carla, how much is your pathetic life worth? Who would pay to save you? When I find you, I'm going to find out."

Cece was mad enough to take the action she threatened. And she would do it even knowing she'd sit in prison. I so regretted that I hadn't brought Coleman into this days ago. If Coleman was here, he'd defuse this whole situation and get Eve to the hospital. I would regret my lack of action for the rest of my life.

Something moved ahead of me and I crouched behind a tree trunk, hoping it wasn't an alligator or wild boar or some other natural predator. I stared into the falling snow, brushing it out of my eyelashes. The figure moving slowly in my direction was slender. Scrawny even. And certainly nothing I was afraid of. I launched myself at Carla and brought her down in a flying tackle. I hit her so hard I heard the breath leave her lungs. When I rolled off her she was still wallowing on the ground gasping for air. No sympathy was forthcoming from me. From my pocket I pulled the bonds Curtis Bromley had used to tie me, flipped her on her stomach, and secured her hands behind her.

"Stop shooting, Cece. I have Carla tied up."

"Good, then I won't miss." Her voice came from right behind me—as did the sound of the gun firing. Shotgun pellets hit the ground and snow flew up not three feet from Carla's head. She screamed in fear but I couldn't hear her. My eardrums were throbbing so hard I couldn't hear anything.

"Dammit, Cece. I'm deaf." I could see her lips moving in response, but I couldn't understand a thing she was saying. I did get it when she chambered another round. I grabbed the gun barrel and pushed it away. "Stop it. Just stop it."

Out of nowhere a burly body came crashing into Cece. The momentum knocked Cece into me and we all three—Cece, me, and Will Falcon—went sprawling in the snow. I was on the bottom of the heap, and now I was the one gasping for air and flopping around. The attacker and Cece got off me, but not soon enough.

"You're under arrest!"

Coleman stood behind Cece and Will, and I could see his lips moving and it wasn't too hard to read what he'd said. He had out his cuffs and snapped them on Will.

"Doc, over here!" Tinkie cried out.

My hearing was returning but I was still having trouble dragging air into my body.

"Doc, we need you right away," Coleman called.

I'd never been so glad to hear those words, and I heaved in some oxygen. I thought maybe my lungs had been permanently crushed. Doc would help me. But instead of coming to tend to me, Doc rushed over to where Tinkie was calling for him.

"The baby is coming. There's too much blood! Help, Doc. Cece, dammit, get over here. Sarah Booth, get off the ground and come help! I don't know a thing about birthin' no babies and I need help!"

Flashlights snapped on and the scene that was illuminated was so surreal I closed my eyes. I'd finally caught a good breath and knew I'd be okay, but my body was still angry at the loss of oxygen. I slowly got to my feet and stumbled toward the gathering of humans that had formed a semicircle around a woman on the ground. The snow had stopped at last, and Tinkie, some man I didn't recognize, and Coleman had taken their coats off and created a litter for the prone woman. Cece held the young woman's head tenderly on her lap and was doing her best to console her. I'd never seen her before but I knew her. Eve Falcon was indeed having her baby. Right at the stroke of midnight on Christmas Eve. And my partner Tinkie was delivering the child with Doc at her side and Cece offering comfort. A young man dropped to his knees beside Eve and reached for her hand. "It's almost over," he whispered.

Eve let out a loud cry, and I thought Tinkie might faint. But she was made of sterner stuff.

"That's it, Tinkie, get ready to support the child," Doc coached.

Coleman handed me his flashlight. "Help Tinkie out. I need to put Carla and Will in the patrol car."

"Sure."

It was such a stunning scene that no one spoke. Eve was as stoic as anyone I'd ever seen. She gasped and struggled, but she never cried out.

I simply hovered as my partner and Doc brought a new life into the world. When I could finally look away, I saw that Coleman, Harold, and Oscar were all in attendance, and they were rounding up the bad guys. They wore their wise men garb, standing behind Cece, except

Coleman's beard was missing. It took me a minute to realize it was stuck to the top of Tinkie's head. She looked like a devotee of a mad bushy squirrel cult. And best of all she had no idea she was wearing a beard on her head.

"You okay, Sarah Booth?" Coleman came up beside me, his arm snaking around my shoulders and pulling me close and easing me back from the scene of the birth.

"I am. Who is that man kneeling beside Eve?" I knew, but I wanted it confirmed.

"It's her brother. They were separated at birth. Will Falcon is the father, but the mother was a woman from Tishomingo County."

I knew all of this, but I didn't have to tell Coleman that. "Who abducted Eve?"

"That I haven't figured out yet, but we'll have a come to Jesus gathering at the hospital and I'll find out. You have my word. First, though, we have to get Eve and the baby to the hospital. There is a lot of blood."

"Are they going to be okay?" I asked.

"Take that up with Doc and Tinkie."

I walked closer and knelt beside Doc, who gave me a tired smile as he rocked back on his heels. "The delivery went off without a hitch, thanks to Tinkie. I might train her for my midwife."

"No thanks," Tinkie said. She had wrapped the baby in Mitch's shirt. "This isn't the most sanitary place to deliver a baby. We need to get to the hospital."

My worry tamped down a little. Doc looked in control and competent, and instead of a frown of worry, he wore a bemused smile. Doc loved delivering babies.

"Where's the ambulance?"

"En route."

Like a miracle I heard the siren as the transport bumped toward us. In another twenty minutes, mother and child would be at the hospital.

Just as the ambulance pulled up, the squall of a baby cut the night. The EMTs came out of the ambulance at a dead run. When I glanced back at the vehicle, for just a moment, I saw Jitty sitting behind the wheel. She gave me a thumbs-up and suddenly the ambulance radio came on.

"Oh, Holy Night, the stars are brightly shining. It is the night of our dear Savior's birth." The carol rang out over the snowy scene, clear as a bell.

"It's a boy!" Tinkie called out. "A healthy baby boy. And Doc says Eve is going to be just fine!"

Tinkie and Cece joined hands and practically danced together. The young man jumped into the back of the ambulance with his sister and the newborn. In another few minutes, the ambulance pulled out, headed to the hospital with its precious cargo.

20

The Christmas decoration in the waiting room at the hospital was one tiny pencil tree with four ornaments remaining. The lower decorations had been picked off by bored children, waiting for good or bad news. Just like us.

As it turned out, Eve and her baby were fine. They had survived the ordeal of birth in the woods, and Doc assured all of us they'd soon be out of the hospital. The same couldn't be said for Mitch and Dara Peterson's little boy, Alfie. The baby was very, very sick, and Carla's greedy scheming had put his life in jeopardy. The specialists said it was touch and go.

Mitch, who, once I had a clear view of him in the light, bore a striking resemblance to his sister Eve, sat with his wife, Dara, and her parents, Matilda and Curtis Bromley. The Petersons and Bromleys were definitely connected, by marriage. Dara Bromley had married Mitch Peterson—who'd been adopted as an infant by the Peterson family who lived not too far upriver from Fortis Landing.

When Alfie had been diagnosed with his illness, Dara and her sister, Mariam, had begun to untangle the story of Mitch's adoption. They'd backtracked, just as I had done, to the birth of twins in a Tishomingo County hospital. Their quest for an organ donor had taken them to Will and Clara Falcon. Will had been agreeable, but Clara had set a high price for a portion of Will's liver. Her hatred of Eve and Cece had dovetailed with her greed, and the scheme to "abduct" Eve and get Cece to pay the ransom had been born. Carla had insisted on the ploy. Her goal had been not only monetary, but a chance to punish everyone. She'd succeeded, but not in the way she'd expected. Everyone had suffered at her hand, but now, she was about to pay the piper.

Will had volunteered his liver—and was being prepped for surgery—for little Alfie, but the child was so sick the odds were fifty-fifty that he would survive the operation. In the waiting room, the seconds ticked by with the creep of cold cane syrup.

Christmas Eve had given way to Christmas Day, and when I went to the window of the waiting room and looked out, the sun on the new snow was a dazzling gold.

I felt a tap on my shoulder and Cece drew me into a hug. "Thank you, Sarah Booth. Thank you."

"Sorry about your aunt," I said. "Wait, that's a lie. I'm not sorry. I hope Carla never sees the light of day again." Carla Falcon was in the Sunflower County jail charged with a number of illegal acts. Will Falcon was in surgery, waiting to donate a portion of his liver to the grandson he'd never been allowed to know. If Alfie's little body could accept the transplant and he was treated for the blood disorder that had caused the damage to his own liver, he stood a chance of having a long, complete life. If the surgery worked. And if the damage to the little boy wasn't too great already.

This was why Eve needed $150,000. Not for the surgery, but to pay Carla Falcon so that she would allow Will to donate a part of his organ. I was still reeling from this revelation.

"I'm glad Carla is in jail," Cece said. "I hope she rots there. All she had to do was ask for the money. I would have gotten it. She's a vile human being."

"Is Will going to be charged, too?" Cece and Coleman had been in a huge confab, and no one had had time to tell me the results.

"I don't know." Cece rubbed the deep furrow between her eyebrows. "I just can't believe he'd let Carla keep him from helping his own grandson. Coleman is also talking to the Tishomingo County authorities. He wants Joanne Woodcock's suicide investigated. And I think he may be on to something. Coleman talked to the nurse who knew Joanne. Yes, Joanne was depressed, but she also said that she believed Will would leave Carla. She was expecting him to visit to see his children. Then suddenly Joanne was dead." Cece shook her head slowly. "Carla is capable of anything."

"Greedy, evil witch." I had no need to mince words.

"I'm going to do everything in my power to see that the prosecutor throws the book at her. If Will goes down with her, so be it." Cece had taken the one big step toward adulthood—she wasn't responsible for the actions of her crazy relatives.

I nodded toward the little group clustered together. "Have you had a chance to talk to Mitch?"

"Not really. He feels terrible about the plot Carla cooked up but he didn't know what else to do."

"He wasn't really in control of that. And I understand, in a way. Carla took control of the situation and manipulated things to suit her. Maybe Mitch should have come to talk to you."

Cece studied the ground for a moment before she settled a clear stare on me. "He didn't think I'd believe him—that he was Eve's brother. He was desperate, Sarah Booth. His baby was going to die, and he had to have that liver. He'd tried to get birth records to prove who he was, but he ran into the same thing we did. There are no records. He figured we'd all assume he was lying, and there wasn't time to get DNA testing done. Alfie was in real danger. He needed that liver yesterday." She turned wistful. "He's such a delicate little boy."

"And Eve's baby is robust and very healthy." I'd seen the little baby—all eight pounds and twenty-three inches of him. She'd named him Jasper, which tickled me.

"Jasper is healthy. He didn't inherit whatever genetic thing made Alfie so sick."

"Thank goodness. And I understand Mitch and Dara's plight, but you have to keep in mind that if Eve had been in real danger out there in the swamp, she might not have made it. Or the baby."

"I know." Cece put her arm around me. "Thank goodness you called Coleman and the cavalry."

"I'm sorry I betrayed your trust."

"You saved us all, Sarah Booth. The only thing I cared about was making sure Eve and her baby were safe. And you did that by following your gut."

I kissed her cheek and turned to the sound of Jaytee calling her name. She ran across the waiting room and into his arms, where she finally allowed herself to really cry.

The worst was over. No one was dead. Carla was in the Sunflower County jail. Will was in surgery giving the gift of life to his grandchild. Eve and Jasper were fine. The Bromleys were down the hall in a waiting room with DeWayne and Budgie watching them until Coleman could assess what charges he'd level. Dara and Mitch were desperately waiting for the outcome of the surgery that could save their son.

I had a few questions for Eve, now that the trauma of childbirth was behind her, and I wanted to ask without Cece in tow. I slipped out of the waiting room and went to her room, my feet dragging with weariness. This was not the Christmas Eve or morning I'd envisioned. Coleman and I had not had a moment alone. Soon, though. Very soon we were going to Dahlia House, my pets, and my bed.

When I tapped on Eve's door, she invited me in. She was a beautiful young woman. Even after the rigors of childbirth, she was still lovely. Almost ethereal. I couldn't help but think of paintings of the Madonna. Eve was nursing a red-faced baby that shook his fists in what I could only assume was eagerness.

"He's perfect," I said.

"He is. And I thought I was having a little girl." She grinned. "Doc Sawyer says he's one hundred percent healthy." She pressed her lips together for a moment. "My brother wasn't so lucky. Alfie wasn't born healthy."

"I know."

"He didn't really kidnap me. If I have to face charges for what I did, I won't fight it. But Mitch doesn't deserve to be punished. He's struggled so hard to provide for Alfie and Dara. When he realized Alfie was so sick, he did everything he knew to do, but there were no matching donors. Then he got the idea that maybe his real father was a match. Sure enough, Dad . . . Will was."

"And Carla intended to charge Mitch for a piece of Will's liver?" She was an awful woman, but could she be that completely soulless? I still had trouble believing it.

"Yes. She did some research and said that $130,000 was the going price. Then she upped it to $150,000."

"And what did Will say?"

Eve blinked back tears. "Nothing. Just like always. Nothing. I don't know if he's afraid of her or if she crushed him so many times he simply quit trying to stand up for himself."

"And it doesn't matter. Alfie is getting the liver."

"And what will happen to Da . . . Will?"

I shook my head slowly. "I don't know. Or the Bromleys. Or Dara and Mitch." I had to say it. "Or you, Eve. You were blackmailing your own cousin. Why didn't you just ask her?"

"It's a long story and I am a fool. I knew Carla hated Cece and wanted to punish her, but . . ."

I suddenly knew the answer. "Carla told you awful things about Cecil, or Cece as she is known now. She made you believe Cece would never willingly pay the ransom. She made you doubt who Cece really was."

"That's it in a nutshell. Why would I ever believe such things about someone I knew to be kind and generous and loving? How could I have betrayed Cece by thinking such horrible things? She'd never given me cause to doubt her. I was just as bad as Carla."

I sat down on the edge of the bed and patted her leg. "No, you weren't. You were a child, Eve. Folks around here have strong opinions about things they know nothing about. Carla played on your lack of experience and also your lack of self-esteem."

"And I was just as bad, willing to believe the worst about Cece." She cried quietly, sending the squirming baby into a spasm of crying. She held the child out to me and I had no choice but to take the baby and do my best to comfort him.

Eve slipped out of the bed and went to the bathroom for some tissue to blow her nose. "I was as low and base as Carla ever dared to be. The apple didn't fall far from the tree. I wasn't Carla's blood but I was a product of her raising."

"And yet you had enough conscience not to ask Cece for money."

She scoffed bitterly. "Yeah, bully for me. I didn't ask outright, I just decided to help Mitch by extorting the money from her. If it matters, I would have paid her back. I was getting a promotion at the bank with a pay increase, and I would have saved every week until I could give every penny back to her."

Whatever sentence was imposed on Eve for her part in the scheme, she would punish herself far worse. I adjusted Jasper in my arms and began the age-old remedy for a cranky baby—walking and gentle rocking motions. To my amazement he quieted and yawned, then reached a tiny baby fist up to touch my cheek. I felt a strange and powerful throb right around my heart.

"Talk to Cece." That was my best bit of advice. "Tell her all of this. We make mistakes, Eve. Every single one of us, every day. The hard thing is to recognize them and learn. I think you've done that."

She reached out for the baby and I returned little Jasper into her arms. "Thank you for understanding. You're a good friend to Cece. She had an awful family, but she's lucky in her friends."

"I think you'll find she wants family. She's beating herself up for not hunting harder for you when you first disappeared. You both carry a lot of unnecessary guilt. Let it go. Live for the moment and don't drag around what you can't change." If only I were smart enough, or strong enough, to live by my own words.

"Merry Christmas, Sarah Booth," Eve said, waving Jasper's little fist at me.

"And you, too, Eve. I'll be in touch." I hesitated. "Who is little Jasper's father?" I asked.

"He's a good man, Sarah Booth. He never knew I was pregnant, and I was never going to tell him, but I've changed my mind. Jasper deserves to know his father, on whatever level of relationship they decide to have. But I'm not telling anyone until I tell him."

"Good plan." I leaned and kissed her forehead. "A very good plan."

It was time for me to go home. It had been a helluva holiday, and I wanted only to light a fire and curl up in front of it with Coleman. When I returned to the waiting room, Tinkie and Oscar had gone home. Coleman had Mitch and Dara's word that they would turn themselves in as soon as the baby's surgery was over—they were huddled in a corner waiting on results. Though Coleman didn't say it, I knew DeWayne and Budgie would stay close.

"Good luck with baby Alfie," I told the young couple. "Do you need me to stay?"

"My parents are in the other room," Dara said. "They'll stay with us. Please keep in mind they were forced into helping with this scheme. It wasn't their idea and they tried to talk us out of it, but Mitch and I had to do what we did for our baby boy. Eve is a victim, too. She found out she had a brother and that her nephew was dying all at the same time. Alfie was so sick and we had to take action. I'm sorry for any pain we caused."

"No judgment from this quarter," I said, and meant it. "Coleman will sort it all out. I know Cece isn't pressing charges. She wants to get to know you, Mitch, and your family. You're her blood."

"I wish I'd known her." Mitch was rueful. "If I had believed she would accept me as family, I would have done things differently. I would never have listened to Carla. All my life I've been shut out of knowing what it's like to have blood."

"Where were you raised?" I asked.

"Here and there. I was adopted as an infant and stayed with the Peterson family until I was fifteen. They were good people, and I took their name. They were kind. But Helena got sick and when she died, Britt just lost his will to continue. They were older, and he had a heart attack. I went back in the system but I was in high school, not the cute infant or toddler that everyone wants. I was lost and angry and I made a lot of mistakes. I came back to

Fortis Landing and started work on the cotton gin. Then I met Dara and her family."

People were capable of overcoming many, many hardships and experiences. We all wore our scars—or hid them. "We'll get this sorted. Now I'm going home to sleep." I'd been up for nearly twenty-six hours.

Coleman was waiting for me in the hall, and I joined him, taking his hand and walking beside him into the sunshine and the snow. My whole world was new and fresh and white. The snow was another Christmas miracle.

"You know I followed your footsteps in the snow to the drop site," Coleman said. "I think about that and how remarkable it is. Snow in Sunflower County."

"I know." I got in the patrol car and left the Roadster in the hospital parking lot, beside Tinkie's caddy. Oscar had driven her home.

"How was the Christmas pageant?" I asked. "I'm sorry I had to miss it."

"Well, Mrs. Hedgepeth was perhaps an unwise choice to play the mother of Jesus."

"What happened?" The hint of gossip perked me up instantly.

"Instead of saying her lines, she went on a tear and listed all of the things that everyone in Zinnia does that make her angry. Your name came up, about a dozen times."

I laughed in the bright sunshine and crisp air. It was wonderful to laugh. "I'll bet it was funny."

"Not to Margaret Welford, who'd worked so hard on the pageant. And Thomas Terrell, who'd written the whole script. They were very upset that Mrs. Hedgepeth had rolled over their entire production just to have her moment of ranting glory." He chuckled as he drove toward Dahlia House. "It was quite a dramatic moment. They had padded Mrs. Hedgepeth's costume to indicate her large pregnancy. When she started on her rant, the padding slipped down a little so she just reached up under her skirt and pulled out that horrible baby doll she insisted had to be Jesus. Mrs. Hart and Mrs. Ninny both screamed and fell backwards. Doc thought they'd had heart attacks and he went to tend to them. Thank goodness they were just swooning from the shock of that delivery."

I couldn't help it. I was laughing out loud. "I'm so sorry I missed this!"

"Then when Mrs. Hedgepeth threw the baby into the audience, well, there was a stampede toward the church door."

"What did you do?"

"Oscar, Harold, and I were hiding behind the choir seats waiting for our cue to come on the scene with our gifts, but once Mrs. Hedgepeth sent the baby Jesus flying into the audience, all bets were off. Neely McDuff had fallen asleep during the service and when that ugly little baby slapped him upside the head, he started screaming and stood up and fell over backwards onto Eunice Dudley. He inadvertently groped Eunice, and she slapped him so hard his glasses flew down the aisle. In the stampede the glasses were broken, and so was Mr. McDuff's arm when Eunice dumped him off her lap."

I tried hard to suppress my mirth, but it was useless. The laughter ripped out of me and I laughed until I cried. "I can't believe I missed all of this."

"You missed a show, but it was videotaped by many."

"Last year, after those bad boys wrecked it with the

pig running through the manger scene and the llamas spitting on everyone, I thought it would be a calm production. Indoors and with only adults participating. Looks like there were several miscalculations."

"Mrs. Hedgepeth was a surprise. Who knew she'd grandstand and go so off script?"

"She is filled with spleen. It has to come out somewhere." But I was laughing still. Mrs. Hedgepeth was way down my list of things to worry about. "Thank you for arriving on time, Coleman."

"I'm glad you called me. It's important to know that you trust my judgment."

"Always. I was caught by a promise to Cece."

"I get it." He pulled me close up against him. "And now we're almost home."

We turned down the drive to Dahlia House and my three horses, blanketed against the cold, met us at the corner of the pasture and raced the car toward the house. They bucked and snorted in the pristine snow that covered the world, hiding all the familiar and ugly flaws. The world was new and fresh and pure.

"I guess DeWayne blanketed the horses again."

"And fed them."

"I need to put him on my payroll."

"Naw, just invite him to ride. He used to as a teen, but he's fallen out of the habit."

"I'd love for him to ride." The suggestion made me smile. Horses were another great way to share good times. "We'll get a group together and maybe ride through one of the state forests. A camping trip in the spring."

"Perfect." Coleman kissed the top of my head just as Dahlia House came into sight.

The cedar and magnolia garlands draped the front

porch, interspersed with large red ribbons. The multi-colored hues of an old-fashioned Christmas came from the front parlor window where someone had plugged in the Christmas tree to welcome us home. With the snow on the ground, it was a picture-perfect moment.

"I wouldn't want to share this with anyone else," I said to Coleman.

"It's like the homecoming I always dreamed of as a kid."

"It would seem," I said as I knelt on the front seat, "that our Christmas dreams have collided." When he parked and turned the car off, I laid a kiss on him that started an instant fire. I'd been tired enough to sleep standing up, but suddenly I was wide awake and hungry for Coleman's touch.

I pulled him into the house, past the Christmas tree and up the stairs to my bedroom.

"What about opening presents?" he asked, pretending to be reluctant.

I arched one eyebrow at him. "You'd rather open presents?"

"Later is good." He grabbed me and tossed me onto the bed. "Now let's get down to some serious Christmas celebrating."

I woke up after the sun had set. Coleman and Sweetie Pie snored softly in a kind of tender harmony. Pluto watched me with his green, green gaze.

I slipped out of bed and went downstairs where the Christmas tree still glowed red, blue, green, and yellow. I stood for a moment and simply drank in the sight. It was good that Jitty had prompted me to put it up and that Coleman and my friends had helped decorate it for me. Christmas Day was gone, but there was still plenty of time to open presents. I suspected that Cece and Jaytee and Tinkie and Oscar were all in bed, too. A night out in the cold and snow had taken the sap out of us. We'd have our celebration later in the week.

I went to the kitchen and poured a glass of water, taking a long slow drink and savoring the simple pleasure of quenching my thirst. So many people were without clean water that flowed out of a tap with the twist of a wrist. For all the things I'd lost, I was a lucky woman.

The strains of *The Nutcracker* came to me and I stepped back into the parlor to see the Sugar Plum Fairy dancing around the entire first floor of Dahlia House. Her elegance stunned me, and the beautiful feathered tutu stood out from her waist and bounced gently with each step she took. I knew that it was Jitty, making one final Christmas appearance, and I didn't care. I simply enjoyed the spectacle of her dancing and the power of her graceful execution of the dance moves. She was a pleasure to watch, and I loved the music. When she finished and took her bows, I applauded softly so as not to disturb Coleman and the pets. I'd whip up something special for my man to regain his strength to open Christmas presents.

Jitty came to me, her skirt bobbing and her hair so perfectly coiffed I was reminded of photographs of Josephine Baker. "You're something else, Jitty. I kind of hate to see this Nutcracker business come to an end."

"You got the message at last. I can move on."

"The message?"

She gave me a peeved look. "Your mama and daddy went to great lengths—Girl, you are a devil."

"I got the message," I admitted.

"Then my work here is done. Until next time."

There was the jingle of Christmas bells as Jitty disappeared in a whirl of snowflakes that dissipated in midair. I walked to the window and looked out on the front porch surrounded by pastures and the long drive between the leafless sycamores. Snow covered the ground. It was the perfect morning for a brisk ride. I had boots for the horses to prevent ice from lodging in their feet and brand-new riding boots for my man. It was time to rouse the sleeping Coleman and the pets and enjoy the sunshine and the magical winter day. After all, I'd gotten the message. Magic, especially at Christmastime, was real. And miracles do happen.

Look for

THE DEVIL'S BONES

the next Sarah Booth Delaney mystery
from Carolyn Haines, available in hardcover
in Spring 2020 from Minotaur Books!